Sapper is the pen nam⟨   888
at the Naval Prison in   was
Governor. He served i   ⟩wn
as 'sappers') from 1907–19, being awarded the Military Cross
during World War I.

He started writing in France, adopting a pen name because
serving officers were not allowed to write under their own
names. When his first stories, about life in the trenches, were
published in 1915, they were an enormous success. But it was his
first thriller, *Bulldog Drummond* (1920), that launched him as
one of the most popular novelists of his generation. It had several
amazingly successful sequels, including *The Black Gang*, *The
Third Round* and *The Final Count*. Another great success was
Jim Maitland (1923), featuring a footloose English sahib in
foreign lands.

Sapper published nearly thirty books in total, and a vast
public mourned his death when he died in 1937, at the early age
of forty-eight. So popular was his 'Bulldog Drummond' series
that his friend, the late Gerard Fairlie, wrote several Bulldog
Drummond stories after his death under the same pen name.

SAPPER

Bulldog Drummond

THE FINAL COUNT

HOUSE OF
STRATUS

This edition published in 2001 by House of Stratus, an imprint of Stratus Holdings plc, 24c Old Burlington Street, London, W1X 1RL, UK.

www.houseofstratus.com

Typeset, printed and bound by House of Stratus.

A catalogue record for this book is available from the British Library.

ISBN 1-84232-548-5

CONTENTS

INTRODUCTION

In endeavouring to put before the public for the first time the truth concerning the amazing happenings of the summer of 1927, I feel myself to be at a disadvantage. In the first place I am no story-teller: so maybe my presentation of the facts will fail to carry conviction. Nay, further: it is more than likely that what I am about to write down will be regarded as a tissue of preposterous lies. And yet to those who condemn me off hand I would say one thing. Take the facts as you know them, and as they appeared in the newspapers, and try to account for them in any other way. You may say that in order to write a book – again, perhaps, a little cheap notoriety – I have taken the ravings of a madman around which to build a fantastic and ridiculous story. You are welcome to your opinion. I can do no more than tell you what I know: I cannot make you believe me.

In one respect, however, I feel that I am in a strong position: my own part was a comparatively small one. And it is therefore from no reason of self-aggrandisement that I write. To one man, and one man only, is praise and honour due, and that is the man who led us – Hugh Drummond. But if unbelievers should go to him for confirmation, it is more than probable they will be disappointed. He will burble at them genially, knock them sense-less with a blow of greeting on the back, and then resuscitate them with a large tankard of ale. And the doubter may well be pardoned for continuing to doubt: I, myself, when I first met Drummond was frankly incredulous as to his capabilities of being anything but a vast and good-natured fool. I disbelieved, politely, the stories his friends told me about him: to be candid, his friends were of very much the same type as himself. There were four of them whom I got to know intimately: Algy Longworth, a tall young man with a slight drawl and an eyeglass; Peter Darrell, who usually came home with the milk each morning, but often turned out to play cricket for Middlesex; Ted Jerningham, who fell in love with a different girl daily; and finally Toby Sinclair, who was responsible for introducing me into the circle.

Finally, there was Drummond himself, of whom a few words of description may not be amiss. He stood just six feet in his socks, and turned the scales at over fourteen stone. And of that fourteen stone not one ounce was made up of superfluous fat. He was hard muscle and bone clean through, and the most powerful man I have ever met in my life. He was a magnificent boxer, a lightning and deadly shot with a revolver, and utterly lovable. Other characteristics I discovered later: his complete absence of fear (though that seemed common to all of them); his cool resourcefulness in danger; and his marvellous gift of silent movement, especially in the dark.

But those traits, as I say, I only found out later: just at first he seemed to me to be a jovial, brainless creature who was married to an adorable wife. It was his face and his boxing abilities that had caused him to be nicknamed Bulldog. His mouth was big, and his nose was small, and he would not have won a prize at a beauty show. In fact, it was only his eyes – clear and steady with a permanent glint of lazy humour in them – that redeemed his face from positive ugliness.

So much, then, for Hugh Drummond, DSO, MO, who was destined to play the leading part in the events of that summer, and to meet again, and for the last time, the devil in human form who was our arch-enemy. And though it is not quite in chronological order, yet I am tempted to say a few words here concerning that monstrous criminal. Often in the earlier stages of our investigations did I hear Drummond mention his name – a name which conveyed nothing to me, but which required no explanation to the others or to his wife. And one day I asked him point blank what he meant.

He smiled slightly, and a dreamy look came into his eyes.

"What do I mean, by saying that I seem to trace the hand of Carl Peterson? I'll tell you. There is a man alive in this world today – at least he's alive as far as I know – who might have risen to any height of greatness. He is possessed of a stupendous brain, unshakable nerve, and unlimited ambition. There is a kink, however, in his brain, which has turned him into an utterly unscrupulous criminal. To him murder means no more than the squashing of a wasp means to you."

He looked at me quietly.

"Understand me: that remark is the literal truth. Three times in the past have he and I met: I'm just wondering if this will prove to be the fourth; if, way back, at the foundation of this ghastly affair, there sits Carl Peterson, or Edward Blackton, or the Comte de Guy, or whatever he calls himself, directing, controlling, organising everything. I haven't seen him now or heard of him for three years, and as I say – I wonder."

At the time, of course, it was Greek to me; but now that the thing is over and the terror is finished, it may be of interest to those who read to know before I start what we did not know at the time: to know that fighting against us with every force at his command was that implacable devil whom I will call Carl Peterson.

I say, we did not *know* it, but I feel that I must mitigate that statement somewhat. Looking back now I think – and Drummond himself admits it – that deep down in his mind there was a feeling almost of certainty that he was up against Peterson. He had no proof: he says that it was just a guess without much foundation – but he was convinced that it was so. And it was that conviction that kept him at it during those weary weeks in London, when all traces seemed to be lost. For if he had relaxed then, as we others did: if he had grown bored, thinking that all was over, a thing would have occurred unparalleled in the annals of crime.

But enough of this introduction: I will begin my story. And in telling it I shall omit nothing: even at the risk of boring my readers I shall give in their proper place extracts from the newspapers of the day which dealt with that part of the affair which is already known to the public. If there is to be a record, let it be a complete one.

CHAPTER 1

In which I hear a cry in the night

It was on a warm evening towards the end of April 1927 that the first act took place, though it is safe to say that there has never been any connection in the public mind up till this day between it and what came after. I was dining at Prince's with Robin Gaunt, a young and extremely brilliant scientist, and a very dear friend of mine. We had been at school together and at Cambridge; and though we had lost sight of one another during the war, the threads of friendship had been picked up again quite easily at the conclusion of that foolish performance. I had joined the Gunners, whilst he, somewhat naturally, had gravitated towards the Royal Engineers. For a year or two, doubtless bearing in mind his really extraordinary gifts, the powers that be ordained that he should make roads, a form of entertainment of which he knew less than nothing. And Robin smiled thoughtfully and made roads. At least he did so officially: in reality he did other things, whilst a sergeant with a penchant for rum superintended the steam roller. And then one day came a peremptory order from GHQ that Lieutenant Robin Gaunt, RE, should cease making roads, and should report himself at the seats of the mighty at once. And Robin, still smiling thoughtfully, reported himself. As I have said, he had been doing other things during that eighteen months, and the fruits of his labours, sent

1

direct and not through the usual official channels, lay on the table in front of the man to whom he reported.

From then on Robin became a mysterious and shadowy figure. I met him once on the leave boat going home, but he was singularly uncommunicative. He was always a silent sort of fellow, though on the rare occasions when he chose to talk he could be brilliant. But during that crossing he was positively taciturn.

He looked ill and I told him so.

"Eighteen hours a day, old John, for eleven months on end. That's what I've been doing, and I'm tired."

He lit a cigarette and stared over the water.

"Can you take it easy now?" I asked him.

He gave a weary little smile.

"If you mean by that, have I finished, then I can – more or less. But if you mean, can I take it easy from a mental point of view, God knows. I'll not have to work eighteen hours a day any more, but there are worse things than physical exhaustion."

And suddenly he laid his hand on my arm.

"I know they're Huns," he said tensely: "I know it's just one's bounden duty to use every gift one has been given to beat 'em. But, damn it, John – they're men too. They go back to their women kind, just as all these fellows on this boat are going back to theirs."

He paused, and I thought he was going to say something more. But he didn't: he just gave a short laugh and led the way through the crowd to the bar.

"A drink, John, and forget what I've been saying."

That was in July '18, and I didn't see him again till after the Armistice. We met in London, and at lunch I started pulling his leg over his eighteen hours' work a day. He listened with a faint smile, and for a long while refused to be drawn. And it was only when the waiter went off to get change for the bill that he made a remark which for many months stuck in my mind.

"There are a few things in my life that I'm thankful for, John," he said quietly. "And the one that I'm most thankful for is that the Boches broke when they did. For if they hadn't…"

"Well – if they hadn't?"

"There wouldn't have been any Boches left to break."

"And a damned good thing too," I exclaimed.

He shrugged his shoulders.

"They're men too, as I said before. However, in Parliamentary parlance the situation does not arise. Wherefore, since it's Tuesday today and Wednesday tomorrow, we might have another brandy."

And with that the conversation closed. Periodically during the next few months that remark of his came back to my mind.

"There wouldn't have been any Boches left to break."

An exaggeration, of course: a figure of speech, and yet Robin Gaunt was not given to the use of vain phrases. Years of scientific training had made him meticulously accurate in his use of words; and, certainly, if one-tenth of the wild rumours that circulated round the military Hush-Hush department was true, there might be some justification for his remark. But after a time I forgot all about it, and when Robin alluded to the matter at dinner on that evening in April I had to rack my brains to remember what he was talking about.

I'd suggested a play, but he had shaken his head.

"I've an appointment, old man, tonight which I can't break. Remember my eighteen hours' work a day that you were so rude about?"

It took me a second or two to get the allusion.

"Great Scott!" I laughed, "that was the war to end war, my boy. To make the world safe for heroes to live in, with further slush *ad nauseam*. You don't mean to say that you are still dabbling in horrors?"

"Not exactly, John," he said gravely. "When the war was over I put the whole of that part of my life behind me. I hoped, as

3

most of us did, that a new era had dawned: now I realise, as all of us realise, that we've merely gone back a few centuries. You know as well as I do that it is merely a question of time before the hatred of Germany for France boils up and cannot be restrained. Any thinking German will tell you so. Don't let's worry about whose fault it is: we're concerned more with effects than causes. But when it does happen, there will be a war which for unparalleled ferocity has never before been thought of. Don't let's worry as to whether we go in, or on whose side we go in: those are problems that don't concern us. Let us merely realise that primitive passions are boiling and seething in Europe, backed by inventions which are the last word in science. Force is the sole arbiter today: force and blazing hate, covered for diplomacy's sake with a pitifully thin veneer of honeyed phrases. I tell you, John, I've just come back from Germany and I was staggered, simply staggered. The French desire for *revanche* in 1870 compared to German feeling today is as a tallow dip to the light of the sun."

He lit a cigar thoughtfully.

"However, all that is neither here nor there. Concentrate on that one idea, that force is the only thing that counts today: concentrate also on the idea that frightfulness in war is inevitable. I've come round to that way of thinking, you know. The more the thing drags on, the more suffering and sorrow to the larger number. Wherefore, pursuing the argument to a logical conclusion, it seems to me that it might be possible to arm a nation with a weapon so frightful, that by its very frightfulness war would be impossible because no other country would dare to fight."

"Frightfulness only breeds frightfulness," I remarked. "You'll always get counter-measures."

"Not always," he said slowly. "Not always. But what's your idea, Robin? What nation would you put in possession of such a weapon – granting for the moment that the weapon is there?"

He looked at me surprised. It was a silly remark, but I was thinking of France and Germany.

"My dear old man – our own, of course. Who else? The policeman of the world. Perhaps America too: the English-speaking peoples. Put them in such a position, John, that they can say, should the necessity arise – ' You shall not fight. You shall not again blacken the world with the hideous suffering of 1914. And since we can't prevent you fighting by words, we'll do it by force.' "

His eyes were gleaming, and I stared at him curiously. That he was in dead earnest was obvious, but the whole thing seemed to me to be preposterous.

"You can't demonstrate the frightfulness of any weapon, my dear fellow," I objected, "unless you go to war yourself. So what the devil is the good of it anyway?"

"Then, if necessary, go to war. Go to war for one day – against both of them. And at the end of that day say to them – ' Now will you stop? If you don't, the same thing will happen to you tomorrow, and the next day, and the next, until you do!' "

"But what will happen to them?" I cried.

"Universal, instantaneous death over as large or as small an area as is desired."

I think it was at that moment that I first began to entertain doubts as to Robin's sanity. Not that people dining near would have noticed anything amiss with him: his voice was low-pitched and quiet. But the whole idea was so utterly far-fetched and fantastic that I couldn't help wondering if his brilliant brain hadn't crossed that tiny bridge which separates genius from insanity. I knew the hideous loathing he had always felt for war: was it possible that continual brooding on the idea had unhinged him?

"It was ready at Armistice time," he continued, "but not in its present form. Today it is perfected."

"But, damn it all, Robin," I said, a little irritably, "what is this IT?"

He smiled and shook his head.

"Not even to you, old man, will I tell that. If I could I would keep it entirely to myself, but I realise that that is impossible. At the moment there is only one other being in this world who knows my secret – the great-hearted pacifist who has financed me. He is an Australian who lost both his sons in Gallipoli, and for the last two years he has given me ceaseless encouragement. Tonight I am meeting him again – I haven't seen him for three months – to tell him that I've succeeded. And tomorrow I've arranged to give a secret demonstration before the Army Council."

He glanced at his watch and stood up.

"I must be off, John. Coming my way?"

Not wanting to go back so early I declined, and I watched his tall spare figure threading its way between the tables. Little did I dream of the circumstances in which I was next to meet him: a knowledge of the future has mercifully been withheld from mortal man. My thoughts as I sat on idly at the table finishing my cigar were confined to what he had been saying. Could it be possible that he had indeed made some stupendous discovery? And if he had, was it conceivable that it could be used in the way he intended and achieve the result he desired? Reason answered in the negative, and yet reason didn't seem quite conclusive.

"Universal, instantaneous death."

Rot and rubbish: it was like the wild figment of a sensational novelist's brain. And yet – I wasn't satisfied.

"Hullo, Stockton! how goes it? Has she left you all alone?"

I glanced up to see Toby Sinclair grinning at me from the other side of the table.

"Sit down and have a spot, old man," I said. "And it wasn't a she, but a he."

For a while we sat on talking, and it was only when the early supper people began to arrive that we left. We both had rooms in Clarges Street, and for some reason or other – I forget why – Sinclair came into mine for a few minutes before going on to his own. I mention it specially, because on that simple little point there hung tremendous issues. Had he not come in – and I think it was the first time he had ever done so: had he not been with me when the telephone rang on my desk, the whole course of events during the next few months would have been changed. But he did come in, so there is no good speculating on what might have happened if he hadn't.

He came in and he helped himself to a whisky-and-soda and he sat down to drink it. And it was just as I was following his example that the telephone went. I remember wondering as I took up the receiver who could be ringing me up at that hour, and then came the sudden paralysing shock.

"John! John! Help. My rooms. Oh! my God."

So much I heard, and then silence. Only a stifled scream, and a strange choking noise came over the wire, but no further words. And the voice had been the voice of Robin Gaunt.

I shouted down the mouthpiece, and Sinclair stared at me in amazement. I feverishly rang exchange, only to be told that the connection was broken and that they could get no reply.

"What the devil is it, man?" cried Sinclair, getting a grip on my arm. "You'll wake the whole bally house in a moment."

A little incoherently I told him what I'd heard, and in an instant the whole look of his face changed. How often in the next few weeks did I see just that same change in the expression of all that amazing gang led by Drummond, when something that necessitated action and suggested danger occurred. But at the moment that was future history: the present concerned that agonised cry for help from the man with whom I had just dined.

"You know his house?" said Sinclair.

Down in Kensington, "I answered, Got a weapon of any sort?"

I rummaged in my desk and produced a Colt revolver – a relic of my Army days.

"Good," he cried. "Stuff some ammunition in your pocket, and we'll get a move on."

But there's no necessity for you to come," I expostulated.

"Go to hell," he remarked tersely, and jammed his top hat on his head. "This is the sort of thing I love. Old Hugh will turn pea-green with jealousy tomorrow when he hears."

We were hurtling West in a taxi, and my thoughts were too occupied with what we were going to find at the other end to inquire whom old Hugh might be. There was but little traffic – the after supper congestion had not begun – and in less than ten minutes we pulled up outside Robin's house.

"Wait here," said Toby to the taxi-driver. "And if you hear or see nothing of us within five minutes, drive like blazes and get a policeman."

"Want any help now, sir?" said the driver excitedly.

"Good lad!" cried Sinclair. "But I think not. Safer to have someone outside. We'll shout if we do."

The house was in complete darkness, as were those on each side. The latter fact was not surprising, as a "To be Sold" notice appeared in front of each of them.

"You know his rooms, don't you? "said Sinclair. "Right! Then what I propose is this. We'll walk straight in as if we're coming to look him up. No good hesitating. And for the love of Allah don't use that gun unless it's necessary."

The front door was not bolted, and for a moment or two we stood listening in the tiny hall. The silence was absolute, and a light from a lamp outside shining through a window showed us the stairs.

"His rooms are on the first floor," I whispered. "Then let's go and have a look at 'em," answered Toby.

With the revolver in my hand I led the way. One or two stairs creaked loudly, and I heard Sinclair cursing under his breath at the noise. But no one appeared, and as we stood outside the door of Robin's sitting-room and laboratory combined, the only sound was our own breathing.

"Come on, old man," said Toby. "The longer we leave it the less we'll like it. I'll open the door, and you cover anyone inside with your gun."

With a quick jerk he flung the door wide open, and we both stood there peering into the room. Darkness again and silence just like the rest of the house. But there was one thing different: a faint, rather bitter smell hung about in the air.

I groped for the switch and found it, and we stood blinking in the sudden light. Then we moved cautiously forward and began an examination.

In the centre of the room stood the desk, littered, as usual, with an untidy array of books and papers. The telephone stood on one corner of it, and I couldn't help thinking of that sudden anguished cry for help that had been shouted down it less than a quarter of an hour before. If only it could speak and tell us what had happened!

"Good Lord! Look at that," muttered Toby. "It's blood, man: the place is running in blood."

It was true. Papers were splashed with it, and a little trickle oozed sluggishly off the desk on to the carpet.

The curtains were drawn, and suddenly Toby picked up a book and hurled it at them.

One of Drummond's little tricks," he remarked. "If there's anyone behind you can spot it at once, and with luck you may hit him in the pit of the stomach."

But there was no one there: there was no one in the room at all.

"Where's that door lead to?" he asked.

9

"Gaunt's bedroom," I answered, and we repeated the performance.

We looked under the bed, and in the cupboard: not a sign of anybody. The bed was turned down ready for the night, with his pyjamas laid in readiness, and in the basin stood a can of hot water covered with a towel. But of Robin or anyone else there was no trace.

"Damned funny," said Toby, as we went back into the sitting room.

"What's that scratching noise?"

It came from behind the desk, and suddenly a little short-tailed, tawny-coloured animal appeared.

"Holy smoke!" cried Toby, "it's a guinea-pig. And there's another of 'em, Stockton: dead."

Sure enough a little black one was lying rigid and stretched out close to the desk.

"Better not touch it," I said warningly. "Leave everything as it is."

And then a thought struck Toby.

"Look here, Stockton, he can't have been whispering down the 'phone. Isn't there anyone else in the house who would have heard him?"

"There is no other lodger," I said. "His landlady is probably down below in the basement, but she's stone deaf. She's so deaf that Gaunt used generally to write things down for her in preference to talking."

"I think we ought to see the old trout, don't you?" he said, and I went over and rang the bell.

"She may or may not hear it," I remarked, as we waited. "Incidentally, what on earth is this strange smell?"

Sinclair shook his head.

"Search me. Though from the look of those bottles and test-tubes and things I assume your pal was a chemist."

A creaking on the stairs, accompanied by the sounds of heavy breathing, announced that the bell had been heard, and a moment later the landlady appeared. She stared at us suspiciously until she recognised me, which seemed to reassure her somewhat.

"Good-evening," I roared. "Have you seen Mr Gaunt tonight?"

"I ain't seen him since yesterday morning," she announced. "But that ain't nothing peculiar. Sometimes I don't see 'im for a week at a time."

"Has he been in the house here since dinner? I went on.

"I dunno, sir," she said. "He comes and he goes, does Mr Gaunt, with 'is own key. And since 'e pays regular, I puts up with 'im in spite of all those 'orrors and chemicals and things. I even puts up with 'is dog, though it does go and cover all the chairs with white 'airs."

"Dog," said Toby thoughtfully. "He'd a dog, had he ?

A wire-haired terrier called Joe," I said. Topping little beast."

"Then I wonder where the dickens it is?" he remarked. "Good Lord! what's all that?"

From the hall below came the sound of many footsteps, and the voice of our taxi-driver.

"This will give the old dame a fit," said Toby with a grin. "I'd forgotten all about our instructions to that stout-hearted Jehu."

There were two policemen and the driver who came crowding into the room amidst the scandalised protests of the landlady.

"Five minutes was up, sir, so I did as you told me," said the driver.

"Splendid fellow," cried Toby. "It's all right, constable: that revolver belongs to my friend."

The policeman, who had picked it up suspiciously from the desk, transferred his attention to me.

"What's all the trouble, sir? "he said. "Don't be alarmed, mother: no one's going to hurt you."

"She's deaf," I told him, and he bellowed in her ear to reassure her.

And then, briefly, I told the two constables exactly what had happened. I told them what I knew of Gaunt's intentions after he had left me, of the cry for help over the telephone, and of our subsequent movements. The only thing I did not feel it incumbent on me to mention was the object of his meeting with the Australian. I felt that their stolid brains would hardly appreciate the matter, so I left it at business.

"Quarter of an hour you say, sir, before you got here. You're sure it was your friend's voice you heard?

"Positive," I answered. "Absolutely positive. He had an unmistakable voice, and I knew him very well."

And at that moment from the window there came a startled exclamation. The second constable had pulled the curtains, and he was standing there staring at the floor.

"Gaw lumme," he remarked. "Look at that." We looked. Lying on the floor, stone dead, and twisted into a terrible attitude was Robin's terrier. We crowded round staring at the poor little chap, and it seemed to me that the strange smell had become much stronger.

Suddenly there came a yell of pain, and one of the policemen, who had bent forward to touch the dog, started swearing vigorously and rubbing his fingers.

"The little beggar is burning hot," he cried. "Like touching a red-hot coal."

He looked at his finger, and then there occurred one of the most terrible things I have ever seen. Literally before our eyes the fingers with which he had touched the dog twisted themselves into knots: then the hand: then the arm. And a moment later he crashed to the ground as if he'd been pole-axed, and lay still.

I don't know if my face was like the others, but they were all as white as a sheet. It was so utterly unexpected, so stunningly sudden. At one moment he had been standing there before us, a great, big, jovial, red-faced man: the next he was lying on the carpet staring at the ceiling with eyes that would never see again.

"Don't touch him," said a hoarse voice which I dimly recognised as my own. "For God's sake, don't touch him. The poor devil is dead anyway." The other policeman, who had gone down on his knees beside the body, looked up stupidly. Ordinary accidents, even straightforward murder, would not have shaken him, but this was something outside his ken.

"I don't understand, sir," he muttered. "What killed him?"

"He was killed because he touched that dead dog," said Sinclair gravely. "We can none of us tell any more than that, officer. And this gentleman is afraid that if you touch him the same thing may happen to you."

"But it's devil's work," cried the constable, getting dazedly to his feet. "It ain't human."

For a while we stood there staring at the dead man, while the landlady rocked hysterically in a chair with her apron over her head. Of the four of us only I had the remotest idea as to what must have happened: to the others it must have seemed not human, as the policeman had said. And even to me with my additional knowledge the thing was almost beyond comprehension.

Robin's wonderful invention; the strange smell which seemed to be growing less, or else I was getting accustomed to it; the dead dog, from which the smell obviously came; and finally the dead policeman, were all jumbled together in my mind in hopeless confusion. That Joe had been killed by this damnable thing his master had perfected was fairly obvious; but why in Heaven's name should Robin have killed a dog whom he adored? The guinea-pig I could understand – but not Joe.

"It looks as you say, constable, like devil's work," I said at length. "But since we know that that does not happen we can only conclude that the devil in this case is human. And I think the best thing to do is to ring up Scotland Yard and get someone in authority here at once. This has become a little above our form."

"I agree," said Sinclair soberly. "Distinctly above our form."

The constable went to the telephone, and the taxi-driver stepped forward.

"If it's all the same to you, gents," he said, "I think I'll wait in the cab outside. I kind of feel safer in the fresh air."

"All right, driver," said Sinclair. "But don't go away: they'll probably want your evidence as well as ours."

"Inspector MacIver coming at once, sir," said the constable, replacing the receiver with a sigh of relief. "And until he comes I think we might as well wait downstairs. Come along, mother: there ain't no good your carrying on like that."

He supported the old landlady from the room, and when we had joined him in the passage he shut and locked the door and slipped the key in his pocket. And then, having sent her down to her basement, we three sat down to wait for the Inspector.

"Cigarette, Bobby?" said Sinclair, holding out his case. "Helps the nerves."

"Thank you, sir: I don't mind if I do. It's fair shook me, that has. I've seen men killed most ways in my time – burned, drowned, hung – not to say nothing of three years in the war; but I've never seen the like of that before. For 'im just to go and touch that there dead dog, and be dead 'imself." He looked at us diffidently. "Have you got any idea, gentlemen, as to what it is that's done it?"

"It's some ghastly form of poison, constable," I said. "Of that I'm pretty certain. But what it is, I know no more than you. Mr Gaunt was a marvellous chemist."

"A damned sight too marvellous," said the policeman savagely. "If it's 'im what's done it I'm thinking he'll find himself in Queer Street when he comes back."

14

"I think it's *if* he comes back," I said. "There's been foul play here – not only with regard to that dog, but also with regard to Mr Gaunt. He idolised that terrier: nothing will induce me to believe that it was he who killed Joe. Don't forget that cry for help over the telephone. Look at all that blood. It's my firm belief that the clue to the whole mystery lies in the Australian gentleman whom he was going to meet tonight. He left me at Prince's to do so. Find that man, and you'll find the solution."

"Have you any idea what he looks like?" asked Toby.

That's the devil of it," I answered. "I haven't the slightest. All I can tell you is that he must be a fairly wealthy man who had two sons killed in Gallipoli."

The policeman nodded his head portentously.

"The Yard has found men with less to go on than that, sir," he remarked. "Very likely he'll be putting up at one of the swell hotels."

"And very likely he won't," put in Toby. "If what Mr Stockton thinks is right, and this unknown Australian is at the bottom of it all, stopping at one of the big hotels is just what he wouldn't do. However, there's a taxi, so presumably it's the Inspector."

The constable hurriedly extinguished his cigarette, and went to the front door to meet MacIver. He was a short, thick-set, powerful man with a pair of shrewd, penetrating eyes. He gave a curt nod to each of us, and listened in silence while I again repeated my story. This time I told it a little more fully, emphasising the fact that Robin Gaunt was at any rate under the impression that he had made a far-reaching discovery which would revolutionise warfare.

" 'What sort of a discovery?" interrupted MacIver.

"I can't tell you, Inspector," I said, "for I don't know. He was employed during the war as a gas expert, and when the Armistice came he had, I believe, invented a particularly deadly form which, of course, was never used. And from what he told me at dinner tonight, this invention was now perfected. He described it to me as causing universal, instantaneous death."

The Inspector fidgeted impatiently: imagination was not his strong point, and I admit it sounded a bit fanciful.

"He left me to come and interview an Australian who has helped him financially. His idea was that the appalling power of this discovery of his could be used to prevent warfare in future, if it was in the sole hands of one nation. He thought that no other nation would then dare to go to war. And his intention was to demonstrate before the Army Council tomorrow, with the idea that England might be that one nation. That is what he told me this evening. How far his claims were justified I don't know. What his discovery was I don't know. But two things I do know: first, that Robin Gaunt is a genius, and second, that his claim can be no more fantastic than what we all of us saw take place before our very eyes half-an-hour ago."

MacIver grunted and rose from his chair.

"Let's go and have a look."

The constable led the way, and once again we entered the room upstairs. Everything was just as we had left it: the dead man still stared horribly at the ceiling: the terrier still lay a little twisted heap in the window: the blood still dripped sluggishly off the desk. But the strange smell we had noticed was considerably less powerful, though the Inspector noticed it at once and sniffed. Then with the method born of long practice he commenced his examination of the room. And it was an education in itself to see him work. He never spoke; and at the end of ten minutes not a corner had been overlooked. Every drawer had been opened, every paper examined and discarded, and the net result was – nothing.

"A very extraordinary affair," he said quietly. "I take it you knew Mr Gaunt fairly intimately?"

He looked at me and I nodded.

"Very intimately," I answered. "We were at school together, and at college, and I've frequently seen him since."

"And you have no idea, beyond what you have already told me, as to what this discovery of his was?"

"None. But I should imagine, Inspector, in view of his appointment with the Army Council tomorrow, that someone at the War Office may be able to tell you something."

"It is, of course, possible that he will keep that appointment," said MacIver. "Though I admit I'm not hopeful."

His eyes were fixed on the dead dog.

"That's what beats me particularly," he remarked. "Why kill the terrier? A possible hypothesis is that he didn't: that the dog was killed accidentally. Let us, for instance, imagine for a moment that your friend was experimenting with this device of his. The dead guinea-pig bears that out. Then some accident occurred. I make no attempt to say what accident, because we have no idea as to the nature of the device. He lost his head, snatched up the telephone, got through to you – and then realising the urgent danger rushed from the room, forgetting all about the dog. And the dog was killed."

"But surely," I objected, "under those circumstances we should find some trace of apparatus. And there's nothing. And why all that blood?"

"He might have snatched it up when he left, and thrown it away somewhere."

"He might," I agreed. "But I can't help thinking, Inspector, that it is more sinister than that. If I may say so, I believe that what happened is this. The Australian whom he was going to meet was not an Australian at all. He was possibly a German or some foreigner, who was deeply interested in this device, and who had deceived Gaunt completely. He came here tonight, and overpowered Gaunt: then he carried out a test on the dog, and found that it acted. After that he, probably with the help of

17

accomplices, removed Gaunt, either with the intention of murdering him at leisure or of keeping him a prisoner."

"Another hypothesis," agreed the Inspector, "but it presents one very big difficulty, Mr Stockton. Your friend must have suspected foul play when he rang you up on the telephone. Now you're on a different exchange, and it must have taken, on a conservative estimate, a quarter of a minute to get through. Are we to assume that during those fifteen seconds this Australian, or whatever he is, and his accomplices stood around and looked at Mr Gaunt doing the one thing they didn't want him to do – getting in touch with the outside world?"

It was perfectly true, and I admit the point had not struck me. And yet in the bottom of my mind I still felt convinced that in the Australian lay the clue to everything, "and I said as much.

"Find that man, Inspector," I repeated, "and you've solved it. There are difficulties, I know, of which not the least is the telephone. Another is the fact that Gaunt is a powerful man: he'd have struggled like a tiger. And except for the blood there's no sign of a struggle."

"They may have tidied up after," put in Toby. "Hullo! what's the matter, constable?

The policeman, who, unnoticed by us, had left the room was standing in the door, obviously much shaken.

"This affair gets worse and worse, sir," he said to MacIver. "Will you just step over the passage here, and have a look in this room?"

We crowded after him into the room opposite – one which belonged to the corresponding suite to Robin's. Instantly the same faint smell became noticeable, but it was not that which riveted our attention. Lying on the floor was a man, and we could see at a glance that he was dead. He was a great big fellow, and his clothes bore witness to the most desperate struggle. His coat was torn, his waistcoat ripped open, and there was a dark purple bruise on his forehead. But in the strange rigidity of his limbs, and in the fixed staring eyes, he resembled exactly the unfortunate constable in the room opposite.

A foot or so away from his head was a broadish-brimmed hat, and MacIver turned it over with his foot. Then he bent down to examine it.

"I'm thinking, Mr Stockton," he remarked grimly, "that we've done what you wanted to do. We've found the Australian. That hat was made in Sydney."

He whistled softly under his breath.

"And that effectively knocks both our hypotheses out of court."

He made a sudden dart into the corner.

"Constable, give me those tongs. I guess I'm not touching anything I can avoid in this house tonight."

He took the tongs and lifted up what appeared to be an india-rubber glove. It was a sort of glazed white in colour, and was obviously new, since the elastic band which fitted round the wrist was quite clean, and there was no sign of scratches or dirt anywhere.

"Put this on the desk in the other room," said MacIver to the policeman. "And now we'll go over every single room in this house."

We did: we explored the attic and the basement, the sitting rooms and the scullery. And it was nearly three before we had finished. But not another thing did we discover: quite obviously everything that had happened had occurred in those two rooms. MacIver grew more and more morose and uncommunicative, and it was obvious that he was completely baffled. Small blame to him: the whole thing seemed like the figment of an incredible nightmare.

And even when Toby Sinclair put forward what seemed on the face of it to be a fairly plausible explanation he merely grunted and expressed no opinion.

"I'll bet you that that's what happened," Toby said, as, the search concluded, we stood once again in Robin's room. "The two of them were in here – Gaunt and the Australian – when they were surprised by someone. The Australian, whom we've suspected unjustly, fought like a tiger, and gained just sufficient time for Gaunt to get through on the telephone. Then they killed the Australian, and got at Gaunt. Don't ask me to explain the dog, for I can't."

It seemed plausible, as I say, and during the drive home behind our patiently waiting taxi-driver I could think of nothing better, We'd both been warned that our evidence would be required the following day, and the constable, reinforced by another, had been left in possession of the house.

"I believe you've hit it, Sinclair," I said, as the car turned into Clarges Street. "But what's worrying me is what has happened to that poor devil Gaunt."

He shrugged his shoulders.

"If I am right, Stockton," he answered gravely, "I'm thinking I wouldn't issue a policy on his life if I was in the insurance business. In fact, what I don't understand is why they didn't kill him then and there."

The car pulled up at the door of my rooms, and I gave the driver a fiver.

"You've been splendid," I said, "and I'm much obliged to you."

"Don't mention it, sir," he answered. "But I guess there's one thing you might like to know."

He pointed to a taxi which had just driven slowly past and was now turning into Curzon Street.

"It's empty; but that there car was down in Kensington all tonight, just about a 'undred yards along the road. You two gents have been followed." He handed me a slip of paper. "And that's the number of the car."

CHAPTER 2

In which I meet Hugh Drummond

I have purposely alluded at some length to that last conversation between Robin Gaunt and myself at Prince's. Apart altogether from the fact that he was my friend, it is only fair that his true character should be known. At the time, it may be remembered, there were all sorts of wild and malicious rumours going round about him. From being an absolutely unknown man as far as the general public was concerned, he attained the notoriety of a popular film star.

It was inevitable, of course: the whole affair was so bizarre and extraordinary that it captivated the popular fancy. And the most favourite explanation was the most unjust of all to Robin. It was that he was a cold-blooded scientist who had been experimenting on his own dog. A sort of super-vivisectionist: a monster without a heart, who had been interrupted in the middle of his abominable work by the Australian, whom he had murdered in a fit of rage; and then, a little alarmed at having killed a man as well as a dog and a guinea-pig, he had rung me up on the telephone as a blind, and fled.

Apart from ignoring the question of the blood, it was ridiculous to anyone who knew him, but there is no doubt that as an explanation of what had occurred it was the one that had most adherents. Certainly the possibility of Robin having killed the Australian – it transpired that he was one David Ganton, a wealthy man, who had been staying at the Ritz – was entertained for a considerable time. Until, in fact… But of that in due course.

I wish now to show how it was that theory started, and why it was that at the inquest I made no mention of the conversation I have recorded. For my lips were sealed by the interview which occurred the following morning. I was rung up on the telephone at eleven o'clock, and an unknown voice spoke from the other end.

"Is that Mr Stockton? It is Major Jackson speaking. I hope it won't be inconvenient for you to come round at once to the War Office in connection with the affair last night. Ask for G branch, Room 38. Instructions will be sent down, so you will have no delay at the door."

To Room 38, G Branch, I accordingly went, there to find four people already assembled. Seated at a desk was a tanned, keen-faced man who had soldier written all over him; whilst standing against the mantelpiece, smoking a cigarette, was a younger man, whom I recognised, as soon as he spoke, as the man who had rung me up. The other two consisted of Inspector MacIver and a thin-lipped man wearing pince-nez whose face seemed vaguely familiar.

"Mr Stockton?" Major Jackson stepped forward and shook hands. "This is General Darton" – he indicated the man at the desk – "and this is Sir John Dallas. Inspector MacIver I think you know."

That was why Sir John's face had seemed familiar. As soon as I heard the name I remembered having seen his photograph in a recent copy of the *Sphere*, as the author of an exhaustive book on toxicology.

Sit down, Mr Stockton," said the General, "and please smoke if you want to. You can guess, of course, the reason we have asked you to come round…"

"I told him, sir," put in Major Jackson.

"Good! Though I expect it was unnecessary. Now, Mr Stockton, we have heard from Inspector MacIver an account of last night and what you told him. But we think it would be more satisfactory if we could hear it from you first hand."

So once again I told them everything I knew. I recalled as far as possible, word for word, my conversation with Robin at dinner, and I noticed that the two officers glanced at one another significantly more than once. But they listened in silence, save for one interruption when I mentioned his notion of fighting indiscriminately against both sides.

It was the General who smiled at that and remarked that as an idea it had at any rate the merit of novelty.

Then I went on and outlined what had happened up till the arrival of the Inspector, paying, naturally, particular attention to the death of the constable. And it was at that point that Sir John spoke for the first time.

"Did you happen to see what part of the dog the constable touched? "he said.

"Roughly, I did, Sir John. He laid his hand on the dog's ribs just above the left shoulder."

He nodded as if satisfied.

"I thought as much. Now another thing. You saw this man die in front of your eyes. Did the manner of his death create any particular impression on your brain apart from its amazing suddenness?"

"It produced the impression that he had acute pain spreading from his fingers up his arm. The whole arm seemed to twist and writhe, and then he was dead."

And once again Sir John nodded as if satisfied.

"There is only one other point which I might mention," I concluded. "The Inspector can tell you everything that happened while he was there. As we got out of our taxi in Clarges Street, another car drove slowly by. And our driver told us that it was the same car that had been standing for hours about a hundred yards further down the road. It was empty, and this is the number." I handed the slip of paper to MacIver, who glanced at it and gave a short laugh. "It struck us both that we might have been followed."

"This car was found deserted in South Audley Street this morning," he said. "Its rightful owner was arrested for being hopelessly drunk in Peckham last night at about half-past nine. And he swears by all his gods that the only drink he'd had was one whisky-and-soda with a man who was a stranger to him. His car was standing in front of the pub at the time, and he remembers nothing more till he woke up in his cell with his boots off."

"That would seem to prove outside influence at work, Inspector," said the General.

"Maybe, sir," said MacIver cautiously. "Maybe not. Though it does point that way."

"But, good Heavens, General," I cried, "surely there can be no doubt about that. What other possible solution can there be?"

For a moment or two he drummed with his fingers on the desk.

"That brings us, Mr Stockton," he said gravely, "to the main reason which made us ask you to come round here this morning. We have decided to take you into our confidence, and rely upon your absolute discretion. I feel sure we can do that."

"Certainly, sir," I said.

"In the first place, then, you must know that the Army Council regard this as a most serious matter. There is no doubt whatever that Gaunt was a most brilliant man: his work during the war proved that. But, as you know yourself, the Armistice prevented any practical test. And there is a vast difference between theory and practice. However, with a man like that one is prepared to take a good deal on trust, and when he asked to be allowed to give us a demonstration today we granted his request at once. I may say that at the time of the Armistice there were still two points where his discovery failed. The first and lesser of the two lay in the stuff itself; the second and greater lay in the method of distributing it. In applying to us for his demonstration he claimed to have overcome both these difficulties.

"At the time when the war ended it was, as you can guess, a very closely guarded secret. Not more than four men knew anything about it. And then, the war over, and the necessity for its use no longer existing, the whole thing was rather pigeon-holed. In fact it was only the day before yesterday, on the receipt of Gaunt's request, that the matter was unearthed again. Naturally we imagined that it was still just as close a secret as ever. The events of last night prove that it cannot have been, unless my alternative theory should prove to be correct. And if that is so, Stockton, we are confronted with the unpleasant fact that someone is in possession of this very dangerous secret. Even in its Armistice stage the matter would be serious enough; but if Gaunt's claims are correct, words are inadequate to express the dangers of the situation. Now, as anyone who is in the slightest degree in touch with the European pulse today knows, we are living on the edge of a volcano. And nothing must be done to start an eruption. Nothing, you understand. All personal feelings must go to the wall. In a moment or two I shall ask Sir John to say a few words, and from him you will realise that the first and lesser of the two points has evidently been rectified by Gaunt. What of the second and greater one? Until we know that, nothing must even be hinted at in the papers as to the nature of the issues at stake. And that brings me to my point. When you give your evidence at the inquest, Stockton, I want you to obliterate from your mind the conversation you had with Gaunt last night. The whole force of Scotland Yard is being employed to try and clear this thing up, and secrecy is essential. And we therefore rely entirely on your discretion and that of your friend, Mr Sinclair."

"You can certainly rely on him, sir," I said, But what am I to say, then? I must give some explanation?"

"Precisely: you must give some explanation," he agreed. "But before I suggest to you what that explanation might be, I will ask Sir John to run over once more the conclusions be has arrived at."

"They are quite obvious," said the celebrated toxicologist. "As you may be aware, the vast majority of poisons must either be swallowed or injected to prove fatal. With the first class we are not concerned, but only with the second. In this second class the primary necessity is the introduction of the poison into a vein. You may have the bite of a snake, the use of a hypodermic syringe, or the prick of a poisoned dart – each of which causes a definite puncture in the skin through which the poison passes into a vein. And in each of those cases the puncture is caused mechanically – by the snake's fang, or the dart, as the case may be.

"Now there is another tiny class of poisons – it is really a subdivision of the second class – of which, frankly, we know very little. Some expert toxicologists are even inclined to dismiss them as legendary. I'm not sure that I myself didn't belong to their number until this morning. Evidence is in existence – but it is not reliable – of the use of these poisons by the Borgias, and by the Aztecs of Mexico. They were reputed to kill by mere external application, without the necessity of a puncture in the skin. They were supposed to generate some strange shattering force, which killed the victim by shock. Now that is absurd: no poison can kill unless it reacts point-blank on the heart. In other words, a puncture is necessary, and this class supplies its own punctures.

"You remember the policeman's last words – 'The dog is burning hot.' What he felt was a mass of small open blisters breaking out on his hand, through which the poison passed into his veins and up his arm to his heart. Had he touched the dog anywhere else nothing would have happened: as bad luck would have it he put his hand on the very spot where the poison had been applied to the dog.

"So much is clear. In all three cases that eruption of open blisters is there: in the dog above its shoulder, in the policeman on his hand, and in the case of the Australian on his right temple. And excepting in those places it is perfectly safe to touch the bodies.

"Now I was in that house at four o'clock this morning: the Inspector, very rightly, judged that time was an important factor and called me up. I took down with me several guinea-pigs, and I carried out a series of tests. I held a guinea-pig against the danger spot in each body, and the three guinea-pigs all died. I did the same an hour later. The one I put against the dog died: the one I put against the policeman's hand died, but the one I put on the Australian's forehead did not. It is possible that that means that the Australian was killed some time before the dog: on the other hand, it may merely prove that the dog's long coat retained the poison more effectively. Finally, I used three more guinea-pigs at six o'clock, and nothing happened to any of them.

"My conclusions, therefore, are as follows: and, needless to say, they concern only the poison itself and not what actually happened last night. Mr Gaunt has discovered a poison which, judging from the few tests I have carried out already, is unknown to science. It kills almost instantaneously when applied externally to the bare skin. Its effect lingers for some time, but only on the actual place on the body where it was applied. And after a lapse of seven or eight hours no further trace of it remains. As to the method of application I can give no positive opinion. One thing, however, is clear: the person using it would have to exercise the utmost caution. If it is fatal to his victim, it is equally fatal to the operator should it touch him. It is therefore probable that the glove found on the floor was worn by the man using the stuff. And I put forward as a possible opinion the idea of something in the nature of a garden syringe which could be used to throw a jet in any required direction."

He paused and glanced at the General.

"I think that that is all I've got to say, except that I propose to carry on with further experiments to see if I can isolate this poison. But I confess that I'm not hopeful. If I was able to obtain some of the liquid neat I should be more confident, but I can only try my best."

"Thank you very much, Sir John," answered the soldier. "Now, Stockton, you see the position. It seems pretty clear, as I said before, that Gaunt has solved one difficulty, by perfecting the stuff: has he solved the other as to the means of distribution? A syringe such as Sir John suggests may be deadly against an individual in a room: used by an army in the field anything of that sort would be useless; just as after the first surprise in the war, flammenwerfer were useless. Until we know that second point, therefore, the less said about this matter the better. And so we come to what you are going to say. It will be distasteful to you, for Gaunt was your friend, but it is your plain and obvious duty. We are faced with the necessity of inventing a plausible explanation, and the Inspector has suggested the following as filling the bill."

And then he put forward the theory to which I have already alluded. He admitted that he didn't believe in it himself: he went so far as to say that he wished to Heaven he could.

"It will, of course, be unnecessary and undesirable for you to advance this theory yourself," he concluded. "All that is required of you is that you should keep your mouth shut when it is advanced. Because the devil of it is, Stockton, that the signs of struggle on the Australian preclude any idea of accident and subsequent loss of head on the part of Gaunt."

For a time I sat in silence whilst they all stared at me. To deliberately allow one's pal to be branded as a murderer is not pleasant. But it was clear that there were bigger issues at stake than that, and at length I rose. What had to be, had to be.

"I quite understand, sir," I said. "And I will get in touch with Sinclair at once, and see that he says nothing."

"Good," said the General, holding out his hand. "I knew I could rely on you."

"Inquest tomorrow," put in MacIver. "I'll notify you as to time and place."

And with that I left and went in search of Toby Sinclair. I found him in his rooms consuming breakfast, whilst, seated in an easy chair with his feet on the mantelpiece, was a vast man whom I had never seen before. It was my first meeting with Drummond.

"Hullo! old man: take a pew," cried Toby, waving half an impaled sausage at a chair. "That little fellow sitting opposite you is Drummond. I think I mentioned him to you last night."

"Morning," said Drummond, uncoiling himself and standing up. We shook hands, and I wished we hadn't. "Hear you had some fun and games last night."

"I've been telling him, Stockton, about our little effort," said Sinclair, lighting a cigarette.

"Well, don't tell anyone else," I remarked. "I've just come from the War Office, and they're somewhat on the buzz. In fact, they regard the matter devilish seriously. It's bound to come out, of course, that a new and deadly form of poison was in action last night, but it's got to rest at that."

I ran briefly over what General Darton and Sir John had said, and they both listened without interruption. And though it did not strike me particularly at the time, one small fact made a subconscious impression on my mind which subsequent knowledge of Drummond was to confirm. As I say, they both listened without interruption, but Drummond listened without movement. From the moment I started speaking till I'd finished he sat motionless in his chair, with his eyes fixed on me, and I don't believe he even blinked.

"What do you think of it, Hugh?" said Sinclair, after I'd finished.

"This beer ain't fit to drink, Toby. That's what I think." He rose and strolled over to the window. "Absolutely not fit to drink."

"Very interesting," I remarked sarcastically. "The point is doubtless of paramount importance, but may I ask you to be good enough to promise me that what you've heard goes no farther. The matter is somewhat serious."

"The matter of this foul ale is a deuced sight more serious," he answered genially. "Toby, old lad, something will have to be done about it. In fact, something is going to be done about it now."

He strolled out of the room, and I looked at Sinclair in blank amazement.

"What on earth is the man up to?" I said angrily. "Does he think this thing is a jest?"

Toby Sinclair was looking a bit surprised himself. "You can never tell what old Hugh thinks," he began apologetically, only to break off as a loud squealing noise was heard on the stairs. And the next moment Drummond entered holding a small and very frightened man by the ear.

"Foul beer, Toby," he remarked. "Almost foul enough for this little lump of intelligence to be made to drink as a punishment. Now, rat face, what excuse have you got to offer for living?"

"You let me go," whined his prisoner, "or I'll 'ave the perlice on yer."

"I think not, little man," said Drummond quietly. "Anyway I'll chance it. Now who told you to watch this house?"

"I ain't watching it, governor: strite I ain't." His shifty eyes were darting this way and that, looking for a way of escape.

"I'm an honest man, I am, and – oh! Gawd, guv'nor, lemme go. You're breaking my arm."

"I asked you a question, you little swine," said Drummond. "And if you don't answer it, I will break your arm. And that thing you call a face as well. Now, who told you to watch this house?"

"A bloke wot I don't know," answered the man sullenly. " 'E promised me 'arf a quid if I did wot 'e told me."

"And what did he tell you to do?"

"Foller that there gent if he went out." He pointed at Sinclair with a grimy finger. "Foller 'im and mark down where 'e went to."

"And how were you to recognise me?" asked Toby.

" 'E showed me a photer, 'e did. A swell photer."

For a moment or two Sinclair stared at the man in amazement: then he crossed over to a writing-table in the corner.

"Well, I'm damned," he muttered, as he opened a big cardboard cover with a photographer's name printed on it. "I'll swear there were six here yesterday, and there are only five now. Was that the photograph he showed you?"

He held one up in front of the man.

That's it, governor: that's the very one."

"There is a certain atmosphere of rapidity about this," murmured Drummond, "that appeals to me."

He thoughtfully contemplated his captive.

"Where were you to report the result of what you found out?" he went on. "Where were you going to meet him, to get your half-quid?"

"Down at the Three Cows in Peckham, guv'nor: tonight at nine."

I gave a little exclamation, and Drummond glanced at me inquiringly.

"Not now," I said. "Afterwards," and he nodded.

31

"Listen here, little man," he remarked quietly. "Do you want to earn a fiver?"

"You bet yer life I do, sir," answered the other earnestly.

"Well, if you do exactly what I tell you to do, you shall. This gentleman whose photo you have seen is shortly going out. He is going to lunch at Hatchett's in Piccadilly. After lunch he will take a little walk in the Park, and after that he will return here. He will probably dine at the Berkeley. At nine o'clock tonight you will be in the Three Cows at Peckham, and you will report this gentleman's movements to the man who promised you half a quid. If you do that – exactly as I have told you – you can come back here tomorrow morning about this time and you'll get a fiver."

"You swear there ain't no catch, guv'nor?" said the other.

"I swear there's no catch," said Drummond quietly.

"Right, sir, I'll do it. Is that all you want with me now?"

"Yes: clear out. And don't make any mistake about what you've got to do."

"Trust me, sir."

He touched a finger to his forehead and dodged out of the room.

"A distinct air of rapidity," repeated Drummond thoughtfully. "I wonder if he'll do it."

"How did you know he was watching the house?" I asked curiously.

"It stuck out a yard," he answered. "He was on the pavement when I came here an hour ago, and he's not a Clarges Street type. What was it hit your fancy over the Three Cows?"

"The real driver of the taxi that followed us last night was drugged in a Peckham pub by a man he didn't know. Presumably it was the Three Cows."

"Then possibly we shall meet the man who followed you last night at nine o'clock this evening. Which will be one step up the ladder at any rate."

He picked up his hat and lit a cigarette. "By the way, what's the number of your house?"

"3–B. It's about ten doors down towards Piccadilly."

And suddenly he gave a grin of pure joy.

"Is it possible, my jovial bucks," he cried, "that once again we are on the war-path? That through the unpleasant object who has lately honoured us with his presence we shall be led to higher and worthier game? Anyway we can but baptise such a wonderful thought in a Martini or even two."

We followed him down the stairs, and Toby smiled as he saw the look on my face.

"It's all right, old man," he remarked. "He's always like this."

"And why not, forsooth?" boomed Drummond, waving his stick joyfully in the air. "Eat, drink and be merry... Don't you agree with me, sir?"

He stopped suddenly in front of a complete stranger, who stared at him in blank amazement.

"Who the devil are you, sir?" he spluttered.

"And what do you mean by speaking to me?"

"I liked your face," said Drummond calmly. "It's the sort of face that inspires confidence in canaries and white mice. Good-morning: sorry I can't ask you to lunch."

"But the man is mad," I murmured helplessly to Toby as we turned into Piccadilly.

"There is generally method therein," he answered, and Drummond smiled.

"He knows not our ways, Toby," he remarked. "But judging by appearances you're evidently the important one, Stockton. That one only stuck out a foot."

"Do you mean to say that that man you spoke to was on the look-out for me?" I stammered.

"What the dickens did you think he was doing? Growing water-cress on the pavement?"

He dismissed the matter with a wave of his hand. "Yes, Toby," he went on. "I have distinct hopes. Matters seem to me to be marching well. And if we adopt reasonable precautions this afternoon it seems to me that they may march even better this evening under the hospitable roof of the Three Cows."

He turned in to Hatchett's.

"We may as well conform to the first part of the programme at any rate. And over some oysters we'll discuss the first move."

"Which is?" I asked.

"How to get you two fellows to my house without your being followed. Because I feel that for any hope of success in the salubrious suburb of Peckham we must effect one or two changes in our personal appearance, and I have all the necessary wherewithal in Brook Street. Toby's little pal, I think, we can neglect: it's that other bloke who is after you that will want watching."

He gave a short laugh.

"Talk of the devil; here he is. Don't look round either of you, but he's taken a table near the door. Well, well: now the fun begins. He is ordering the *plat du jour* and a whisky-and-soda: moreover, he is adopting the somewhat unusual custom of paying in advance. Most thoughtful of him. It goes to my heart to think that his money will be wasted."

He signalled to the head waiter, who came at once.

Add this little lot to my account," said Drummond. "We've suddenly remembered we're supposed to be lunching in Hampstead. Now, you two – up the stairs: through Burlington Arcade, into a taxi and straight to Brook Street. I'll deal with this bloke."

Looking back on things now after the lapse of many months, one of the strangest things to me is the habit of unquestioning obedience to Drummond into which I dropped at once. If someone tells me to do a thing, my nature as a general rule impels me to do the exact reverse. In the Army I never took kindly to discipline. And yet when Drummond gave an order I never questioned, I never hesitated. I mention this fact merely to emphasise the peculiar influence he had on people with whom he came in contact, and the extraordinary personality which he tried to obscure by an air of fatuous nonsense. And though it took me some weeks to realise it, yet the fact remains that that first day I met him I did what he said with the same readiness as I did in days to come after I had grown to know him better.

And I remember another thing which struck me very forcibly that day. I stopped at the top of the stairs for a moment or two to see the fun. Drummond was half-way up when he dropped his stick. And in stooping to pick it up he completely blocked the gangway. Behind him, dancing furiously from side to side in his endeavours to pass, was the other man.

"Why, it's the man with the charming face," cried Drummond genially. "But I wish you wouldn't hop, laddie. It's so damned bad for the tum-tum."

I heard no more: Toby Sinclair, swearing vigorously under his breath, dragged me into Piccadilly.

"Confound you, Stockton, why the devil don't you do what you're told? I was half-way along Burlington Arcade before I realised you weren't there. You'd better take it here and now that if Hugh tells you to do a thing he means it to be done exactly as he said. And he said nothing about standing and watching him."

"Damn Drummond and everything connected with him," I said irritably. "Who is he anyway to give me orders?"

He laughed quietly as we got into the taxi.

"I'm sorry, old man," he said. "I was forgetting for the moment that you only met him for the first time today. You'll laugh yourself in a few days when you recall that remark of yours."

I did; but at the time I was peevish.

"If there's a man living in England today," he went on, "who is more capable than Hugh of finding out what happened last night I'd like to meet him."

And I smiled my incredulity. To tell the truth, the things that had happened since my return from the War Office had rather driven that interview from my mind. But now I had leisure to recall it, and the more I thought of it the less I liked it. It is all very well in theory to say that there are occasions when an individual must suffer for the good of the state, but in practice it is most unpleasant when that individual is your own particular friend. Your friend, too, who has called to you for help and whom you have failed. Mercifully Robin had neither kith nor kin, which eased my mind a certain amount: by allowing this false impression to be given at the inquest I was harming no one, except Robin himself. And if he was dead, sooner or later his body would be found, which would prove beyond a doubt that he was not the original culprit: whereas if he was alive the time would come when I should be able to explain. For all that, nothing could alter the fact that I disliked my role, and not the less because it was compulsory.

I said as much that afternoon as we sat in Drummond's study. He had come in about two hours after us, and he seemed a bit silent and thoughtful.

"You can't help it, Stockton," he said. "And probably Gaunt if he knew would be the first man to realise the necessity. It's not that that's worrying me." He rose and went to the window. "I'm thinking I've made a fool of myself. I don't see a sign of anyone: I haven't for the last hour – and I took Ted's car out of St James's Square, and have been all round London in it; but I'm afraid I've transferred attention to myself. There was just a second or two on the stairs at Hatchett's when our little lad of the genial face looked at me with the utmost suspicion."

He resumed his chair and stretched out his legs. "However, we can but chance it. It may lead to something."

"It's very good of you," I said a little doubtfully. "But I really don't know if – I mean, the police and all that, don't you know. They've got the thing in hand."

He gazed at me in genuine amazement.

"Good Lord! my dear man," he remarked, "if you want to leave the thing to old MacIver and Co., say the word. I mean it's your palaver, and I wouldn't butt in for the world. Or if you want to handle the thing yourself I'm away out from this moment. And you can have the free run of my various wardrobes if you want to go to Peckham tonight."

I couldn't help it: I burst out laughing.

"Frankly, it would never have dawned on me to go to Peckham tonight," I said. "Incidentally if it hadn't been for you I shouldn't have known anything about Peckham, for I should never have had the nerve to pull that little blighter into Toby's rooms even if I'd realised he was watching the house – which I shouldn't have. What I meant was that it seemed very good of you to worry over a thing like this – seeing that you don't even know Gaunt."

An expression of profound relief had replaced the amazement.

"By Jove! old man," he remarked, "you gave me a nasty fright then. What on earth does it matter if I know Gaunt or not? Opportunities of this sort are far too rare to stand on ceremony. What I was afraid of was that you might want to keep it all for yourself. And I can assure you that lots of amusing little shows I've had in the past have started much less promisingly than this. You get Toby to tell you about 'em while I go and rout out some togs for tonight."

"What an amazing bloke he is," I said as the door closed behind him. And Toby Sinclair smiled thoughtfully.

"In the words of the American philosopher, you have delivered yourself of a perfectly true mouthful. And now, if you take my advice, you'll get some sleep. For with Hugh on the warpath, and if we have any luck, you won't get much tonight."

He curled himself up in a chair, and in a few minutes be was fast asleep. But try as I would I could not follow his example. There was a sense of unreality about the whole thing: events seemed to be moving with that queer, jumbled incoherence that belongs to a dream. Robin's despairing cry: the policeman crashing to the floor like a bullock in a slaughterhouse: the dead Australian who had fought so fiercely. And against whom? Who was it who had come into that room the night before? What was happening there even as Robin got through to me on the phone?

And suddenly I seemed to see it all. The door was opening slowly, and Robin was staring at it. For a moment or two we watched it, and then I could bear the suspense no longer. I hurled myself forward, to find myself in the grip of a huge black bearded man with a yellow handkerchief knotted round his throat.

"You swine," I shouted, and then I looked round stupidly.

For the room had changed, and the noise of a passing taxi came from Brook Street.

"Three hours of the best," said the big man genially, and a nasty-looking little Jew clerk behind him laughed. "It's half-past seven, and time you altered your appearance."

"Good Lord!" I muttered with an attempt at a grin. "I'm awfully sorry: I must have been dreaming."

"It was a deuced agile dream," answered Drummond. "My right sock suspender is embedded about half-an-inch in my legs. Toby saw you coming and dodged."

He turned to the little Jew, who was lighting a cigarette.

"Make some cocktails, old man, while I rig up Stockton."

"Great Scott!" I said. "I'd never have known either of you."

"You won't know yourself in twenty minutes," answered Drummond. "You're going to be a mechanic with Communistic tendencies, and my third revolver."

CHAPTER 3

In which some excellent advice is followed

The Three Cows at Peckham proved an unprepossessing spot. It was a quarter to nine when we entered the public bar, and the place was crowded. The atmosphere reeked of tobacco-smoke and humanity, and in one corner stood one of those diabolical machines in which, for the price of one penny, a large metal disc rotates and delivers itself of an appalling noise.

Involuntarily I hesitated for a moment; then seeing that Drummond had elbowed his way to the bar and that Toby was standing behind him, I reluctantly followed. I really had half a mind to chuck up the whole thing: after all the police were already on the matter. What on earth was the use of this amateur dressing-up business?

"Three of four-'alf, please, Miss," said Drummond, plonking down a shilling on the counter. "Blest if you ain't got much thinner since I was last 'ere."

"Come off it," returned the sixteen-stone maiden tersely. "You ain't a blinking telegraph pole yourself. Three whiskies and splash, and a Guinness. All right! All right! I've only got two hands, ain't I?"

She turned away, and I stared round the place with an increasing feeling of disgust. Racing touts, loafers, riff-raff of all descriptions filled the room, and the hoarse hum of conversation, punctuated by the ceaseless popping of corks for the drinkers of

Bass, half deafened one. But of either of our friends of the morning there was no sign.

I took a sip out of the glass in front of me. Drummond was engaged with a horsy-looking gentleman spotting winners for next day; on my other side Toby Sinclair, in the intervals of dispassionately picking his teeth, was chaffing the sixteen-stoner's elderly companion. And I wondered if I appeared as completely at ease in my surroundings and as little noticeable as they did. A cigarette might help, I reflected, and I lit one. And a moment or two later Drummond turned round.

" 'Ear that," he remarked in a confidential whisper. "Strite from the stables. Why the devil don't you smoke a Corona Corona, you fool! Put out that Turk. And try and look a bit less like a countryman seeing London for the first time. Absolutely strite from the stables. Stargazer – for the two-thirty. 'E can't lose."

"Like to back yer fancy, Mister?" The horsy-looking gent leaned forward with a wink.

"What's that? I mean – er..." I broke off, completely bewildered. Mechanically I put out my cigarette. For Drummond's words had confused me. They both laughed.

" 'E ain't been long in London, 'ave yer, mate?" said Drummond. " 'E comes from up North somewhere. What this gentleman means is that if you'd like to 'ave five bob or 'alf a Bradbury on a 'orse for tomorrer 'e can arrange it for yer."

"And wot's more," said the horsy man, "I can give you the winner of the Derby. As sure as my name is Joe Bloggs I can give you the winner. You may not believe it, but I 'ad it direct from the stewards of the Jockey Club themselves. 'Bloggs,' they says to me, they says, 'it ain't everyone as we'd tell this to. But you're different; we knows you're a gentleman.' "

"Did they now?" said Drummond in an awed voice.

"But wot they said to me was this. 'We don't object to your a passing of it on, if you can find men wot you trust. But it ain't fair to give anyone this information for nothing. We don't want the money, but there are 'orspitals that do. The price to you, Bloggs, is one thick 'un; to be paid to the London 'Orspital.' So I said to 'em, I said – 'Done with you, your Graces; a thick 'un it is. And at 'ome, mates, now – locked up along with my marriage lines and the youngster's christening certificate is a receipt for one pound from the London 'Orspital. I shall taike it with me to Epsom, and it'll be a proud day for me if I can taike receipts for two more. It's yer chance, boys. Hand over a couple of Brads, and the hinformation is yours – hinformation which the King himself don't know!"

"I'll bet 'e doesn't," agreed Drummond. "It's a pleasure to 'ave met yer, Mr Bloggs. 'Ave another gargle? I guess me and my mate 'ere will come in on that little deal. Money for nothing, I calls it."

It was at that moment that I saw them enter the bar – the man who had been in Hatchett's, and another one. Of the squealing little specimen who had been dragged into Toby's room I saw no sign, but doubtless he would come later. However, the great point was that the others had arrived, and I glanced at Drummond to make sure he had noticed the fact.

To my amazement he was leaning over the bar calling for Mother to replenish his glass and that of his new friend. So I dug him in the ribs covertly, at the same time keeping a careful eye on the two new-comers. It was easy to watch them unperceived, as they were talking most earnestly together. And by the most extraordinary piece of good fortune they found a vacant place at the bar itself just beside the horsy man.

Again I dug Drummond in the ribs, and he looked at me knowingly.

"All right, mate, o' course we'll take it. But wot I was just wondering was whether, seeing as 'ow there are the two of us like, this gentleman wouldn't let us 'ave his hinformation for thirty bob. Yer see, guv'nor, it's this way. You tells me the name of the 'orse, and I pays you a quid. Wot's to prevent me passing it on to him for nothing, once I knows it?"

"The 'Orspital, mate. Them poor wasted 'uman beings wot looks to us for 'elp in their sufferings. As the Duke of Sussex said to me, 'Bloggs!' 'e said – ' old friend of my youth…' "

I could stand it no longer: I leant over and whispered in Drummond's ear – "Do you see who has just come in? Standing next this awful stiff."

He nodded portentously.

"I quite agree with you, mate. Excuse me one moment, Mr Bloggs."

He turned to me, and his expression never varied an iota.

"Laddie," be murmured wearily, "I saw them ten minutes ago. I felt London shake when you gave your little start of surprise on seeing them yourself. With pain and gloom I have watched you regarding them as a lion regards the keeper at feeding time at the Zoo. All that remains is for you to go up to them and let them know whom we are. Then we'll all sing 'Auld Lang Syne' and go home. Well, then, that's agreed. Seeing as 'ow it's for an 'orspital, Mr Bloggs, my mate 'ere says 'e'll spring a thick 'un."

"Good for both of yer," cried the tipster. "And you may take it from me, boys, that it's dirt cheap at the price."

"Come in 'ere between us, Mr Bloggs," said Drummond confidentially. "It wouldn't do for no one else to 'ear anything about it. We don't want no shortening of the odds."

"I sees you knows the game, mate," said the other appreciatively as they changed places, thereby bringing Drummond next to our quarry. "You're right: the Duke would never forgive me if we was to do that. 'Spread your money amongst all yer bookmakers, Joe, and keep them damned stiffs from bilking 'onest men like you and me,' – them were his very words."

"Wait a moment, mate," cried Drummond. "Mother – give me a pencil and a bit o' paper, will yer? I've got a shocking memory,

Mr Bloggs, and I'd like to 'ave this 'ere 'orse's name down in writing, seeing as 'ow I'm springing a quid for it. There it is, and now let's 'ear.'"

He produced a one-pound note which he laid on the bar, from which it disappeared, with a speed worthy of Maskelyne and Cook, into Mr Bloggs' pocket. And then the momentous secret was whispered in his ear.

"You don't say," said Drummond. "Well, I never did."

"And if yer gets on now yer gets on at 66 to 1," said the tipster triumphantly.

"Lumme! it's like stealing the cat's milk." Drummond seemed suddenly to be struck with an idea. "Why, blow my dickey, if I 'ain't been and forgotten young Isaac. 'E's careful with 'is money, Mr Bloggs, is Isaac – but for a cert like this 'e might spring a quid too. Isaac – 'ere."

"Whath the matter?" said Toby, glancing round.

"Do you want the winner of the Derby 'orserace, my boy? That's the matter."

"Go on," said Toby suspiciously. "I've heard that stuffh before."

"It's the goods this time, my boy," said Mr Bloggs impressively. "Strite from my old pal the Duke of Essex – I mean – er – Sussex – 'imself."

His back was turned to Drummond, and the movement of Drummond's face was almost imperceptible. But its meaning was clear: Toby was to accept the offer. And for the life of me, as I stood there feeling bored and puzzled, I couldn't make out the object of all this tomfoolery. This palpable fraud had served his purpose; what on earth was the use of losing another pound for no rhyme or reason? The two men behind Drummond were engrossed in conversation, and there was still no sign of the third.

For a moment or two I listened half mechanically to Toby bargaining for better terms, and then something drew my attention to a man seated by himself in a corner, he had a tankard of beer at his side, and his appearance was quite inconspicuous. He was a thick-set burly man, who might have been an engine-driver off duty or something of that sort. And yet he seemed to me to be studying the occupants of the bar in a curiously intent manner. At any ordinary time I probably shouldn't have noticed him; but then at any ordinary time I shouldn't have been in the Three Cows. And after a while I began to watch him covertly, until I grew convinced that my suspicions were correct. He was watching us. Once or twice I caught his eye fixed on me with an expression which left no doubt whatever in my mind that his presence there was not accidental. And though I immediately looked away, lest he should think I had noticed anything, I began to feel certain that he was another of the gang – possibly the very one we had come to find. Moreover, my certainty was increased by the fact that never once, as far as I could see, did the two men standing next to Drummond glance in his direction.

Drummond noticed nothing: he and Toby were still occupied in haggling with the Duke of Sussex's pal. And I couldn't help smiling slightly to myself as I realised the futility of all this ridiculous masquerade. However, I duly paid my pound, as I didn't want to let them down in their little game, and thought out one or two sarcastic phrases to put across at Drummond later. Though I had said nothing at the time I had not been amused by his remark about "Auld Lang Syne."

And then another idea dawned on me – why should I say anything about it? Though I would never have thought it, there was a certain amount of fun in this dressing-up game. And one thing seemed pretty obvious without any suggestion of self-conceit. If Drummond could succeed at it, I certainly could. An excellent fellow doubtless, and one possessed of great strength – but there it ended. And I even began to wonder if he really had spotted the arrival of the two men until I told him. It's easy to be wise after the event, and there is such a thing as jealousy. So I decided that I would have a shot at it myself the following evening. At the moment I was not very busy, and doubtless I'd be able to borrow my present disguise from Drummond. After all he'd offered to lend it to me whenever I wanted it, and even to give me the run of his wardrobe.

"Well, I'm off." It was Toby speaking, and with a nod that included all of us he slouched out of the bar, to be followed shortly afterwards by Mr Bloggs.

"Don't forget, mate," said that worthy to me earnestly as he put down his empty glass, "that it's the goods: 66 to 1 is the price today, so that if yer backs it each way you lands a matter of eighty quid, which is better than being 'it in the eye with a rotten hegg."

I agreed suitably with this profound philosophical fact, and omitted to tell him that I hadn't even heard the name of this fortune-maker, owing to slight deafness in the ear which I had presented to him.

"One of the lads," remarked Drummond, as the swing-doors closed behind Mr Bloggs and our three quid. "Another of the same, Mother, and a drop of port for yourself."

"Closing time," bellowed a raucous voice, and a general move towards the door took place. The two men next to Drummond finished their drinks, and then, still engrossed in conversation, went out into the street along with the rest, but he made no movement to follow them, which rather surprised me. In fact, he seemed to have completely lost all interest in them, and he stayed on chaffing the two women behind the bar until a general turning down of lights showed that it was closing time in earnest.

And since my principal interest lay in the thickset burly man, who was one of the last to leave, it suited me very well. In him I felt convinced lay the first clue to what we wanted, and when I saw a second man, whom I had not previously noticed, and who had been sitting in another corner of the bar, whisper something in his ear as he went out, it seemed proof positive. However, true to my decision, I said nothing about what I had discovered, and, smiling inwardly, I waited to hear what Drummond proposed to do.

"Not bad," he remarked in his normal voice, as we strolled towards the nearest Tube station. "Almost too good. In fact – I wonder."

"Whether the London Hospital will benefit to the extent of three pounds," I remarked sarcastically, and he laughed.

"He was one of mother's bright boys, wasn't he? It was a bit too blatant, Stockton. That's the trouble."

"As I'm afraid I didn't even catch the name of the horse I can't argue the point."

"The name of the horse was 10 Ashworth Gardens," he answered.

"What on earth do you mean?" I remarked, staring at him blankly.

"10 Ashworth Gardens," he repeated, "wherever that may be. Shortly we will get into a taxi and follow Toby there."

"I say, do you mind explaining?" I demanded. "Is that what that tout fellow told you?"

He laughed again, and hailed a passing taxi.

"Victoria Station, mate – Brighton Line. And 'op it. Now," he continued, as the man turned his car, "I will endeavour to elucidate. Just before Mr Joe Bloggs gave me a whisky shower-bath in the ear, and told me that my uncle's horse, which was scratched late this afternoon, was the winner, our two friends on my right mentioned that address. They mentioned it again when I changed my position and stood next to them. Now my experience is that people don't shout important addresses at one another in public – at least not people of that type. That's why I said that it struck me as being a little too blatant. However, it may have been that they thought they were perfectly safe, so that it's worth trying."

He put his head through the window.

"I've changed my mind, mate. I want to go to Hashworth Gardens. Know 'em?"

"Know my face," answered the other. "Of course I do. Up Euston way."

"Well, stop afore you get there, and me and my pal will walk."

"So that was what you wrote on the paper and showed Sinclair," I exclaimed as he resumed his seat.

"Bright lad," said Drummond, and relapsed into silence.

For a while I hesitated as to whether I should tell him of my suspicions, but I still felt a bit riled at what I regarded as his offhand manner. So I didn't, and we sat in silence till Piccadilly Circus and Shaftesbury Avenue were left behind us.

"Look here, Stockton," said Drummond suddenly, "this is your palaver principally, so you'd better decide. We're being followed."

He pointed at the little mirror in front of the driver.

"I rather expected we might be, and now I'm sure. So what do you propose to do? It's only fair to warn you that we may be putting our noses into a deliberate and carefully prepared trap."

"What would you do yourself if I wasn't here?" I remarked.

"Put my nose there, of course," he answered.

"Then mine goes too," I said.

"Good man," he cried. "You'll be one of the firm in no time."

"Tell me," I said, laughing, "do you do this sort of thing often? I mean in this case, for no rhyme or reason as far as I can see, you are running the risk of certain death."

"Oh! I dunno," he answered casually. "Probably not as bad as that. Might lead to a scrap or something of that sort, which helps to pass away the time. And, really, when you come to think of it, Stockton, this show was positively asking for it. When a man whose lunch you have spoilt literally bawls an address in your ear, it's not decent to disregard it. Incidentally, I wonder if little rat face will have the gall to come and demand his fiver tomorrow."

The car pulled up and the driver stuck his head round the door.

"Second on the left up that road," he said, and we watched his red tail lamp disappearing down the almost deserted street. At the far end just before a turn stood another stationary car, and Drummond gave a sudden little chuckle.

Our followers, unless I'm much mistaken. Let's get a move on, Stockton, and see what there is to be seen before they arrive."

He swung off down the turning, and at the corner of Ashworth Gardens a figure detached itself from the shadows. It was Toby Sinclair.

"Fourth house down on the left, Hugh," he said. "And there's something damned funny going on there. I haven't seen the sign of a soul, but there's the most extraordinary sort of sound coming from a room on the first floor. Just as if a sack was swinging against the blind."

It was an eerie sort of noise, such as you may hear sometimes in old houses in the country when the wind is blowing. Creak, shuffle, thud – creak, shuffle, thud, and every now and then a sort of drumming noise such as a man's heels might make against woodwork. For a while we stood listening, and once it seemed to me that the blind bulged outwards with the pressure of something behind it.

"My God! you fellows," said Drummond quietly, "that's no sack. I'm going in, trap or no trap; there's foul play inside that room."

Without a second's hesitation he walked up the steps and tried the front door. It was open, and Sinclair whistled under his breath.

"It is a trap, Hugh," he whispered.

"Stop here, both of you," he answered. "I'm going to see."

We stood there waiting in the hall, and I have no hesitation in confessing that the back of my scalp was beginning to prick uncomfortably. The silence was absolute: the noise had entirely ceased. Just once a stair creaked above us, and then very faintly we heard the sound of a door opening. Simultaneously the noise began again – thud, shuffle, creak – thud, shuffle, creak, and the next moment we heard Drummond's voice.

"Come up – both of you."

We dashed up the stairs, and into the room with the open door. At first I could hardly see in the faint light from a street lamp outside, and then things became clearer. I made out Drummond holding something in his arms by the window, and then Toby flashed on his torch.

"Cut the rope," said Drummond curtly. "I've freed him from the strain."

It was Toby who cut it: I just stood there feeling dazed and sick. For the sack was no sack, but our rat-faced man of the morning. He was hanging from a hook in the ceiling, and his face was glazed and purple, while his eyes stared horribly. His hands were lashed behind his back and a handkerchief had been thrust into his mouth.

"Lock the door," ordered Drummond, as he laid the poor devil down on the floor. "He's not quite dead, and I'm going to bring him round if every crook in London is in the house. Keep your guns handy and your ears skinned."

He unknotted the rope and pulled out the gag, and after ten minutes or so the breathing grew less stertorous and the face more normal in colour.

"Take a turn, Stockton," said Drummond at length. "Just ordinary artificial respiration. I want to explore a bit."

I knelt down beside the man on the floor and continued the necessary motions mechanically. It was obvious now that he was going to pull round, and if anything was going to be discovered I wanted to be in on the fun. Sinclair had lit a cracked incandescent light which hung from the middle of the ceiling, and by its light it was possible to examine the room. There was very little furniture: a drunken-looking horse-hair sofa, two or three chairs and a rickety table comprised the lot. But on one wall, not far from where I knelt, there was hanging a somewhat incongruous piece of stuff. Not that it was valuable, but it seemed to have no reason for its existence. It was the sort of thing one might put up to cover a mark on the wall, or behind a washstand to prevent splashing the paper – but why there? Someone upset the ink, perhaps: someone…

My artificial respiration ceased, and my mouth grew dry. For the bit of stuff was moving: it was being pushed aside, and something was appearing round the edge. Something that looked like a small-calibre revolver, and it was pointed straight at me. No, not a revolver: it was a small squirt or syringe, and behind it was a big white disc. Into my mind there flashed the words of Sir John Dallas only that morning – "Something in the nature of a garden syringe" – and with a great effort I forced myself to act. I rolled over towards the window, and what happened then is still more or less a blur in my mind. A thin jet of liquid shot through the air, and hit the carpet just behind where I'd been kneeling, and at the same moment there came the crack of a revolver, followed by a scream and a heavy fall. I looked up to see Drummond ejecting a spent cartridge, and then I scrambled to my feet.

"What the devil," I muttered stupidly.

"Follow it up," snapped Drummond, "and shoot on sight."

He was out in the passage like a flash, with Toby and I at his heels. The door of the next room was locked, but it lasted only one charge of Drummond's. And then for a moment or two we stood peering into the darkness – at least I did. The others did not, which is how one lives and learns.

I never heard them: I never even realised they had left me, and when two torches were flashed on from the other side of the room, I shrank back into the passage.

"Come in, man, come in," muttered Drummond. "Never stand in a doorway like that. Ah!"

He drew in his breath sharply as the beam of his torch picked up the thing on the floor. It was the man who had been in Hatchett's that morning, the man who had stood behind him at the Three Cows, and he was dead. The same terrible distortion and rigour was visible: the cause of death was obvious.

"Don't touch him, for Heaven's sake," I cried, as Drummond bent forward. "It's the same death as we saw last night?"

"And you were darned nearly the victim, old man," said Drummond grimly.

"By Jove! Hugh, it was a good shot," said Toby. "You hit the syringe itself, and the stuff splashed on his face. You can see the mark."

It was true: in the middle of his right cheek was an angry red circle, in which it was possible to see an eruption of tiny blisters. And the same strange, sweet smell hung heavily about the air.

On each hand was a white glove of the same type as the one we had found the previous night, and it was evidently that which had seemed to me like a white disc around the syringe.

"So things begin to move," said Drummond quietly. "The whole thing was a trap, as I thought. They evidently seem to want you pretty badly, Stockton."

"But why?" I asked angrily. "What the devil have I got to do with it?"

He shrugged his shoulders.

"They may think you know too much; that Gaunt told you things."

"But why hang that poor little toad in the next room?" said Toby.

"Ask me another," answered Drummond. "Possibly they found out we'd got at him, and they hanged him as a punishment for treachery: possibly to ensure our remaining here some time to bring him round. And incidentally – who hanged him? The occupants of the car that followed us couldn't have got to this house before we did, and he was triced up before Toby arrived here. That means there were people here before, and the occupants of that car have yet to arrive."

Suddenly his torch went out, and I felt his hand on my arm warningly.

"And unless I mistake," he whispered, "they've just come. Stick by me, Stockton: you're new to this game. Get to the window, Toby, and keep against the wall."

A half-breathed "Right" came from the darkness, and I felt myself led somewhere. Once the guiding hand drew me to the right, and I realised that I had just missed a chair. And then I felt the wall at my back, and a faint light coming round the blind showed the window close by. It was shut, and I could see the outline of Drummond's head as he peered through it.

What had caused his sudden action, I wondered? I hadn't heard a sound, and at that time I had yet to find out his almost uncanny gift of hearing. To me the house was in absolute silence; the only sound was the heavy pounding of my own heart. And then a stair creaked as it had creaked when Drummond left us in the hall.

I glanced at Drummond: his hand was feeling for the window-catch. With a little click it went back, and once more he crouched motionless. Again the stair creaked, and yet again, and I thought I heard men whispering outside the door. Suddenly with a crash that almost startled me out of my senses Drummond flung up the sash and the whispering ceased.

"Stand by to jump, when I give the word," muttered Drummond, "and then run like hell. There's about a dozen of 'em."

He was crouching below the level of the window-sill; dimly on his other side I could see Toby Sinclair. And then the whispering started again; men were coming into the room. There was a stifled curse as someone stumbled against a chair, and at that moment Drummond shouted "Jump."

Just for a second I almost obeyed him, for my leg was over the sill. And then I heard him fighting desperately in the room behind. He was covering our retreat, a thing which no man could allow.

There may have been a dozen in all: I know there were three of them on me. Chairs went over as we fought on in the dark, and all the time I was thinking of the liquid on the floor and the dead man's face and what would happen if we touched it. And as if in answer to my thoughts there came Drummond's voice.

"I have one of you here powerless," he said. "In this room is a dead man who died you know how. Unless my other two friends are allowed to go at once I will put this man's hand against the dead man's cheek. And that means death."

"Who is that speaking?" came another voice out of the darkness.

"Great Scott!" Drummond's gasp of surprise was obvious. "Is that you, MacIver?"

"Switch on the lights," returned the other voice angrily.

And there stood my burly thick-set man of the Three Cows.

"What is the meaning of this damned foolishness?" he snarled. He glared furiously at Drummond and then at me. "Why are you masquerading in that rig, Mr Stockton?" he went on suspiciously. And then his eyes fell on the dead man. "How did this happen?"

But Drummond sprawling in a chair was laughing helplessly.

"Rich," he remarked, "extremely rich. Not to say ripe and fruity, old friend of my youth. Sorry, Mac" – the detective was glowering at him furiously – "but my style of conversation has become infected by a gent with whom I dallied awhile earlier in the evening."

"I didn't recognise you at the Three Cows, Captain Drummond," said MacIver ominously.

"Nor I you," conceded Drummond. "Otherwise we'd have had a spot together."

"But I think it's only right to warn you that you're mixing yourself up in a very serious matter. Into Mr Stockton's conduct I propose to inquire later." Once again he looked at me suspiciously. "Just at the moment, however, I should like to know how this man died."

Drummond nodded and grew serious.

"Quite right, MacIver. We were in the next room – all three of us... Good Lord! I wonder what's happened to rat face. You see, an unfortunate little bloke had been hanged in the next room..."

"What?" shouted MacIver, darting out into the passage. We followed, crowding after him, only to stand in amazement at the door. The light was still burning; the rope still lay on the carpet, but of the man we had cut down from the ceiling there was no sign. He had absolutely disappeared.

"Well, I'm damned," muttered Drummond. "This beats cock-fighting. Wouldn't have missed it for a thousand. Look out! Don't go near that pool on the floor. That's some of the juice."

He stared round the room, and then he lit a cigarette.

"There's no good you looking at me like that, MacIver," he went on quietly. "There's the hook, my dear fellow; there's the rope. I'm not lying. We cut him down, and we laid him on the floor just there. He was nearly dead, but not quite. For ten minutes or so I put him through artificial respiration – then Mr Stockton took it on. And it was while he was doing it – kneeling down beside him – that that bit of curtain stuff moved. I'd be careful how you touch it; there may be some of that liquid on it."

He drew it back, covering his hand with the table-cloth.

"You see there's a hole in the wall communicating with the next room. Through that hole the man who is now lying dead next door let drive with his diabolical liquid at Mr Stockton. By the mercy of Allah he rolled over in time, and the stuff hit the carpet – you can see it there, that dark stain. So then it was my turn, and I let drive with my revolver."

"We heard a shot," said MacIver.

54

"That's his syringe, or whatever you like to call the implement," continued Drummond.

"And it obviously wasn't empty, for some of the contents splashed back in his face. The result you see in the next room, and I can't say I regret it."

"But this man whom you say was hanging? What on earth has become of him?"

"Search me," said Drummond. "The only conclusion I can come to is that he recovered after we had left the room, and decided to clear out. When all is said and done he can't have had an overpowering affection for the house, and he probably heard the shindy in the next room and did a bolt."

MacIver grunted: he was obviously in an extremely bad temper. And the presence of his large group of stolid subordinates, who were evidently waiting for orders in a situation that bewildered them, did not tend to soothe him.

"Go and search the house," he snapped. "Every room. And if you find anything suspicious, don't touch it, but call me."

He waited till they had all left the room; then he turned to Drummond.

"Now, sir," he said. "I want to get to the bottom of this. In the first place, what brought you to this house?"

"The bird in the next room shouted the address in my ear," returned Drummond, "that time we were having one at the Three Cows."

"Damn it," exploded MacIver, "what took you to the Three Cows? In disguise too."

"Just vulgar curiosity, Mac," said Drummond airily. "And we felt that our presence in evening clothes might excite rude comment."

"Your presence in that rig excites my comment," snapped the detective.

"Undoubtedly, old lad," said Drummond soothingly. "But there's no law against toddling round in fancy dress as far as I know, and you ought to be very grateful to us for bringing you here. We've presented you with a new specimen, in a better state of preservation than the others you've got. Moreover, he's the only one who deserved his fate. The fact of the matter, MacIver, is that we're up against some pretty unscrupulous swine. Their object tonight was to kill Mr Stockton, and they very nearly succeeded. Why they should view him with dislike is beyond me, but the fact remains that they do. They set a deliberate trap for us, and we walked into it with our eyes open. You followed on, and in the darkness everybody mistook everybody else."

The detective transferred his gaze to Toby Sinclair.

"You're Mr Sinclair, ain't you?"

"I am," returned Toby affably.

"I thought you were both of you told not to pass this matter on. How is it that Captain Drummond comes to know of it?"

"My fault entirely, Inspector," said Toby. "I'd already told him before Mr Stockton returned from the War Office this morning."

"So I thought I'd help you unofficially," murmured Drummond, "the same as I did at the time of the Black Gang."

MacIver's scowl grew positively ferocious.

"I don't want your help," he snarled. "And in future keep out of this matter or you'll find yourself in trouble."

"Well!" He swung round as some of his men came into the room.

"Nothing, sir. The house is empty."

"Then, since the hour is late, I think we'll leave you," remarked Drummond. "You know where to find me, Mac; and you'd better let me know what I'm to say about that bloke's death. From now on, I may say, we shall drop this, and concentrate exclusively on the breeding of white mice."

For a moment I thought MacIver was going to stop us; then apparently he thought better of it. He favoured us with a parting scowl, and with that we left him. By luck we found a taxi, and Drummond gave his own address.

"There are one or two things we might discuss," he said quietly, as we got into the car. "MacIver's arrival is an undoubted complication. I wonder how he spotted you, Stockton."

"That's what beats me," I remarked. "I spotted him – not as MacIver, of course – down at the Three Cows. He struck me as a suspicious character, so I kept my eye on him casually while you were talking to that racing tout."

"Oh! Lord!" Drummond began to laugh. "Then that accounts for it. The effect of your casual eye would make an archbishop feel he'd committed bigamy. It has a sledge-hammer action about it, old man, that would make a nun confess to murder."

"I'm very sorry," I said huffily. "But please remember that this sort of thing is quite new to me. And the practical result seems to be that we've got ourselves into a very nasty hole. Why – that confounded Inspector man suspects me."

"He doesn't really," said Drummond reassuringly. "He was merely as mad as thunder at having made an ass of himself."

And then he started laughing again.

"Poor old Mac! Do you remember when we laid him out to cool on his own doorstep, Toby?"

"I do," returned Sinclair. "And I further noticed that your allusion to the Black Gang was not popular. But, joking apart, Hugh – what's the next move?"

"It rests on a slender hope, old boy," said Drummond. "And even then it may lead to nothing. It rests on the reappearance of little rat face. Of course he may be able to tell us nothing: on the other hand, there must have been some reason for tricing him up. And that reason may throw some light on the situation."

"But are you really going on with it?" I asked. They both stared at me in amazement.

"Going on with it!" cried Drummond. "What a question, my dear man. Of course we are. Apart altogether from the fact that they're bound to have another shot at you, and probably at us too, there is all the makings of a really sporting show in this affair. Wash out MacIver's unfortunate entrance for the moment, and concentrate on the other aspects of the case. Evidently what I feared this afternoon was correct, and our friend at Hatchett's – now defunct – got on to us at Brook Street. He may have asked the head waiter whom I was – that's a detail. He follows us to the Three Cows; he lays a deliberate trap into which we fall – admittedly with our eyes open. The sole object of that plot is to kill you and possibly us. It fails, and somewhat stickily for the originator. But you don't imagine that we can allow the matter to rest there, do you? It wouldn't be decent."

"Still," I persisted, "it seems to me that we may be getting ourselves into hot water with the police if we go on."

Drummond laid his hand reassuringly on my knee.

"It's not the first time, old lad," he remarked. "Mac and I are really bosom friends. Still, if you feel doubtful, you can back out. Personally I propose to continue the good work."

"Oh! if you're going on I'm with you," I said, a little ungraciously. "Only please don't forget I'm reputed to be a lawyer."

"Magnificent," returned Drummond imperturbably. "We'll come to you for legal advice."

The car pulled up in front of his house and we got out.

"Come in and change," he went on, "and we'll have a nightcap."

I noticed that his eyes were searching the street. The hour was two, and as far as I could see it was deserted. And yet I couldn't help a distinct feeling of relief as the stout front door shut behind us. It gave one a feeling of safety and security which had been singularly lacking during the preceding part of the evening: no one could get at us there.

I lit one of my prohibited Turkish cigarettes, and as I did so I saw that Drummond was staring with curious intentness at a letter and a parcel that lay on the hall table. The parcel was about the size of a cigar box, and the label outside proclaimed that it came from Asprey's.

He led the way upstairs, carrying them both with him. And then having drawn himself some beer, and waved his hand at the cask in the corner for us to help ourselves, he slit the envelope open with a paper knife.

"I thought as much," he said after he had read the contents. "But how very crude; and how very untruthful. Though it shows they possess a confidence in their ability, which is not so far justified by results."

We looked over his shoulder at the typewritten slip he held in his hand. It ran as follows

Mr Stockton is dead because he knew too much: a traitor is dead because he was a traitor. Unless you stop at once, a fool will die because he was a fool.

"How crude," he repeated. "How very crude. I'm afraid our opponents are not very clever. They must have been going to the movies or something. It is rare to find three lies in such a short space. Toby, bring me a basin chock-full of water, will you? There's one in the bathroom."

His eyes were fixed on the parcel, and he was smiling grimly.

"To be certain of success is an admirable trait, Stockton," he murmured, "if you succeed. If, on the contrary, you fail, it is ill-advised to put your convictions on paper. Almost as ill-advised, in fact, as to send live-stock disguised as a cigarette case."

"What on earth do you mean?" I asked.

"Put your ear against that parcel and listen," he answered shortly.

And suddenly I heard it – a faint rustling, and then a gentle scraping noise.

"You're having an excellent blooding to this sort of game," he laughed. "In fact, I've rarely known events come crowding so thick and fast. But crude – oh! so crude, as I said before."

"Here you are, old man. Is there enough water?"

Toby had re-entered the room with the basin.

"Ample," answered Drummond, picking up the parcel and holding it under the surface. "Give me that paper-weight, Stockton, and then we can resume our beer."

Fascinated I watched the bubbles rise to the surface. At first they came slowly, then as the water permeated the wrappings they rose in a steady stream. And then clear and distinct there came a dreadful hissing noise, and the surface of the water became blurred with a faint tremor as if the box itself was shaking.

"A pleasant little pet," murmured Drummond, watching the basin with interest. "There's no doubt about it, you fellows, that the air of rapidity grows more and more marked."

At last the bubbles ceased; the whole parcel was water-logged.

"We'll give it five minutes," said Drummond, "before inspecting Asprey's latest."

We waited, I at any rate with ill-concealed impatience, till the time was up and Drummond took the parcel out of the water. He cut the string and removed the paper. Inside was a wooden box with holes drilled in it, and the water was draining out of it back into the basin.

With the paper-knife he prised open the lid, and even he gave a startled exclamation when he saw what was inside. Personally it filled me with a feeling of nausea, and I saw Toby Sinclair clutch the table.

It was a spider of sorts, but such a spider as I have never dreamed of in my wildest nightmares. Its body was the size of a hen's egg; its six legs the size of a crab's. And it was covered with coarse black hair. Even in death it looked the manifestation of all evil, with its great protruding eyes and short sharp jaws, and with a shudder I turned away.

"A jest I do not like," said Drummond quietly, tipping the corpse out into the basin. "Hullo! Another note."

He was staring at the bottom of the box, and there sure enough was an envelope. It was sodden with water, but the letter inside was legible. And for a while we stared at it uncomprehendingly.

This is to introduce William. If you decide to keep him, his favourite diet is one of small birds and mice. He is a married man, and since I hated to part him from his wife I have sent her along too. She is addressed to the most suitable person in the house to receive a lady.

As I say, for a moment or two we stared at the note uncomprehendingly, and then Drummond gave a sudden strangled grunt in his throat and dashed from the room.

"Phyllis," he flung at us hoarsely, from the door. "Good Lord! his wife," cried Toby, and with sick fear in our hearts we followed him.

"It's all right, darling," came his voice from above us, but there was no answer. And when we got to the open door and looked into the room the silence was not surprising.

Cowering in a corner, her eyes dilated with horror, there stood a girl. She was staring at something on the carpet – something that was hidden from us by the bed. Her lips were moving, but no sound came from them, and she never even lifted her eyes to look at her husband.

And I don't wonder. Even now, though eighteen months have passed, my skin still creeps as I recall that moment. If the dead thing below had been horrible, what words can I use for the living? As with many spiders, the female was larger than the male, and the thing which stood on its six great legs about a yard

61

from her feet looked the size of a puppy. It was squat and utterly loathsome, and as Drummond with the poker in his hand dashed towards it, it scuttled under the bed, hissing loudly.

It was I who caught Mrs Drummond as she pitched forward in a dead faint, and I held her whilst her husband went berserk. It was my first acquaintance with his amazing strength. He hurled heavy pieces of furniture about as if they were out of a doll's house. The two beds flew apart with a crash and the foul brute he was after sidled under a wardrobe. And then the wardrobe moved like Kipling's piano, save that there was only one man behind and not several.

But at last he had it, and with a grunt of rage he hit it with the poker between the beady staring eyes. He hit it again and again and then he turned round and stared at us.

"If ever I lay hands on the man who sent these brutes," he said quietly, "I will do the same to him."

He took his wife from me and picked her up in his arms.

"Let's go out of here before she comes to," he went on. "Poor kid; poor little kid!"

He carried her downstairs, and a few minutes later she opened her eyes. Stark horror still shone in them, and for a while she sobbed hysterically.

But at length she grew calmer, and disjointedly, with many pauses, she told us what had happened.

She'd come in from a dance, and seen the two boxes lying on the hall table. She'd taken hers upstairs, thinking it was a present from her husband. And she'd opened it at her dressing-table. And then she'd seen this awful monster staring at her. Her maid had gone to bed, and suddenly it had scrambled out of the box and flopped off the table on to the floor at her feet.

"I tried to scream, Hugh, and I couldn't. I think I was half mesmerised. I just rushed blindly away, and I went to the wrong corner. Instead of going to the door, I went to the other. And it followed me. And when I stopped it stopped."

She began to shudder uncontrollably; then she pulled herself together again.

"It just squatted there on the floor and its eyes seemed to grow bigger and bigger. And once I found myself bending right forward towards it, as if I was forced against my will. I think if it had touched me I should have gone mad. Who sent it, Hugh: who was the brute who sent it?"

"If ever I find that out," said Drummond grimly, "he will curse the day that he was born. But just now, darling, I want you to take some sleep dope and go to bed."

"I couldn't," she cried. "I couldn't sleep with a double dose."

"Right ho!" he answered. "Then stop down here and talk to us. By the way, you don't know Mr Stockton, do you? He's really quite good-looking when you see his real face."

"I'm afraid, Mrs Drummond," I said apologetically, "that I am indirectly responsible for those two brutes being sent to you tonight."

"Two," she cried. "Your parcel had one too?"

"Yes, my dear, it did," said Drummond. "Only I took the precaution of drowning mine before inspecting it."

"Look here, Hugh," cried his wife, "I know you're on the war-path again. Well, I tell you straight I can stand most things – you've already given me three goes of Peterson – but I can't stand spiders. If I get any more of them I shall sue for divorce."

Her husband grinned and she turned to me pathetically.

"You wouldn't believe what he's like, Mr Stockton, once he gets going."

"I can hazard a pretty shrewd guess," I returned. "We haven't exactly been at a Sunday School treat this evening."

"Life is real and life is earnest," chanted her husband. "And Stockton's becoming one of the boys, my pet. We've had a really first-class show tonight. I've got the winner of the Derby, if it hadn't been scratched a little tactlessly by old Uncle Bob. And

MacIver – you remember that shining light of Scotland Yard – has chased us all over London, and is very angry in consequence.

"And – oh! well, lots of other things. What's that you're grasping in your hand, Toby?"

"Another note, old boy. He's a literary gent, is our spider friend."

"Where did you find it?"

"In the box on Phyllis' dressing-table. And I don't think it will amuse you."

It did not.

A little nervy? Lost your temper? Well, well! They were quite harmless, both of them, though I admit Mary's claim to beauty must not be judged by ordinary standards. But let that be enough. I don't want meddlers. Next time I shall remove you without mercy. So cease being stupid.

"An amazingly poor judge of human nature," said Drummond softly. "Quite amazingly so. I wonder which of the two it was. I trust with all my heart that it was not our friend of Hatchett's and Ashworth Gardens. I should hate to think we would never meet again."

"But why won't you?" said his wife hopefully. "Well, we had a little game tonight, darling," answered Drummond. "And he has taken his own excellent advice. He has ceased being stupid."

CHAPTER 4

In which Hugh Drummond discovers a new aunt

And at this point I feel that I owe my readers an apology. In fact, Hugh Drummond, who has just read the last chapter, insists on it.

"What an appalling song and dance about nothing at all," is the tenor of his criticism. "My dear fellow, concentrate on the big thing."

Well, I admit that in comparison with what was to come it was nothing at all. And yet I don't know. After all, the first shell that bursts near one affects the individual more than a bombardment later on. And the events I have described constituted my first shell, so that on that score alone I crave indulgence.

But there is another reason too which, in my opinion, renders it impossible to concentrate only on the big thing. Had these words been penned at the time, much that I am writing now would have been dismissed in a few lines, simply because the position of certain episodes in the chain of events would not have been obvious. But now looking back, and armed with one's present knowledge, it is easy to see how they all fitted in; and how the two chains of events, the big one and the one that Drummond calls little, ran side by side till they finally met. And so I will give them both, merely remarking that if certain things appear obscure to the reader, they appeared even more obscure to us at the time.

We were confronted then, on the morning after our visit to the Three Cows, with the following position of affairs. The secret of a singularly deadly poison had been stolen, and in the process of the theft the inventor of the poison had disappeared, his dog had been killed, and the man who, according to his own story, had not only been his friend but had also been financing his experiments, had been murdered. The death of the constable was an extraneous matter, and therefore did not affect the position, save that it afforded proof, if further proof was needed, of the deadliness of the poison.

Sinclair and I, owing to the fact that we had come to Gaunt's rooms, had been followed; and, of the two of us, I was regarded as the more dangerous. So much the more dangerous, in fact, that my death had been deliberately decided on under circumstances which our enemies imagined did not admit of failure.

They had clearly added Drummond to our list, probably, as he surmised, owing to the incident at Hatchett's. And the fact that the head waiter knew him rendered his efforts to throw them off his track abortive. We were undoubtedly followed to the Three Cows, with the idea of inveigling us to Ashworth Gardens. MacIver was there simply and solely because he knew it was the pub in which the taxi-driver had been drugged the night before, and he hoped to pick up a thread to follow.

And there came our first query. Did MacIver recognise the two men, and did they recognise him? To the first of these questions we unhesitatingly answered – No. There was no reason that he should know them at all as far as we could see; and the fact that MacIver's worst suspicions were at once concentrated on me rendered it less probable that he would notice them. To the other question we again answered – No, but with less certainty. It didn't appear a very important one, anyway, but it struck us that it would be taking an unnecessary and dangerous risk on their part to carry on with their programme if they thought they were being watched. And human nature being what it is, they would, with their guilty conscience, if they had recognised MacIver, have assumed he was after them.

As far as we were concerned they didn't care – in fact, they wanted to be recognised. They wanted us to assume that they didn't know us – that our disguises were perfect. And so what more natural than that they should discuss things openly in our hearing? In fact, they had been very sure of themselves, had those two gentlemen.

All that was clear: it was over the subsequent events that there rested the fog of war. Why hang the poor little brute when obviously they had a supply of the poison? If they wished to kill him, that would have been a far surer and more efficacious method. And why the spiders?

We were holding a council of war, I remember, at which I met Peter Darrell and Algy Longworth for the first time, and we discussed those two points from every angle. And it was Drummond who stuck out for the simplest explanation.

"You're being too deep, old lads," he remarked. "The whole of this thing has been done with one idea, and one idea only – to frighten us. They think I'm a positive poop – a congenital whatnot. They intended to kill Stockton, whom they are afraid knows too much; and they intended to inspire in me a desire to hire two nurses and a bath-chair and trot up and down the front at Bournemouth. The mere fact that they have brought off a double event in the bloomer line doesn't alter the motive."

He rose and pressed the bell, and in a moment or two his butler entered.

"Did you take in those two parcels from Asprey's last night, Denny?"

"I did, sir."

"What time did they come?"

"About midnight, sir."

"Who brought 'em?"

"A man, sir."

"You blithering juggins, I didn't suppose it was a tame rhinoceros. What sort of a man?"

"Don't know that I noticed him particularly, sir. He just handed 'em in and said you'd understand."

Drummond dismissed him with a wave of his hand.

"No help there," he remarked. "Except as to time. Obviously they had everything prepared. As soon as they saw we were going to Ashworth Gardens, one of them came here, and the other followed us."

"Granted all that, old bean," said Toby. "But why hang rat face? that's what beats me."

Drummond lit a cigarette before replying.

"There's a far more interesting point than that," he remarked. "And I mentioned it last night. *Who* hanged him? There were people in that house before we got there: men don't hang themselves as a general rule. Those people left that house before we arrived there, just as the man who tried to murder Stockton got there after we arrived there. And on one thing I'll stake my hat: the latter gentleman did not come up the stairs, or I'd have heard him. If he didn't come up the stairs he entered by some unusual method: presumably the same as that by which the others left, or else Toby would have seen them. And houses with unusual entrances always interest me."

"There's generally a back door," said Algy Longworth.

"But only one staircase, laddie," returned Drummond. "And the man I killed did not come up that staircase. No: the old brain has seethed, and I'm open to a small bet that what they intended to do is clear. They meant to kill Stockton, and then they assumed that Toby and I would dash into the next room to catch the fellow who did it. Owing to the door being locked he would have time to get away. Then probably we should go for the police. And when we got back I'm wondering if we would have found either body there. On the other hand, we should have had to admit that we were masquerading in disguise, and doubts as to our sanity if nothing worse would be entertained. That, coupled with the spiders, they thought would put me off. Instead of that, however, he didn't kill Stockton and got killed himself. Moreover, the police came without our asking, and found a dead body."

"But look here, Hugh," interrupted Peter Darrell, "you said he'd have time to get away. How? The door is off, and if he'd jumped out of the window you could have followed him."

Drummond grinned placidly.

"The window was shut and bolted, Peter. That's why I think I shall return to Ashworth Gardens in the very near future."

"You mean to go back to the house?" I cried.

"No – not to Number 10," he answered. "I'm going to Number 12 – next door. And there's very little time to be lost."

He stood up and his eyes were glistening with anticipation.

"It's clear, boys: it must be. Either I'm a damned fool, or those blokes belong to the genus. If only old MacIver hadn't arrived last night we could have followed it through then. There must be a means of communication between the two houses, and in Number 12 we may find some amusement. Anyway it's worth trying. But, as I say, there's no time to be lost. They've brought the police down on themselves in a way that shows no traces of insanity on our part, and they'll change their quarters. In fact, I wouldn't be surprised if they've done so already."

"You aren't coming to the inquest?" said Toby.

Drummond shook his head.

"I haven't been warned to attend. And when it comes to the turn of our friend last night, doubtless MacIver will tell me what to say."

The door opened and Denny entered.

"Inspector MacIver would like to see you, sir."

"Show him up. Dash it all – that's a nuisance. It means more delay."

However, his smile was geniality itself as the detective entered.

"Good-morning, Inspector. Just in time for a spot of ale."

But our visitor was evidently in no mood for spots of ale.

"Look here, Captain Drummond," he said curtly, "have you been up to your fool tricks again?"

"Good Lord! what's happened now?" said Drummond, staring at him in surprise.

"The body of the man you killed last night has completely disappeared," answered MacIver, and Drummond whistled softly.

"The devil it has," he muttered. And then he began to laugh. "You don't imagine, do you, my dear fellow, that I've got it lying about in the bathroom here? But how did it happen?"

"If I knew that I shouldn't be here," snapped the Inspector, and then, with the spot of ale literally forced on him, he proceeded to tell all that he did know.

Three of his men had been left in the house, and owing to the smell from the poison they had none of them been in the room with the dead man. Also the window had been left open and the door locked. MacIver had left to ring up Sir John Dallas, but he was out of London. And when he finally got through to the house of a well-known scientist in Hampshire where Sir John was staying for the night, in order, as it transpired, to discuss the very matter of this poison, it was nearly five o'clock in the morning. And Sir John had decided that so much time had already elapsed that the chances of his being able to discover anything new were remote. So he had adhered to his original plan and come up by an early train, which the Inspector met at Waterloo. Together they went to 10 Ashworth Gardens, and MacIver unlocked the door. And the room was empty: the body had disappeared.

The three men who had been left behind all swore that they hadn't heard a sound. The front door had been locked all the night, and the men had patrolled the house at intervals.

" 'Pon my soul," cried MacIver, "this case is getting on my nerves. That house is like a cupboard at a conjuring show. Whatever you put inside disappears."

I glanced at Drummond, and I thought I detected a certain suppressed excitement in his manner. But there was no trace of it in his voice.

"It is possible, of course," he remarked, "that the man wasn't dead. He came to: found the door locked and escaped through the window."

MacIver nodded his head portentously.

"That point of view naturally suggests itself. And, taking everything into account, I am inclined to think that it must be the solution."

"You didn't think of finding out if the blokes next door heard anything?" said Drummond casually.

"My dear Captain Drummond!" MacIver smiled tolerantly. "Of course I made inquiries about the occupants of neighbouring houses."

"You did, did you?" said Drummond softly. "On one side is a clerk in Lloyd's with his wife and two children; on the other is an elderly maiden lady. She is an invalid, and, at the moment, has a doctor actually in the house."

"Which is in Number 12?" asked Drummond. "She is: her name is Miss Simpson. However, the point is this, Captain Drummond. There will now, of course, be no inquest as far as the affair of last night is concerned."

"Precisely," murmured Drummond. "That is the point, as you say."

"So there will be no necessity…"

"For us to concoct the same lie," said Drummond, smiling. "Just as well, old policeman, don't you think? It's really saved everyone a lot of bother."

MacIver frowned, and finished his beer.

"At the same time you must clearly understand that Scotland Yard will not tolerate any further activities on your part."

"From now on I collect butterflies," said Drummond gravely. "Have some more beer?"

"I thank you – no," said MacIver stiffly, and with a curt nod to us all he left the room.

"Poor old MacIver's boots are fuller of feet than usual this morning," laughed Drummond as the door closed. "He simply doesn't know which end up he is."

"A rum development that, Hugh," said Sinclair. "Think so, old man? I don't know. Once you've granted what I maintain – namely, that there's some means of communication between the two houses – I don't think it's at all rum. Just as MacIver said – the point is that there will be no inquest. Inquests mean notoriety: newspaper reporters, crowds of people standing outside the house staring at it. If I'm right that's the one thing that the occupants of Number 12 want to avoid."

"But dash it all, Hugh," cried Darrell, "you don't suggest that the invalid Miss Simpson – "

"To blazes with the invalid," said Drummond. "How do we know it's an invalid? They may have killed the old dear, for all we know, and buried her under the cucumber frame. Of course, that man was dead: I've never seen a deader. Well, dead bodies don't walk. Either he went out through the window, or he went into Number 12. The first would be an appalling risk, seeing it was broad daylight; in fact, without making the devil of a shindy it would be an impossibility. So that's where I get the bulge on MacIver. I can go into Number 12, and he can't without a warrant. That's so, isn't it, lawyer man?"

"He certainly can't enter the house without a warrant," I agreed. "But I don't see that you can go at all."

"My dear old lad," he answered, "I am Miss Simpson's long-lost nephew from Australia. If she is all that she pretends to be, I shall buy her some muscatel grapes, kiss her heartily on each cheek and fade gracefully away. But if she isn't..."

"Well," I said curiously. "If she isn't?"

"Then there will be two damned liars in the house, and that's always a sound strategical position if you're the lesser of them. So-long, boys. Tell me all about the inquest, and stand by for a show tonight."

He lounged out of the room, and I sat looking after him a little helplessly. His complete disregard for any normal methods of procedure, his absolute lack of any conventionality, nonplussed me. And yet I couldn't help admitting to myself that what he said was perfectly correct. If she was the genuine article he merely retired gracefully: if she wasn't, he held the whip hand, since the last thing the occupants of the house could do was to send for the police. And after a time I began to find myself hoping that she would prove to be an impostor, and that there would be another show tonight. It struck me as being more exciting than the legal profession...

But at this point, in order to keep to the sequence of events, I must digress for the moment and allude to the inquest. It was an affair of surpassing dullness, chiefly remarkable for the complete suppression of almost all the facts that mattered. I realised, of course, that it was part of the prearranged plan: though even I, knowing as I did that there is a definite understanding between the coroner and the police in all inquests where murder has occurred, was surprised at the result when compared to the facts.

But bald as that result was, the reporters got hold of it. The few central facts which concerned the death of the policeman and the finding of the dead bodies of the dog and the Australian had to come out. Also the disappearance of Robin Gaunt. (In fact, as anyone who cares to look up the account can see for himself, no mention occurred of the War Office or things military throughout the whole of the proceeding. I saw Major Jackson in the body of the court, but, since he was in mufti, he was indistinguishable from any ordinary spectator.)

I told of the cry over the telephone; and, in short, I told with the omissions I have mentioned the story I have already put down in these pages up to the moment when Inspector MacIver arrived. And Toby Sinclair confirmed it.

Then Sir John Dallas gave his evidence, which consisted of a series of statements of fact. The deaths had been due to an unknown poison administered externally: he was unable to say how it had been applied. He could give no opinion as to the nature of the poison, beyond saying that it punctured the skin and passed up an artery to the heart. He was continuing his experiments in the hopes of isolating it.

Then MacIver was called, and I must say that I admired the almost diabolical cunning with which he slurred over the truth, and advanced the theory that had been decided upon. He didn't say much, but the reporters seized it with avidity, and turned it from a weakly infant into a lusty child.

"No trace has been discovered of Mr Gaunt?" said the coroner.

"None," admitted MacIver.

Though naturally a full description had been circulated all over the country.

The verdict, as may be remembered, was "Wilful murder by some person or persons unknown" in the case of the Australian – David Gayton: and "Death by misadventure" in the case of the constable. And in the latter case expressions of sympathy were tendered to his widow.

"Well done, Stockton." Major Jackson and I went out of the court together.

"I suppose you know they had a shot at me last night," I said.

"The devil they did," he remarked, looking thoughtful. "Where?"

"It's too long a story to tell," I answered.

"Have you heard anything about the selling of the secret abroad?"

"Couldn't have yet," he said. "Of course, strictly between ourselves, we're on to it in every country that counts. But the devil of it all is that unless old Dallas can isolate this poison, the mere fact of finding out that some other Power has got the secret isn't going to help, because we can't make it ourselves. We've given him all the data we possess at the War House, but he says it isn't enough. He maintains, in fact, that if that formula represents the whole of Gaunt's discovery at the time of the Armistice, then it would have been a failure."

"Gaunt said he'd perfected it," I remarked.

"Quite," answered Jackson. "But, according to Dallas, it isn't merely a process of growth along existing lines, but the introduction of something completely new. I'm no chemist, so I can't say if the old boy is talking out of the back of his neck or not."

He hailed a passing taxi.

"It's serious, Stockton; deuced serious. Our only hope lies, as the General said yesterday, in the fact that the distribution question may defeat them. Because we've gone through every single available paper of Gaunt's, and that point doesn't appear anywhere. You see" – his voice dropped to a whisper – "aeroplanes are impracticable – they travel too fast, and they couldn't take up sufficient bulk. And a dirigible – well, you remember sausage balloons, don't you, falling in flames like manna from the heavens in France? One incendiary bullet – and finish. That's the point, but don't pass it on. Has he solved that? If so..."

With a shrug of his shoulders he left his sentence uncompleted, and I stood watching the car as it drove away towards Whitehall.

"Universal, instantaneous death."

Robin's words came back to me, and they continued to come back to me all through the day, when, for very shame's sake, I was making a pretence of work. They danced between my eyes and the brief in front of me, till in despair I gave up trying to concentrate on it.

"Universal, instantaneous death."

I lit a pipe and fell to reviewing the events of the past few days. And after a time the humour of the situation struck me. My elderly clerk, I felt, regarded me with displeasure: evidently he thought that a man of law displayed carelessness in getting mixed up in such a matter. As a set-off against that, however, I realised that I had seriously jeopardised Douglas Fairbanks in the office boy's estimation.

But the point I had to consider was my own future action. It was all very well for Hugh Drummond and a crowd of his irresponsible friends to go about committing breaches of the peace if they chose to: it was a very different matter for me. And Inspector MacIver had definitely told him that such activities were to cease. Yet, dash it all...

I took a pull at myself and lit another pipe. Undoubtedly it was folly on my part to continue. The police had it in hand: almost certainly I should be getting myself into trouble. Yes, I'd be firm: I'd point out exactly to Drummond and the others how matters stood: my reputation as a lawyer and the impossibility of my countenancing such irregularities. Besides, this brief...

And at that stage of my deliberations I heard a loud and well-known voice in the office outside.

"Is Mr Stockton in? I can't help it if he is busy. I've just killed my grandmother and I want his advice."

I went to the door and opened it. Drummond stood there beaming cheerfully at my outraged clerk, and as soon as he saw me he waved his hand.

"Bolted the badger," he cried. "My boy, I must have words with you. Yonder stout-hearted lad says you're busy."

"A brief," I said a little doubtfully, "which I ought to get on with. However, come in."

"Blow your old brief," he answered. "Give the poor girl custody of the children and be done with it."

He sat down and put his legs on the desk, whilst I, with a glance at my clerk's face of scandalised horror, hurriedly shut the door.

"Look here, Stockton," said Drummond, lowering his voice. "I thought I'd rout you out here, because it was a bit too long to say over the telephone. And since you're really the principal in this affair, you ought to know at once. To start at the end of the matter, I haven't the faintest doubt in my own mind now that my suspicions about Number 12 are correct."

He lit a cigarette and I felt my determination weakening. At any rate I wasn't committed to anything by hearing what he had to say.

"As you know," he continued, "I went up to see my long-lost aunt – Miss Simpson. I put on a slouch hat, and made one or two slight alterations in my appearance. The first thing I did was to call at one or two of the local food shops, and at the greengrocer's who supplied the house. I discovered her name was Amelia. Apparently she sometimes paid by cheque – in fact, they'd had one only last week."

"Well, that was a bit of a jolt to start off with: however, I thought I'd have a shot at it since I'd got so far. So off I strolled to Number 12. Two of the most obvious policemen I've ever seen in my life are watching Number 10, but they paid no attention to me as I went past.

"I rang the bell, and for some time nothing happened. And then a curtain in the room next to the front door moved slightly. I was being inspected, so I rang again to show there was no ill-feeling. An unpleasant-looking female opened the door about four inches, and regarded me balefully.

" 'Good-morning,' I remarked, getting my foot wedged in that four inches. 'I've come to see Aunt Amelia.'

" 'Who are you?' she said suspiciously.

" 'Aunt Amelia's nephew,' I answered. 'It's ten years now since my father – that's her brother Harry – died, and his last words to me were, "Wallie, my boy, if ever you go back to England, you look up sister Amelia." '

"You see, Stockton, I'd already decided that if it was a genuine show I'd get out of it by pretending that it must be another Miss Simpson.

" 'Miss Amelia's ill,' said the woman angrily.

" 'Too bad,' I said. 'I reckon that seeing me will be just the thing to cheer her up.'

" 'She's not seeing anyone, I tell you,' she went on. 'She'll see little Wallie,' I said. 'Why, according to my father, she was clean gone on me when I was a child. Used to give me my bath, and doses of dill-water. Fair potty about me was Aunt Amelia. Besides, I've got a little memento for her that my father gave me to hand over to her.'

"As a matter of fact I'd bought a small pearl necklace on the way up.

" 'I tell you she can't see you,' snapped the woman. 'She's ill. You come back next week and she may be better.'

"Well, there was nothing for it: I leaned against the door and the door opened. And I tell you, Stockton, I got the shock of my life. Standing at the foot of the stairs was a man with the most staggering face I've ever thought of. Tufts of hair sprouted from it like whin bushes on a seaside links: he was the King Emperor of Beavers. But it wasn't that that stopped me in my tracks, it was the look of diabolical fury in his eyes. He came towards me – and he was a heavy-weight all right – with a pair of great black hairy fists clenched at his sides. And what he resembled most was a dressed-up gorilla.

" 'What the devil do you want?' he snarled at me from the range of about a foot.

" 'Aunt Amelia,' I said, staring him in the eyes. 'And I reckon you're not the lady in question.'

"I saw the veins beginning to swell in his neck, and the part of his face not covered with vegetation turned a rich magenta.

" 'You infernal puppy,' he shouted. 'Didn't you hear that Miss Simpson was ill?'

" 'The fact is hardly to be wondered at with you about the house,' I retorted, getting ready, I don't mind telling you, Stockton, for the father and mother of scraps.

"But he didn't hit me: he made a desperate effort and controlled himself.

" 'I am Miss Simpson's doctor,' he said, 'and I will tell her of your visit. If you leave your address I will see that you are communicated with as soon as she is fit to receive visitors.'

"Now that told one beyond dispute that there was something wrong. If he really had been the old lady's doctor: if she really was ill upstairs, my intentionally insulting remark could only have been received as vulgar and gratuitous impertinence. So I thought I'd try another.

" 'If this is a sample of your bedside manner,' I said, 'she won't be fit to receive visitors for several years.'

"And once again I thought he was going to hit me, but he didn't.

" 'If you come back tomorrow morning at this hour,' he remarked, 'I think your aunt may be fit to receive you. At the moment I fear I must forbid it.'

"Well, I did some pretty rapid thinking. In the first place I knew the man was lying: he probably wasn't a doctor at all. No man with a face like that could be a doctor: all his patients would have died of shock. In the second place I'd had a fleeting glimpse out of the corner of my eye of a couple of men upstairs who were examining me through a mirror hanging on the wall – a mirror obviously placed for that very purpose with regard to visitors.

"And another thing stuck out a yard: throughout the whole of our conversation he had kept between me and the stairs. Of course it might have been accidental: on the other hand, it might not. The way it struck me, however, was that he was afraid, seeing that I was obviously a breezy customer, that I might make a dash for it. And I damned nearly did, Stockton – damned nearly.

"However, not quite. I'd seen two men upstairs and there might be more: moreover, the bird I was talking to – if he was as strong as he looked – would have been an ugly customer by himself. And even if I'd got to the top and been able to explore the rooms, it wouldn't have done much good. I couldn't have tackled the show single handed.

"So I pulled myself together, and did my best to appear convinced.

" 'Well, I'm real sorry Aunt Amelia's so sick,' I said. 'And I'll come round tomorrow as you say, Doctor. Just give her my love, will you, and on my way back I'll call in and tell 'em to send along some grapes.'

"His mouth cracked in what I presume was a genial smile.

" 'That is very good of you,' he answered. 'I feel sure Miss Simpson will appreciate your kind attention.'

"And with that I hopped it, sent up some grapes, and that's that."

He lit a cigarette and stared at me with a smile. "But didn't you tell the police?" I cried excitedly.

"Tell 'em what?" he answered.

"Why, that there's foul play going on there," I almost shouted.

"Steady, old man," he said quietly. "Your lad outside will die of a rush of blood to the head if he hears you."

"No, but look here, Drummond," I said, lowering my voice, "you may have hit on the key of the whole affair."

"I think it's more than probable that I have," he answered calmly. "But that seems to me to be quite an unnecessary reason to go trotting off to the police."

"But I say, old man," I began feebly, mindful of my previous resolutions. And then the darned fellow grinned at me in that lazy way of his, and I laughed.

"What do you propose to do? "I said at length.

"Anticipate the visit to Aunt Amelia by some nine or ten hours, and go there tonight. Are you on?"

"Confound you," I said, "of course I am."

"Good fellow," he cried. "I knew you'd do it." He took his feet off the desk and leaned towards me.

"Stockton," he said quietly, "we're hot on the track. I know we are. Whether or not we shall find that unfortunate old lady upstairs I haven't a notion. True she signed a cheque quite recently, but there's such a thing in this world as forgery. And murder. What induced them to select that particular house and her I know not. But one thing I do know. Tonight is going to be a pretty stiff show. Be round in Brook Street at eight o'clock."

CHAPTER 5

In which we pay the aunt an informal visit

I was there to the minute. For a while after Drummond had gone, I told myself that I would have nothing more to do with the business, but it was a feeble struggle. The excitement of the thing had got hold of me, and poor old Stevens – my clerk – had never seemed so intolerably prosy and longwinded.

"Splendid," said Drummond as I walked in. "That completes us. Stockton, this is Ted Jerningham, a lad of repulsive morals but distinctly quick on the uptake."

He brought our numbers up to six, and when I look back now and think of the odds against which, in all ignorance, we were pitting ourselves I could almost laugh. And yet I know one thing. Even had Drummond realised what those odds were, it would not have made an iota of difference to him. With him it was always a question of the more the merrier.

"We will now run over the plan of operations," he went on, when I had removed two dogs from a chair and sat down. "I've told these birds what I told you this afternoon, Stockton, so it only remains to discuss tonight. In the first place we've had a stroke of luck which is a good omen. The street running parallel to Ashworth Gardens is called Jersey Street. And the back of Number 13 Jersey Street looks on to the back of 12 Ashworth Gardens. Moreover, the female who owns Number 13 Jersey Street lets rooms, and I have taken those rooms. In fact, I've taken the whole bally house for a week – rent paid in advance – for a party of divinity students who have come up to this maelstrom of vice to see the Mint and Madame Tussaud's and generally be inconceivably naughty.

"Separating the backs of the houses are two brown patches of mud with a low wall in the middle which a child of four could climb with ease. And since there is no moon tonight, there oughtn't to be much difficulty in getting over that wall unseen – should the necessity arise.

"And since the spectacle of four of you dashing down the stairs and out of the old girl's back door might rouse unworthy suspicions in her breast, I have stipulated that we must have the use of a ground floor sitting-room at the back of the house. She doesn't usually let it, but I assured her that the wild distractions of Jersey Street would seriously interfere with our meditations."

"Four?" interrupted Jerningham. "Why four?"

"I'm coming to that," said Drummond. "I want someone with me in Number 12. And since the sport will probably be there, I think it's only fair to let Stockton have it, as this is really his show."

A chorus of assent greeted his remark, and for the life of me I couldn't help laughing. I had formed a mental picture of Drummond's pal of the afternoon with the whin bushes sprouting from his face, and I could see him being my portion for the evening. But the whole tone of the meeting was one of the most serious gravity: it might have been a discussion before a shoot when the principal guest was being given the best position. So I suppressed the laugh and accepted with becoming gratitude.

"Right," said Drummond. "Then that's settled. Now to the next point."

He picked up from his desk a cowl-shaped black mask, and regarded it reminiscently.

"Lucky I kept a few of these: do you remember 'em, you fellows? Stockton wouldn't, of course."

He turned to me.

"Years ago we had an amusing little show rounding up Communists and other unwashed people of that type. We called ourselves the Black Gang, and it was a great sport while it lasted."

"Good Heavens!" I said, staring at him. "I dimly remember reading something about it in the papers. I thought the whole thing was a hoax."

They all laughed.

"That's when we chloroformed your pal MacIver and left him to cool on his own doorstep. Happy days, laddie: happy days. However, taking everything into account, the going at the moment might be worse. And it struck me that these things might come in handy tonight. If we wear our old black gauntlets, and these masks well tucked in round the collar, it will afford us some protection if they start any monkey tricks with that filthy juice of theirs. At any rate there is no harm in having them with us in case of accidents: they don't take up much room and we can easily slip them into our pockets. So it all boils down to this. Stockton and I will deposit you four in Jersey Street, where you will take up a firm position in the back sitting room. Bearing in mind that you are destined for the Church, and the penchant of landladies for keyholes, you will refrain from your usual conversation. Under no circumstances is Toby to tell any of his stories, nor is Ruff's Guide to be placed in a prominent position on the table when she brings you in your warm milk at ten. Rather should there be an attitude of devotion: possibly a note-book or two in which you are entering up your impressions of the Wallace Collection – "

A struggling mass of men at length grew quiescent in a corner, with Drummond underneath.

"It takes five of us to do it," panted Darrell to me. "And last time the chandelier in the room below fell on Denny's head."

84

"That being quite clear," pursued Drummond from his place on the floor, "we will pass on. Should you hear shouts as of men in pain from the house opposite; or should you, on glancing through the crack of the blind, see me signalling you will abandon your attitude of devotion and leg it like hell over the wall. Because we may want you damned quick. Wear your masks: Ted to be in 'charge', and I leave it to you as to what to do once you arrive in Number 12."

"And if we neither hear nor see anything?" asked Jerningham. "How long are we to give you?"

They had resumed their normal positions, and Drummond thoughtfully lit a cigarette.

"I think, old boy," he remarked, "that half-an-hour should be long enough. In fact," he added, rubbing his hands together in anticipation, "I'm not at all certain it won't be twenty-nine minutes too long. Let's get on with it."

We pocketed our masks and gauntlets and went downstairs. There was no turning back for me now: I was definitely committed to go through with it. But I have no hesitation in admitting that our taxi-drive seemed to me the shortest on record. We had two cars, and Drummond stopped them several hundred yards short of our objective. Then leading the way with me we walked in pairs to Jersey Street.

Number 13 was typical of all the houses in the neighbourhood – an ordinary drab London lodging house of the cheaper type. But the landlady, when she finally emerged, was affability itself. The strong odour of gin that emerged with her showed that the rent had not been wasted, and led us to hope that sleep would shortly overcome her. At the moment it had merely made her thoroughly garrulous, and only the timely advent of an acute attack of hiccoughs stemmed the reminiscences of her girlhood's happy days. But at last she went, and instantly Drummond was at the window peering through a chink in the blind.

"Lower the light, someone, and then come and reconnoitre. There's the house facing you: there's the wall. No lights: I wonder if the birds have flown. No, by Jove! I saw a gleam then from that upstairs window. There it is again."

Sure enough a light was showing in one of the rooms, and I thought I saw a shadow move across the blind. Downstairs all was dark, and after a few moments' inspection Drummond stepped back into the room.

"Come on, Stockton," he said. "We'll go round by the front door. Don't forget I'm an Australian, and you're a pal of mine whom I met unexpectedly in London today. And if I pretend to be a little blotto – pugnaciously so – back me up. Ted – half-an-hour; but keep your eye glued on the house in case we want you sooner."

"Right ho! old man. Good luck."

We walked through the hall cautiously, but the door leading to our landlady's quarters was shut. And in three minutes we were striding down Ashworth Gardens. A figure detached itself from the shadows outside the scene of last night's adventure, and glanced at us suspiciously. But Drummond was talking loudly as we passed him of his voyage home, and the man made no effort to detain us.

"One of MacIver's men," he muttered to me as we turned into Number 12. "Now, old man, we're for it. If I can I'm going to walk straight in."

But the front door was bolted, and perforce we had to ring. Once more he started talking in the aggressive way of a man who has had something to drink, and I noticed that the detective was listening.

"I tell you my Aunt Amelia will just be charmed to see you, boy. Any pal of mine is a pal of hers. And I haven't come twelve thousand miles to be told that my father's sister isn't well enough to see Wallie. No, sir – I have not."

The door suddenly opened and a man stood there looking at us angrily.

"What do you want?" he snapped. "Are you aware, sir, that there is an invalid in this house?"

"I'm perfectly well aware of it," said Drummond loudly. "But what I'm not aware of – and what I'm going to be aware of – is how that invalid, who is my aunt, is being treated. I'm not satisfied with the attention she is receiving" – out of the corner, of my eyes I saw the detective drawing closer – "not at all satisfied. And I and my friend here are not going to leave this house until Aunt Amelia tells me that she's being well looked after. There's such a thing as the police, sir, I tell you..."

"What on earth are you talking about?" said the man savagely, and I noticed he was looking over our shoulders at the detective, who was now listening openly. "However, you'd better come inside, and I'll consult the doctor in charge."

He closed the door behind us, and Drummond gave me an imperceptible wink. Then he went on again aggressively: "How many doctors are there in this house? I saw a man this afternoon with a face like a hearthrug – is he here? And do you all live here? I tell you I'm not satisfied. And until I see my Aunt Amelia..."

A door opened and the man whom Drummond had described to me in my office came out into the hall.

"How dare you return here, sir?" he shouted. "You're the insolent, interfering young swine who was here this afternoon, and if you aren't out of this house in two seconds I'll throw you out."

"You'd better try," answered Drummond calmly. "And why don't you let your face out as a grouse moor? I'm your patient's nephew and I want to know what all you ugly-looking swabs are doing in this house?"

With a quick movement he stepped past the man into the room beyond, and I followed him. Three other men were there sitting round a table, and they rose as we entered. Two packed suit-cases lay on the floor waiting to be strapped up, and on the table were five glasses and a half-empty bottle of whisky.

"Five of you," continued Drummond. "I suppose you'll be telling me next that my aunt runs a boys' school. Now then, face fungus, what the hell does it mean?"

"It means that if you continue to make such a row your aunt's death will probably be at your door," answered the other.

"I noticed that you were whispering yourself in the hall," said Drummond. "You're a liar, and a damned bad liar at that. You aren't doctors, any of you."

The men were glancing at one another uneasily, and suddenly the whole beauty of the situation flashed on me. They knew as well as we did that there was a Scotland Yard man outside the house, and the fact was completely tying their hands. Whatever they may have suspected concerning Drummond's alleged relationship, we were, as he had himself remarked, in the sound strategical position of being the lesser liars of the two. Our opponents could do nothing, and the fact that they were utterly nonplussed showed on their faces. And I waited with interest to see what their next move would be. What answer were they going to make to Drummond's definite charge that they were none of them doctors?

They were saved the trouble, and in, to me at any rate, the most unexpected way. In my own mind I was firmly convinced by this time that there was no Miss Simpson, and that even if there was she was no sickly invalid ailing in bed. And yet at that moment there came a weak querulous woman's voice from the landing upstairs.

"Doctor Helias! Doctor Helias, I've been woken up again just as I was going off to sleep. Who is it making that terrible noise downstairs?"

The black-haired man swung round on Drummond.

"Now are you satisfied?" he said savagely. "And if my patient has a relapse and dies, by Heavens! I'll make it hot for you at the inquest."

He strode to the door, and we heard him speaking from the foot of the stairs.

"It's the nephew I told you about, Miss Simpson, who called to see you this afternoon. He seems to be afraid you aren't being properly looked after. Now I must insist on your going back to bed at once."

He went up the stairs, and I glanced at Drummond. His eyes had narrowed as if he too was puzzled, and he told me afterwards that a woman's voice was the last thing he expected to hear. But his voice was perfectly casual as he addressed the room at large.

"Dangerous place London must be. Do you – er – doctors always carry revolvers with you?"

"What the devil are you talking about?" snapped the man who had let us in.

Without a word Drummond pointed to one of the suit-cases, where the butt of an automatic Colt was plainly visible.

"I suppose when your surgical skill fails you merely shoot your patients," went on Drummond affably. "Very kind and merciful of you, I call it."

"Look here," said the other grimly, "we've had about enough of you, young man. You've forced your way into this house: you've insulted us repeatedly, and I'm thinking it's about time you went."

"Are you?" said Drummond. "Then you'd better think all over again."

"Do you mean to say that now you've heard what your aunt has said to Doctor Helias, you still are not satisfied?"

"Never been less so in my life," he replied genially. "This house reeks of crooks like a seaside boarding-house of cabbage at lunch-time. And since we've wakened poor Auntie up between us, I'm going to see her before I go."

"By all manner of means," said Doctor Helias quietly. He was standing in the door, and his voice was genial. "Your aunt would like to see you and your friend. But you must not alarm her or excite her in any way. And incidentally, when your interview is over, I shall await an apology for your grossly insulting remarks."

He stood aside and I followed Drummond into the passage.

"The first door on the left," murmured the doctor. "You will find your aunt in bed."

"For God's sake, keep your eyes skinned, Stockton," whispered Drummond as we went up the stairs. "There is some trap here, or I'll eat my hat."

But there was no sign of anything out of the ordinary as we entered the room. A shaded lamp was beside the bed, and the invalid was in shadow. But even in the dim light one could see that she was a frail old lady, with the ravages of pain and disease on her face.

"My nephew," she said in a gentle voice. "My brother Harry's boy! Well, well – how time does pass. Come here, nephew, and let me see what you've grown into."

With an emaciated hand she held up the electric lamp so that its rays fell on Drummond. And the next instant the lamp had crashed to the floor. I bent quickly and picked it up, and as I did so the light for a moment shone on her face. And I could have sworn that the look in her eyes during that brief instant was one of sheer, stark terror… So vivid was the impression that I stared at her in amazement. True, the look was gone at once, but I knew I had not been mistaken. The sight of Drummond's face had terrified the woman in the bed. Why? Crooked or not crooked, it seemed unaccountable.

"I'm so weak," she said apologetically. "Thank you, sir – thank you." She was speaking to me, as if she realised that I was staring at her curiously. "It was quite a shock to me to see my nephew grown into such a big man. I should never have known him, but that's only natural. You must come again when I'm better, nephew, and tell me all about your poor dear father."

"I certainly will, Aunt Amelia," said Drummond thoughtfully.

"Harry was always a little wild, but such a dear lovable boy," went on the old lady. "You're not very like him, nephew."

"So I've been told," murmured Drummond, and I saw his mouth beginning to twitch. "I'm much more like my mother. She'd just about have been the same age as you, Auntie, if she'd been alive. You remember her, don't you – Jenny Douglas that was, from Cirencester?"

"It's a long time ago, nephew."

"But my father always said that you two were such friends!"

For a moment the woman hesitated, and from downstairs came the sound of an electric bell rung twice.

"Why, of course," she said, "I remember her well."

"Then you must have a darned good memory, Auntie," said Drummond grimly. "It was conceivable that you might have had a brother called Harry who went to Australia, though I did happen to invent him. But by no possible stretch of imagination could you have had a sister-in-law called Jenny Douglas from Cirencester, for I've just invented her too."

"Look out, Drummond," I shouted, and he swung round. Stealing across the floor towards us was the black-haired Doctor Helias with a piece of gas-piping in his hand, and behind him were three of the others.

And then like a flash it happened. It was the men we were watching; we'd forgotten the invalid in bed. I had a momentary glimpse of bed-clothes being hurled off, and a woman fully dressed springing at Drummond from behind. In her hand was something that gleamed, and suddenly the overpowering smell of ammonia filled the room. But it was Drummond who got it straight in the face. In an instant he was helpless from the fumes, lurching and staggering about blindly, and even as I sprang forward to help him I heard the woman's voice –

"Put him out, you fool, and do it quick."

And the black-haired man put him out easily and scientifically. He was obviously an expert, for he didn't appear to use much force. He just applied his piece of piping to the base of Drummond's skull, and it was over. He went down as if he was pole-axed and lay still.

"My God!" I muttered, "you've killed him."

And that was my last remark for some hours. The three men who applied themselves to me were also experts in their line, and I estimated it at half-a-minute before I was gagged and trussed up, and thrown into a corner. But I was still able to hear and see.

"You damned fool," said the woman to the man called Doctor Helias. "Why didn't you tell me it was him?"

She was pointing at Drummond, and he stared at her in surprise.

"What do you mean?" he answered. "I don't know who he is any more than you do. Isn't he the nephew?"

She gave a short laugh.

"No more than I am. And you can take it from me I know him only too well. He suspected, of course: that's why I rang."

She flung the water pistol which had contained the ammonia on to a table, and going to the cupboard took out a hat.

"Put 'em both below, and for Heaven's sake get a move on. Is he dead?" Once again she pointed at Drummond, and the big man shook his head. "If I'd known he was coming I'd have been out of this house four hours ago. Mon Dieu! Helias – you have bungled this show."

"But I don't understand," stammered the other. "Throw 'em below," she stormed at him. "With your brain you wouldn't understand anything."

"Take 'em downstairs," snarled Helias to the others. He was glaring sullenly at the woman, but he was evidently too afraid of her to resent her insults. "Hurry, curse you."

And at that moment the fifth man dashed into the room.

"Men coming across the wall at the back," he said breathlessly. "Listen: they're getting in now."

From below came the sound of a window opening, and muttered voices.

"Police?" whispered the woman tensely.

"Don't know: couldn't see."

"How many?"

"Three or four."

"Out with the light. Whoever they are – do 'em down one by one as they come into the room. But no noise."

And then ensued the most agonising minute I have ever spent in my life. Helpless, unable to do anything to warn them, I lay in the corner. It was Ted Jerningham, of course, and the others – I knew that, and they were walking straight into a trap. The room was dark: the door was open, and outlined against the light from the passage I could see the huge form of Doctor Helias crouching in readiness. Dimly I saw the others waiting behind him, and then the woman moved forward and joined them. But before she did so I had seen her stand on a chair and remove the bulb from the central electric light.

The steps on the stairs came nearer, and now the shadow of the two leaders fell on the wall. There was a click as the switch was turned on – and then, when nothing happened, they both sprang into the room. For a moment they were clearly visible against the light, and even I gave a momentary start at their appearance. In the excitement of the past few minutes I had forgotten about the black masks, and they looked like two monstrous spectres from another world. The woman gave a little scream, and then the other two came through the door.

Thud! Thud! Swiftly Helias' arm rose and fell with that deadly piece of piping in his hand, and the two last arrivals pitched forward on the floor without a sound.

"At him, Peter." It was Jerningham's voice muffled by the covering over his face, and I saw the two of them spring at the doctor.

But it was hopeless from the start. Two to five: the odds were impossible, especially when one of the five was a man with the strength of three. It may have been half-a-minute, but it certainly wasn't more before the bunch of struggling men straightened up, and two more unconscious and black-cowled figures lay motionless.

With a feeling of sick despair I watched the woman put back the bulb and flood the room with light. What an ignominious conclusion to the night's work. And what was going to happen now? We were utterly powerless, and our captors were not overburdened with scruples.

Already Helias had taken off the masks, and was staring at the unconscious men on the floor with a savage scowl.

"What's all this damned tomfoolery?" he muttered. "Who are these young fools, and why are they rigged up like that?"

And then something made me look at the woman. She was leaning against the table, and in her eyes was something of that same look of terror that I had seen before.

"Kill them. Kill them all: now – at once."

Her voice was harsh and metallic, and the others stared at her in amazement.

"Impossible, Madame," said Helias sharply. "It would be an act of inconceivable folly."

She turned on him furiously.

"It would be an act of inconceivable folly not to. I tell you they are more dangerous by far, these men, than all the police of England."

"Well, they are not particularly dangerous at the moment," said the other soothingly. "Think, Madame: reflect for a moment. We have difficulties already, severe enough in all conscience. And are we to add to those difficulties by murdering six young fools in cold blood?"

"I tell you, I know these men," she stormed. "And that one" – she pointed to Drummond – "is the devil himself."

"I can't help it, Madame," returned the doctor firmly. "I have no scruples as you know, but I am not a fool. And to kill these men or any of them would be the act of a fool. We have to get away at once: there is no possible method of disposing of the bodies. Sooner or later they are bound to be discovered in this house, and a hue and cry will start, which is the last thing we want. Pitch them into the cellar below and leave them there, by all means. But no unnecessary killing."

For a moment I thought she was going to continue the argument: then with a little shrug of her shoulders she turned away.

"Perhaps you're right," she remarked. "But, mon Dieu! I would sooner have seen all Scotland Yard here than that man."

"Who is he?" said Helias curiously.

"His name is Drummond," answered the woman. "Get on with it, and put them below."

And from the darkness of the cellar where they pitched us I listened to the sounds of their departure. How long it was before the last footstep ceased above I don't know, but at length the house was silent. The stertorous breathing of the unconscious men around me was the only sound, and after a while I fell into an uneasy doze.

I woke with a start. Outside a wagon was rumbling past, but it was not that which had disturbed me: it was something nearer at hand.

"Peter! Algy!"

It was Ted Jerningham's voice, and I gave two strangled grunts by way of reply.

"Who's there?"

Once more I grunted, and after a pause I heard him say, "I'm going to strike a match."

The feeble light flickered up and he gave a gasp of astonishment. Sprawling over the floor just where they had been thrown lay the others, and as the match spluttered and went out Algy Longworth groaned and turned over.

"Holy smoke!" came his voice plaintively: "have I been passed over by a motor bus or have I not?"

It was Drummond himself who had taken it worst. The cowls had broken the force of the blows in the case of the others, whilst I had come off almost scot free. But Drummond, poor devil, was in a really bad way. His face was burnt and scalded by the ammonia, and the slightest movement of his head hurt him intolerably. In fact it was a distinctly pessimistic party that assembled upstairs at half-past six in the morning. We none of us asked anything better than to go home to bed – none of us, that is, save the most damaged one. Drummond wouldn't hear of it.

"We're here now," he said doggedly, "and even if my neck is broken, which is more than likely by the feel of it, we're going to see if we can find any clue to put us on the track of that bunch. For if it takes me five years, I'll get even with that damned gorse bush."

"I think the lady disliked us more than he did," I remarked. "Especially you. She went so far as to suggest killing the lot of us."

"The devil she did," grunted Drummond.

"She knew you. She knew your name. I think she knew all of you fellows by sight, but she certainly knew Drummond."

"The devil she did," he grunted again, and stared at me thoughtfully out of the one eye that still functioned. "You're certain of that?"

"Absolutely. You remember she dropped the lamp in her agitation when she first saw your face. I saw the look in her eyes as I picked it up: it was terror."

And now they were all staring at me.

"Why," I went on, "she alluded to you as the devil himself."

"Good Lord!" said Drummond softly, "it can't be... Surely, it can't be..."

"There's no reason why it shouldn't," said Jerningham. "It's big enough for them to handle."

"We're talking of things unknown to you, Stockton," explained Drummond. "But in view of what you saw and heard, it may be that a very extraordinary thing has taken place... Confound my neck!..."

He rubbed it gently, and then went on again.

"As far as I know there is only one woman in the world who is likely to regard me as the devil himself, and be kind enough to suggest killing me. And if it is her... Great Scott! boys – what stupendous luck."

"Marvellous!" I ejaculated. "She must love you to distraction."

But he was beyond my mild sarcasm.

"If it's her – then Helias...oh! my sainted aunt! don't tell me that old gorse bush was Carl Peterson."

"I don't know anything about Carl Peterson," I said. "But it was old gorse bush, as you call him, who flatly refused to kill you and us as well. Moreover, he didn't know you."

"Then gorse bush wasn't Carl. But the woman... Ye Gods! I wonder. Just think of the humour of it, if it really was Irma. Not knowing it was me, she thought I possibly was the genuine article – the real Australian nephew. She made herself up into a passable imitation of Aunt Amelia, kept the light away from her face, and trusted to luck. Then she recognised me, and saw at once that I was as big a fraud as she was, and that the game was up."

"I don't know your pals, as I said before," I put in, "but that's exactly what did happen."

"If I'm right, Stockton, you'll know 'em soon enough. And furthermore, if I'm right my debt of gratitude to you for putting me in the way of this little show will be increased a thousand-fold."

His voice was almost solemn, and I began to laugh. "Mrs Drummond's debt of gratitude will wilt a bit when she sees your face," I said. "Don't you think you'd better get home and have it attended to?"

"Not on your life," he remarked. "My face can wait: examining this house can't. So let us, with due care as befits five blinking cripples, see what we can find. Then a bottle of Elliman's embrocation and bed."

"Damnation!" roared a furious voice from the door. "What the devil are you doing here again?"

"MacIver's little twitter," said Drummond. "I would know that fairy voice anywhere."

He rose cautiously and turned round.

"Mac, we have all taken it in the neck, not only metaphorically but literally. Any sudden movement produces on the spot an immediate desire for death. So be gentle with us, and kind and forbearing. Otherwise you will see the heartrending spectacle of six men bursting into tears."

"What on earth has happened to your face?" demanded the detective.

"Aunt Amelia sprayed it with ammonia from point-blank range," said Drummond. "A darned unfriendly act I think you'll agree. And then a nasty man covered with black hair took advantage of my helpless condition to sandbag me. Mac, my lad, in the course of a long and blameless career I've never been so badly stung as I was last night."

"What do you mean by Aunt Amelia?" growled the other.

"The official occupant of this house, Mac."

"Miss Simpson. Where is she?"

"I know not. But somehow I feel that the sweet woman I interviewed in bed last night was not Miss Amelia." Then with a sudden change of tone – "Have you found the communication between the two houses?"

"How do you know there is one?"

"Because I'm not a damned fool," said Drummond. "It was principally to find it that I came here."

He glanced at the detective's suspicious face and began to laugh.

"Lord! man: it's obvious. That fellow the other night was dead, so how did the body disappear? It couldn't have gone out by the window in broad daylight, and unless your men were liars or asleep it couldn't have gone out by the door. So there must have been some way of communication."

"I found it by accident a few minutes ago from the next house," said MacIver. "It opens into the bedroom above."

"I thought it must," said Drummond. "And I wouldn't be surprised if dear Aunt Amelia's bed was up against the opening."

"There was a woman here, was there?"

"There was." For a moment or two Drummond hesitated. "Look here, MacIver," he said slowly, "we've had one or two amusing little episodes together in the past, and I'm going to tell you something. After they knocked me out last night, Mr Stockton, who was only bound and gagged, heard one or two very strange things. This woman who was here masquerading as Miss Simpson evidently knew me. She further evinced a strong wish to have me killed then and there. Now who can she have been? MacIver, I believe – and mark you, there is nothing inherently improbable in it – I believe that once more we are up against Peterson. He wasn't here; but the girl – his mistress – was. I may be wrong, but here and now I'd take an even pony on it."

"Perhaps you're right," acknowledged the other. "We've heard nothing of the gentleman for two or three years."

"And if we are, MacIver," continued Drummond gravely, "this whole show, serious as it is at the moment, becomes ten times more so."

"If only I could begin to understand it," said the detective angrily. "The whole thing seems so utterly disconnected and pointless."

"And it will probably remain so until we reach the end, if we ever do reach the end," said Drummond. "One thing is pretty clear: this house was evidently the headquarters of that part of the gang which lived in London."

"I'm getting into touch with Miss Simpson at once," said MacIver.

Drummond nodded.

"She may or may not be perfectly innocent."

"And two of my fellows are searching this house now," went on the detective. "But damn it, Captain Drummond, I'm defeated – absolutely defeated. If whoever is running this show wanted to get away with Gaunt's secret – why all this? Why didn't they go at once? Why waste time?"

He swung round as one of his men came into the room. He was carrying in his arms a metal tank of about four gallons capacity, which was evidently intended to be strapped to a man's back. To the bottom was attached a length of rubber tubing, at the end of which was fixed a long brass nozzle with a little tap attached. On one side of the tank a small pump was placed, and we crowded round to examine it as he placed it on the table.

"Two or three more of them in the cellar below, sir," said the man.

"Pretty clear what they are intended for," said Drummond gravely. "It's nothing more nor less than a glorified fruit sprayer. And with that liquid of theirs inside..."

"There is this too that I found," went on the man.

"I'd like you to come yourself, sir, and see. There was blood on the walls and on the floor – and this – "

From his pocket he took a handkerchief, and it was stained an ominous red. It was quite dry, and MacIver opened it out and laid it beside the tank.

"Hullo!" he muttered, "what's this mean?"

Scrawled over part of the material were some red letters. The ink used had been blood: the pen might have been the writer's finger.

3 P 7 A N T

A smear completed it: evidently he'd collapsed or been interrupted.

"I found it in a crack in the wall, sir," said the man. "It had been pushed in hard."

MacIver's eyes had narrowed, and without a word he pointed to the corner of the handkerchief. Clearly visible through the blood were two small black letters. And the letters were R G.

CHAPTER 6

In which we get a message from Robin Gaunt

Robin Gaunt! It was his blood-soaked handkerchief that lay in front of us. He too had been thrown into the same cellar where we had spent the night. And where was he now?

I picked up the handkerchief, and a sudden wave of bitterness swept over me. I pictured him, wounded – perhaps dying – scrawling his message down there in the darkness, whilst outside men said vile things about him and papers fanned the flame.

"Your super-vivisector, Inspector," I remarked. "It's damned well not fair."

"But just at present it's necessary, Mr Stockton," he answered. "By Jove! if only that handkerchief could speak! 3 P 7 A N T... What on earth was he trying to write?"

He turned and went briskly out of the room.

"Show me exactly where you found it," he said to his subordinate.

We all trooped after him, and by the light of an electric torch we explored the cellar. The officer pointed to the crack in the wall where he had found the handkerchief, and to the dark stains just below and on the floor.

"I'm thinking," said Drummond gravely, "that the poor devil was in a pretty bad way."

Torch in hand MacIver was carrying out his examination systematically. An opening in one wall led to a smaller cellar, and it was there that three other spraying cisterns, similar to the one upstairs, were standing. They differed in small details, but their method of action was the same. In each design there was a pump for producing the necessary pressure, and a small stopcock at the end of the spraying pipe which allowed the jet of liquid to be turned on or off at will.

The main points of difference lay in the arrangement of the straps for securing the reservoirs to the shoulders, and the shape and size of the reservoirs themselves. Also the rubber piping varied considerably in length in the different models.

"Take these upstairs," said MacIver to the officer, "and put them alongside the other one."

Once more he resumed his examination, only to stop abruptly at the startled exclamation that came from his man. He was standing at the top of the cellar steps tugging at the door.

"It's locked, sir," he cried. "I can't make it budge."

"Locked!" shouted MacIver. "Who the devil locked it?"

"It's been locked from the other side, and the key is not in the keyhole."

MacIver darted up the steps, and switched his torch on to the door.

"Who came in last?" he demanded.

"I did," said Toby Sinclair. "And I left the door wide open. I can swear to it."

In a frenzy of rage the Inspector hurled himself against it, but the result was nil.

"Not in a hundred years, Mac," said Drummond quietly. "No man can open a door as stout as that at the top of a flight of stairs. You can't get any weight behind your shoulder."

"But, damn it, man," cried the other, "we haven't been down here ten minutes. Whoever locked it must be in the house now."

"Bexton is there too, sir," said the officer. "He was exploring upstairs."

"Bexton!" bellowed the Inspector, through the keyhole. "Bexton! Lord! is the man deaf? Bexton – you fool: come here."

But there was no answer.

"Steady, MacIver," said Drummond, "you'll have a rush of blood to the head in a minute. He's possibly up at the top of the house, and we'll get him as soon as he comes down. No good getting needlessly excited."

"But who has locked this door? "demanded the other. "That's what I want to know."

"Precisely, old lad," agreed Drummond soothingly. "That's what we all want to know. But before we have any chance of knowing, we've got to get to the other side. And since we can't blow the blamed thing down there's no good going on shouting. Let's have a look at it: I'm a bit of an authority on doors."

He went up the stairs, and after a brief examination he gave a short laugh.

"My dear Mac – short of a crowbar and a pickaxe we're stung. And since we've none of us got either in our waistcoat pockets there's no good worrying. The bolt goes actually into the brickwork: you can see it there. And the lock on the door has been put on from the other side, so a screw-driver is no good."

He came down again laughing.

"I can't help it – I like these people. They are birds after my own heart. They've bitten us properly, and got away with their expensive set of uppers and lowers completely intact. I shall sit down and ruminate on life, and if anyone feels strong enough to massage my neck, I shall raise no objections. Lord! what a game we'll have when I meet gorse bush again."

He lit a cigarette, and deposited himself on the floor with his back against the wall.

"Mac, if that's our only means of illumination you'd better switch it off. We may want it later – you never know."

"Bexton must be down in a moment or two," said the Inspector angrily.

"True," answered Drummond. "Unless he's down already."

"What do you mean?"

"I mean that there are some people knocking about in this district who are no slouches in the sand-bag game. And I should think it was quite on the cards that the worthy Bexton has already discovered the fact."

"If that's the case we're here for hours."

"Just so," agreed Drummond. "Which is all the more reason for preserving that air of masterly tranquillity which is the hall-mark of the Anglo-Saxon in times of stress. Men have won prizes ranging from bull's-eyes to grand pianos for sentiments less profound than that. We are stung, Mac: we are locked in, and we shall remain locked in until some kindly soul comes along to let us out. And since the betting is that the key has been dropped down the nearest drain-pipe, and that our Mr Bexton has taken it good and hard where I took it last night, I think we can resign ourselves to a fairly lengthy period of rest and meditation… Damn my neck!"

"Supposing we all shouted together," I suggested, after we had sat in silence for several minutes. "Somebody must hear surely."

We let out a series of deafening bellows, and at length our efforts were rewarded. A heavy blow was struck on the other side of the door, and an infuriated voice shouted through the keyhole.

"Stop that filthy row. You'll have plenty of time to sing glees when you're breaking stones on Dartmoor. If you do it any more now I'll turn a hose on you."

We heard the sound of retreating footsteps, and MacIver gave a gasp of amazement.

"Am I mad?" he spluttered. "Am I completely insane? That was Fosdick's voice – the man on duty next door."

And then every semblance of self-control left him, and he raved like a lunatic.

"I'll sack the fellow! I'll have him out of the force in disgrace. He's been drinking: the fool's drunk. Fosdick – come here, damn you, Fosdick!"

He went on shouting and beating on the door with one of the tin reservoirs, till once again came a blow from the other side followed by Fosdick's voice.

"Look 'ere, you bally twitterer: I'm getting fair fed up with you. There's a crowd outside the door now asking when the performing hyenas are going to be let out. Now listen to me. Every time I 'ears a sound from any of you, you stops down there another 'alf-hour without your breakfasts. The van when she comes can easily wait, and I ain't in no hurry."

"Listen, you fool," roared MacIver. "You're drunk: you've gone mad. I order you to open the door. it's me – Inspector MacIver."

"Inspector my aunt," came the impassive reply. "Now don't you forget what I said. The van oughtn't to be long now."

"The van," said MacIver weakly, as the footsteps outside departed. "What van? In the name of Heaven, what is the man talking about?"

"Oh! Lord, Mac," cried Drummond helplessly, "don't make me laugh any more. As it is I've got the most infernal stitch."

"I fail to see the slightest humour in the situation," said MacIver acidly. "The only possible conclusion I can come to is that Fosdick has suddenly lost his reason. And in the meantime I, sir, am locked in here at a time when every moment is of value. In the whole of my career such a timing has never happened."

"There's no doubt about it, old man," agreed Drummond in a shaking voice, "that up-to-date our investigations have not yet met with that measure of success which they justly deserve. We can muster between us five stiff necks, one parboiled face, and an excessively uncomfortable floor to sit on."

"The whole thing is entirely owing to your unwarrantable interference," snapped the detective.

"My dear Mac," said Drummond, "if, as you think, your bloke Fosdick has gone off the deep end you really can't blame me. Personally I don't think he has."

"Then perhaps you'd be good enough to explain what he's doing this for," said MacIver sarcastically. "A little game, I suppose."

"Nothing of the sort," answered Drummond. "My dear man, cease going off like a steam-engine and think for a moment. The whole thing is perfectly obvious. The van is to take us to prison."

"What on earth…" stuttered MacIver.

"No more and no less," went on Drummond calmly. "Yonder stout-hearted warrior is under the firm impression that he has a band of bloodthirsty criminals safe under lock and key. He sees promotion in store for him: dazzling heights – "

"Inspector MacIver! Inspector MacIver. Are you there?"

It was Fosdick's agitated voice from the other side of the door.

"I should rather think I am," said MacIver grimly. "Open this door, you perishing fool…"

"I will, sir, at once. It's all a mistake."

"Damn your mistakes! Open the door."

"But I haven't got the key. Wait a bit, sir, I'll get a screwdriver."

"Hurry," roared MacIver. "May Heaven help that man when I get at him."

"I wouldn't be too hasty if I was you, Mac," said Drummond quietly. "Better men than he have been caught napping."

It was a quarter of an hour before the door was opened and we trooped upstairs, followed by the trembling Fosdick.

"Now, you fool," said MacIver, "will you kindly explain this little jest of yours?"

"Well, sir," answered the man. "I'm very sorry, I'm sure – but I acted for the best."

"Get on with it," stormed the Inspector. "I was on duty outside Number 10, when I saw you come out of the house."

"You saw me come out of this house? Why, you blithering idiot, I've been locked up in the cellar all the morning."

"I know that now, sir, but at the time I thought it was you. You passed me, sir – at least the man did – and you said to me, 'We've got the whole bunch.' It was your voice, sir; your voice exactly. 'They're in the cellar in Number 12 – locked in, and I've got the key. I'm going round to the Yard now, and I'll send a van up for 'em. They can't get out, but they may make a row.' And then you went on – or rather the other man did – 'By Jove! this is a big thing. I've got one of 'em in there that the police of Europe and America are looking for. I had him once before – and do you know how he got away? Why, by imitating my voice over the telephone so well that my man thought it was me!' "

"How perfectly gorgeous," said Drummond ecstatically.

"And then you see, sir, when I heard your voice in that there cellar I thought it was this other bloke imitating you."

"I see." Despite himself MacIver's lips were beginning to twitch. "And what finally made you decide that I wasn't imitating my own voice?"

"Well, sir, I waited and waited and the van never came – and then I went upstairs. They've knocked out Bexton, sir; I found him unconscious on the floor in the room above. So then I rang up the Yard: nothing had been heard of you. And then I knew I'd been hoaxed. But I swear, sir, that bloke would have deceived Mrs MacIver herself."

"He certainly put it across you all right," said MacIver grimly. "I'd give quite a lot to meet the gentleman."

"I wonder what the inducement was," said Drummond. "No man was going to run such an infernal risk for fun."

"By Jove!" cried MacIver, "that cistern is gone. It's lucky I had the handkerchief in my pocket."

"He was carrying a tin with straps on it when he spoke to me," said Fosdick, and MacIver groaned.

"Literally through our fingers," he said. "However, we've got the other three cisterns. Though I'd much sooner have had the man."

"Anyway that's a point cleared up," remarked Drummond cheerfully. "We know why he came here – "

"We don't," snapped MacIver. "The fact that he took the blamed thing is no proof that he came for that purpose."

"True, my dear old policeman," said Drummond. "But it is, as they say, a possible hypothesis. And, as I remarked before, he didn't come here for fun, so in default of further information we may as well assume that he came for the cistern. In the hurry of their departure last night they forgot these little fellows down in the cellar, so someone came back to get them. He found one nicely put out for him on the table, and a personally conducted Cook's party in the cellar inspecting the others. So in addition to taking his property he locked the cellar door. Easy, laddie: easy."

"Yes; isn't it?" said MacIver sarcastically. "And perhaps you'll explain what he'd have done if we hadn't been in the cellar."

"My dear Mac, what's the good of making it harder? I haven't the faintest idea what he'd have done. Stood on his head and given an imitation of a flower-pot. He *did* find us in the cellar, and that's all we're concerned with. He took a chance – and a darned sporting chance – and it came off. You're up against something pretty warm, old lad. I don't pretend to be a blinking genius, but if my reconstruction of what has happened up to date is right, I take off my hat to 'em for their nerve."

" 'What is your reconstruction?" said MacIver quietly, and I noticed his look of keen attention. Whatever may have been his official opinion of our interference, it was pretty clear that unofficially he was under no delusions with regard to Drummond. In fact, as he told me many months later, there was no one he knew who had such an uncanny faculty for hitting the nail on the head.

"Well, this is how I see it," said Drummond. "Their first jolt was the fact that Gaunt managed to get through on the telephone to Stockton. Had that not happened they'd have been in clover. It might have been a couple of days before the Australian was found dead in that house. The old woman is deaf, and probably the first thing she'd have known about it was when she showed a prospective lodger a dead man in her best bedroom and a dead dog across the passage. But Gaunt getting through on the phone started it all, and everything that has happened since is due, I'm certain, to their endeavour to fit in their previous arrangements with this unexpected development. They brought Gaunt here: that's obvious. Why did they bring Gaunt here particularly? Well – why not? They had to take him somewhere. They couldn't leave him lying about in Piccadilly Circus.

"They brought him here, and then for reasons best known to themselves they decided to murder Stockton. Well, we all know what happened then, and it was another unexpected development for them. The last thing they wanted was your arrival on the scene. And you wouldn't have arrived, Mac – unless you'd followed Stockton. That's what huffed 'em: old Stockton giving his celebrated rendering of a mechanic at the Three Cows. Naturally you suspected him at once: it was without exception the most appalling exhibition of futility I've ever seen."

"Thanks so much," I murmured.

"That's all right, old bean," he said affably. "I expect you're the hell of a lawyer. However, to continue. You arrived, Mac, with most of the police force of London next door – and you can bet your life the people in here began to sweat some. Why didn't they go away at once, you say? I don't know. Instead of their quiet little backwater the whole glare of Scotland Yard was beating on the next-door house. And what was even worse for them was, that not only had they failed to murder Stockton before you came, but one of their own men was dead. Inquests: newspaper publicity. All the more reason for them to go at once.

Why didn't they? What was their reason for stopping on when they must have realised their danger? I don't know; but it must have been a pretty strong one. Anyway they chanced it – and, by Jove! they've pulled it off. That's why I take off my hat to 'em. They were ready to go last night, and they went last night, and the last twenty-four hours they spent in this house must have been pretty nerve-racking."

"May I ask what you are doing in my house?" came in an infuriated female voice from the door.

A tall, thin, acidulated woman was standing there regarding us balefully, and MacIver swung round.

"May I ask your name, madam?"

"Simpson is my name, sir. And who may you be?"

"I'm Inspector MacIver from Scotland Yard, and I must ask you to answer a few questions."

"Scotland Yard!" cried Miss Simpson shrilly. "Then you're the very man I want to see. I have been the victim of a monstrous outrage."

"Indeed," remarked MacIver. "I'm sorry about that. What has happened?"

"Three weeks ago a female person called to see me in this house. She wished to know if I would let it furnished for a month. I refused, and told her that I considered her request very surprising, as I had not told any house-agent that I wanted to let. I further asked her why she had picked on my house particularly. She told me that she had just returned from Australia, and was spending a month in London. She further said that before going to Australia she had lived with her father in this house, and that since he was now dead she wished to spend the month under the old roof for remembrance' sake. However, I told her it was impossible, and she went away. Two days afterwards occurred the outrage. Outrage, sir – abominable outrage, and if there is any justice in England the miscreants should be brought to justice. I was kidnapped, sir – abducted by a man."

"Is that so?" said MacIver gravely. "How did it happen, Miss Simpson?"

"In a way, sir, that reflects the gravest discredit on the police. I was returning from the Tube station late in the evening – I had been to a theatre – and as I reached the end of the road a taxi drew up beside me. At the time the road was deserted: as usual no adequate protection by the police was available against gangs of footpads and robbers. From the taxi stepped a man, and before I had time to scream, or even guess their fell intention, I was bundled inside by him and the driver – a handkerchief was bound round my mouth and another round my eyes and we were off."

"You have no idea, of course, who the men were?" said MacIver.

"Absolutely none," she remarked indignantly. "Do you imagine, sir, that I should number among my acquaintances men capable of such a dastardly act?"

"No one who knew you would ever be likely to abduct you," agreed Drummond soothingly. "Er – that is, in such a violent manner, don't you know. What I was going to say" – he went on hurriedly – "is what about the servants? Didn't they start running round in circles when you failed to roll up?"

"That is one of the very points I wish to clear up," she said. "Jane – I keep only one maid – had received a telegram only that morning stating that her mother in Devonshire was ill. So she had gone off, and there was therefore no one in the house. But that was three weeks ago. Surely she must have returned in that time, and if so, when she failed to find me here, why did she say nothing to the police?"

"An interesting point, Miss Simpson," said MacIver, "and one that we will endeavour to clear up. However, let's get on now with what happened to you. I hope these men used no unnecessary violence."

"Beyond forcibly placing me in the car," she conceded, "they did not. And I may say that during the whole period of my imprisonment I was treated very well."

"Where did they take you? "demanded MacIver eagerly.

"I don't know: I can't tell you. It was a house in the country: that's all I can say. It stood by itself amongst some trees – but I was blindfolded the whole way there. And when they brought me back this morning I was again blindfolded. They brought me as far as the Euston Road: whipped off the handkerchief from my eyes, pushed me out on the pavement, and then drove off at a furious rate. Now, sir, what is the meaning of this inconceivable treatment?"

"If you'll come upstairs, Miss Simpson, you'll understand," answered MacIver. "The meaning of the whole thing is that you happened to be living in this house. And it wasn't you they wanted: it was the house. Had you agreed to let it to that woman who called to see you, none of this would have happened."

"But why did they want the house?"

"That's why."

MacIver stepped into the room where Drummond and I had interviewed the bogus invalid, and pointed to an opening in the wall.

"You knew nothing of that, of course?"

"Good Heavens! no." She was staring at it in amazement. "What's through on the other side?"

"The next house: Number 10."

"And that's been there all these years. Why! I might have been murdered in my bed."

"It's a carefully done job, MacIver," said Drummond, and the detective nodded.

The wall of each room consisted of imitation oak boarding, and the opening was made by means of two sliding panels. The brickwork between them had been removed to form the passage, and the opening thus made crowned with a small iron girder. The

113

two panels moved in grooves which had been recently oiled, and when closed it was impossible to notice anything unusual.

"A bolt-hole, Miss Simpson," explained MacIver. "A bolt-hole, the existence of which was known to the gang that abducted you. And a bolt-hole is very useful at times. That's why they wanted your house."

"Do you mean to say that a gang of criminals has been living in my house?"

"That is just what I do mean," said MacIver. "But I don't think they are likely to return. If they intended to do so they wouldn't have let you go. They lived here and they used the empty house next door. The thing I'm going to find out now is the name of your predecessor. Can you tell me the agent through whom you got this house?"

"Paul & Paul in the Euston Road."

"Good. That saves time."

"And now I shall be glad, sir, if you would kindly go," she said. "I presume I may expect to hear in time that the police have a clue to account for my treatment. It would be too much to expect any more. But at the moment my house resembles a bear garden, and I would like to start putting it into some semblance of order – "

And then occurred a most embarrassing incident. It was so sudden and unexpected that it took us all by surprise, and it was over before anyone could intervene.

Drummond became light-headed. We heard a dreadful noise from an adjoining room: he had burst into song. And the next moment – to our horror – he came dancing through the door, and made a bee-line for Miss Simpson.

"My Tootles," he cried jovially. "My little flower of the east."

Miss Simpson screamed: Ted Jerningham gave an uncontrollable guffaw.

"Dance with me, my poppet," chanted Drummond, seizing her firmly round the waist.

Protesting shrilly, the unfortunate woman was dragged round the room, until between us we managed to get hold of Drummond. The poor chap was completely delirious, but fortunately for all concerned not violent. We explained to the almost hysterical woman that he had had a very bad blow on the head the preceding night, from one of the same gang of scoundrels who had abducted her – and that, of course, he was suffering from concussion. And then we got him downstairs and into a taxi. He was still humming gently to himself, and playing with a piece of string, but he offered no resistance.

"Extraordinary thing his going like that so suddenly," I said to Darrell, who was sitting opposite.

"Frightfully so," agreed Drummond. "Just hold that end of the string."

"Good Lord!" I stammered. "Do you mean to say…"

"Hold the end," he said tersely. "I want to see something."

With his fingers outstretched he measured the distance between my end and the point he was holding, whilst I still stared at him in amazement.

"I thought as much," he said quietly. "Tell the taxi to stop at the first small hotel we come to. You go back, Peter, and bring MacIver along there at once. Tell him it's urgent, but don't let that woman hear you."

"Who – Miss Simpson?"

"She's no more Miss Simpson than I am."

The car pulled up, and we all got out.

"Go back in it, Peter: make any old excuse. Say I left my hat – but get MacIver quickly. Now, Stockton – let's have a drink, and think things over."

"I say, Drummond," I said weakly, "do you mind explaining?"

"All in good time, old man – all in good time. I refuse to utter until I've got outside a pint."

"What on earth is the meaning of this?" said MacIver a few minutes later as he came into the room where we were sitting.

"Only that you apologised for my attack of insanity so convincingly that I think the lady believed it. I sincerely hope so at any rate. While you were holding forth, Mac, about the secret opening I went on a little voyage of exploration. And I found a cupboard full of female clothes. They were all marked A. Simpson, and right in front three or four skirts were hanging. I don't know why exactly, but it suddenly occurred to me that the skirts seemed singularly short for the lady. So I took one down and measured it round the waist-band. And allowing the span of my hand to be about ten inches I found that Miss Simpson's waist was approximately forty inches. Now that woman is thinner than my wife – but I thought I'd make sure. I took her measurement with this bit of string when I was dancing with her, and if that is Amelia Simpson she's shrunk thirteen inches round the tum-tum. Laddie – it can't be done. But, by Jove, it was a fine piece of acting. She's got every man jack of us out of the house as easily as peeling a banana."

MacIver rose and walked towards the door.

"What are you going to do?" said Drummond.

"Have that woman identified by somebody," answered the detective. "Ask her some more questions, and if the answers aren't satisfactory, clap her under lock and key at once."

"Far be it from me to call you an ass, dear boy, but that doesn't alter the fact that you are one. At least you will be if you arrest that woman."

"Well, what do you suggest? We'll have got one of them anyway."

"And if you give her sufficient rope, we may get a lot more. Think, man, just think. What did that fellow who impersonated you run his head into a noose for this morning? Not for the pleasure of locking us into a cellar. What has that woman turned up for so quickly, pretending she is the rightful owner? If those garments belong to Miss Simpson – as they surely must do – the two women must be utterly unlike. True, they would assume – and rightly so as it happened – that none of us had ever seen Miss Simpson. All the same, if they hadn't been in a tearing hurry they would surely have sent someone a little less dissimilar. They are in a tearing hurry – but what for? There's something in that house that they want – and want quickly: something they forgot last night when they all flitted. And when that woman finds it – or if she finds it – she'll go with it – to them. And we shall follow her. Do you get me, Steve? We can watch the house in front from Number 10. We can watch it from behind from Number 13 Jersey Street, in which six respectable divinity students have taken rooms for the week. We are the noble half-dozen. Let's get rid of the young army that we've had tracking around up to date, and be nice and matey. But we insist, Mac, on seeing the fun. Out of the kindness of my heart I've put you wise as to what I discovered, and you've got to play the game. You and I and Stockton will go to Number 10; Ted, Peter and Algy to Jersey Street. Toby, you trot back and tell Phyllis what is happening – and tell her to put up some sandwiches and half a dozen Mumm '13. Then come back to Jersey Street, and tell the old geyser there that it's a new form of Apenta Water. And send all the rest of your birds home to bed, Mac."

"It's strictly irregular," he said, grinning, "but, dash it all, Captain Drummond, I'll do it."

"Good fellow!" cried Drummond. "Let's get on with it."

"I'll keep a couple of my men below in 10 to follow her if she goes out," went on MacIver.

"Excellent," said Drummond. "And Toby can tell my chauffeur to bring the Hispano up to Jersey Street. For I'll guarantee to keep in sight of anything in England in her."

And so, once more, we returned to Number 10. No one had entered the house next door during our absence – and no one had come out, at any rate at the front. Of that Fosdick, who was still on duty, was sure. And then there commenced a weary vigil. Personally, I make no bones about it, I dozed through most of the afternoon. We were in the room which communicated with Number 12, but though we pulled back the panel on our side, no sound came from the next house. If she was carrying out her intention of restoring some semblance of order she was being very quiet about it.

Just once we heard the noise of drawers being pulled out, and what sounded like their contents being scattered on the floor; and later on footsteps in the next room caused MacIver to noiselessly slide back the panel into its closed position. But that was all we heard, while the sleepy afternoon drowsed on and the shadows outside grew longer and longer.

I think MacIver was nodding himself when there suddenly came the sound that banished all sleep. It was a scream – a woman's scream – curiously muffled, and it came from Number 12. It was not repeated, and as we dashed open the other panel the house was as silent as before. We rushed through into the passage and thence into the bedrooms: everywhere the same scene of disorder. Clothes thrown here and there: bedclothes ripped off and scattered on the floor.

"She's restored a semblance of order all right," said MacIver grimly, as we went downstairs.

And then he paused: a light was filtering out from the half-opened cellar door.

"The end of the search, Mac," said Drummond. "Go easy."

At first as we stood on the top of the stairs we could see nothing. A solitary candle guttered on the floor, throwing monstrous shadows in all directions : and then we smelt it once again – that strange bitter sweet smell – the smell of death.

MacIver's torch flashed out – to circle round and finally concentrate on something that lay just beyond the buttress wall still stained with Robin Gaunt's blood. And there was no need to ask what that something was: the poison had claimed another victim.

She lay there – the woman who had taken Miss Simpson's place – and the scream we had heard had been with her last breath. The same dreadful distortion: the same staring look of horror in the eyes – everything was just the same as in the other cases. But somehow with a woman it seemed more horrible.

"My God! but it's diabolical stuff," cried MacIver fiercely as he bent over the woman. "How did it happen, I wonder?"

"It's on her hand," said Drummond. "She's cut it on something. Look, man – there's a bit of a broken bottle beside her with liquid in it. For Heaven's sake be careful: the whole place is saturated with the stuff."

"We'll leave the body exactly as it is," said the Inspector, "until Sir John Dallas comes. I'll go and telephone him now. Captain Drummond, will you and Mr Stockton mount guard until I return?"

"Certainly," answered Drummond, and we followed the Inspector up the stairs.

"So that's what they came to look for," I remarked as the front door closed behind MacIver.

"Seems like it," agreed Drummond, lighting a cigarette thoughtfully. "And yet it's all a little difficult. A fellow may quite easily forget his handkerchief when he goes out, but he ain't likely to forget his trousers. What I mean, Stockton, is this. The whole thing has been done from the very beginning with the sole idea of getting the secret of that poison. Are we really to believe that after committing half-a-dozen murders and a few trifles of that description they went off and left it behind? Is that the only sample in existence? And if it isn't, what is the good of worrying about it? Why send back for it at all? It looked as if it was quite a small bottle.

"There's another point," he went on after a moment. "Where was that bottle this morning? I'll stake my dying oath that it

119

wasn't lying about in the cellar. It was either hidden there somewhere, or that woman took it down there with her. Great Scott! but it's a baffling show!"

We sat on in silence, each busy with his own thoughts. For me it was Robin who filled them: what had happened to him – where was be now? Or had they killed him? Or had he died as the result of his injuries? It was a possible solution to many things.

"If Gaunt is dead, Drummond," I said after a while, "it may account for a lot. It's not likely that he had very large supplies of the stuff in his rooms. And we know anyway that a lot of it was wasted when you shot our friend the night before last. So it seems to me to be perfectly feasible that that bottle down below contained the only existing sample – which in the event of Gaunt's death would become invaluable to them. They may not know his secret: in which case their only hope would be to get a sample."

"But why leave it behind?" he objected. "Why go to the worry and trouble of hiding it in the cellar? For I think it must have been hidden there: the idea that that unfortunate woman should have carried it down there seems pointless. It's just my trouser example, Stockton."

"Each one may have thought the other had it," I said, but he shook his head.

"You may be right," he remarked, "but I don't believe it was that that she was looking for. And my opinion is that the clue to the whole thing is contained in that blood-stained handkerchief, if only one could interpret it. 3 P 7 A N T. It's directions for something: it can't be meaningless."

Once again we relapsed into silence, until the sound of a taxi outside announced the arrival of someone. It was MacIver, and with him was Sir John carrying some guinea-pigs in cases.

"Sorry to have been so long," said the Inspector, "but I couldn't get Sir John on the telephone, so I had to go and find him. Anything happened?"

"Not a thing," said Drummond.

MacIver had brought another torch and several candles, and by their light Sir John proceeded to make his examination. He had donned a pair of stout India-rubber gloves, but even with their protection he handled things very gingerly.

First he poured what was left of the poison into another bottle, and corked it with a rubber cork. Then he took a sample of the dead woman's blood, which he placed in a test-tube and carefully stoppered. And finally, after a minute examination of the cut in her hand and the terrible staring eyes, he rose to his feet.

"We can now carry her upstairs," he remarked. "There is nothing more to be seen here. But on your life don't touch her hand."

We lifted her up, and MacIver gave a sudden exclamation. Underneath where the body had been lying, and so unseen by us until then, was a hole in the floor. It had been made by removing a brick, and the brick, itself, which had been concealed by the body, lay beside the hole. At the bottom of the hole was some broken glass and the neck of the bottle from the base of which Sir John had removed the poison. So it was obviously the place where the poison had been hidden. But who had hidden it – and why?

"Obviously not a member of the gang," said MacIver, "or she would have known where it was and not wasted time ransacking the house."

"Therefore obviously Gaunt himself," said Drummond. "Great Scott! man," he added, "it's the third brick from the wall. Give me your stick, Sir John. The handkerchief, MacIver – 3 and 7."

He tapped on the seventh brick, and sure enough it sounded hollow. With growing excitement we crowded round as he endeavoured to prise it up.

"Careful – careful," cried Sir John anxiously. "If there's another bottle we don't want any risk of another casualty. Let me: I've got gloves on."

And sure enough when the seventh brick was removed, a similar hole was disclosed, at the bottom of which lay a small cardboard pill-box. With the utmost care he lifted it out, and removed the lid. It was filled with a white paste, which looked like boracic ointment.

"Hullo!" he said after he'd sniffed it. "What fresh development have we here?"

And suddenly Drummond gave a shout of comprehension.

"I've got it. It's the message on the handkerchief. 3 P. The third brick – poison: 7 A N T – the seventh brick, antidote. That's the antidote, Sir John, you've got in your hand; and that's what they've been after. That woman came down to look for it – and she only found the poison. Gaunt must have hidden them both while he was a prisoner down here, and then left that last despairing message of his…"

"We'll try at once," said Sir John quietly.

He handed me the pill-box, and took the poison himself.

"Take a little of the ointment on the end of a match," he said, "and I'll take a little of the poison. You hold one of the guinea-pigs, MacIver. Now the instant I have applied the poison, you follow it up with your stuff in the same place, Stockton."

But the experiment was valueless. With a sudden convulsive shudder the little animal died, and when we tried with another the result was the same.

"Not a very effective antidote," said Sir John sarcastically.

"Nevertheless," said Drummond doggedly, "I'll bet you it is the antidote. Couldn't you analyse it, Sir John?"

"Of course I can analyse it," snapped the other. "And I shall analyse it."

He slipped the box into his bag, followed by the bottle of poison.

"I wonder if I might make a suggestion," said Drummond. "I don't want to seem unduly alarmist, but I think we've seen enough to realise that we are up against a pretty tough proposition. Now do you think it's wise to have all one's eggs in one basket, or rather all that snuff in one box? It might get lost: it might be stolen. Wouldn't it be safer, Sir John, to give, say, half of it to MacIver – until at any rate your analysis is concluded? I see you have a spare box in your bag."

We were going up the steps as he spoke and he was in front. And suddenly he paused for a moment or two and stared at the door. Then he went on into the hall, and I noticed that he glanced round him in all directions.

"A most sensible suggestion," said Sir John, "with which I fully agree."

"Then come in here, Sir John," said Drummond. He led the way into one of the downstairs rooms, and shut the door. And it seemed to me that he was looking unduly grave. He watched the transfer of half the paste to another box, and he waited till MacIver had it in his pocket. Then – "Please send for Fosdick, MacIver."

A little surprised, the Inspector stepped to the window and beckoned to the man outside.

"Anyone been in this house, Fosdick, during the last half-hour? "said Drummond.

"Only Sir John's assistant, sir."

"I haven't got an assistant," snapped Sir John. "My sainted aunt, Mac," said Drummond grimly, "we're up against the real thing this time. He's gone, I suppose?"

"Yes, sir," said Fosdick. "About ten minutes ago."

"Then I tell you, Sir John, your life is not safe. It's the stuff in the pill-box that they are after. Perhaps we've put it on wrong: perhaps you've got to eat it. Anyway that man who posed as your assistant knows you've got it. I beg of you to put yourself under police protection day and night. If possible, at any rate, until you have analysed the stuff don't go near your house. Remain inside Scotland Yard itself."

But what Sir John lacked in inches he made up for in pugnacity.

"If you imagine, sir," he snapped, "that I am going to be kept out of my own laboratory by a gang of dirty poisoners you're wrong. If the Inspector here considers it necessary he can send one of his men to stand outside the house. But not one jot will I deviate from my ordinary method of life for twenty would-be murderers. Incidentally" – he added curiously – "how did you know a man had been here?"

"The position of the cellar door," answered Drummond. "It's a heavy door, and I know how I left it when we went in. It was a foot farther open when we came out – and there is no draught."

Sir John nodded approvingly.

"Quick: I like quickness. What in the name of fortune have you done to your face?"

"Don't you worry about my face, Sir John," said Drummond quietly: "you concentrate on your own life."

"And you mind your own business, young man," snapped the other angrily. "My life is my own affair."

"It isn't," answered Drummond. "It's the nation's – until you've analysed that stuff. After that, I agree with you: no one is likely to care two hoots."

Sir John turned purple.

"You insolent young puppy," he stuttered. "Cut it out, you silly little man," said Drummond wearily. "But don't forget – I've warned you. Come on, Stockton: we'll rope in the others and push off. Mount Street finds me, Mac; but I must have some sleep. Let me know how things go, like a good fellow."

"Sorry I lost my temper with the little bloke," he said to me, as he spun the Hispano into the Euston Road. "But really, old man, this stunt of yours is enough to try anybody's nerves."

The other four were behind, all more or less asleep, and I was nodding myself. In fact I hardly noticed where he was taking us until we pulled up in front of his house.

"My warrior can take you round and drop you," he said, yawning prodigiously. "And tomorrow we might resume the good work."

Personally I didn't even get as far as bed. I just fell asleep in an easy-chair in my room, until I woke with a start to find the lights lit and someone shaking me by the shoulder.

It was Drummond, and the look on his face made me sit up quickly.

"They've got him," he said, "as I knew they would. Sir John was stabbed through the heart in his laboratory an hour ago."

"My God!" I muttered. "How do you know?"

"MacIver has just rung up. Stockton – as I've said before – we're up against the real thing this time."

CHAPTER 7

In which I appear to become irrelevant

I think it was the method of the murder of Sir John that brought home to me most forcibly the nerve of the gang that confronted us. And though there will be many people who remember the affair, yet, for the benefit of those who do not, I will set forth what happened as detailed in the papers of the following day. The cutting is before me as I write.

"Another astounding and cold-blooded murder occurred between the hours of nine and ten last night. Sir John Dallas, the well-known scientist and authority on toxicology, was stabbed through the heart in his own laboratory.

"The following are the facts of the case. Sir John, as our readers will remember, gave evidence as recently as the day before yesterday in the sensational Robin Gaunt affair. He described in court the action of the new and deadly poison, by means of which the dog, the policeman and the Australian – David Ganton – had been killed. He also stated that he was endeavouring to analyse the drug, and there can be little doubt that he was engaged on that very work when he met his end.

"It appears that yesterday afternoon a further and, at present, secret development occurred which caused Sir John to feel hopeful of success. He returned to his house in Eaton Square in time for dinner, which he had served in his study – the usual course of procedure when he was busy. At eight-thirty he rang the bell and Elizabeth Perkins, the parlour-maid, came and removed the tray. He was apparently completely absorbed in his research at that time, since he failed to answer her twice repeated question as to what time he would like his milk. On the desk in front of him was a bottle containing a colourless liquid which looked like water, and a small cardboard box.

"These facts are interesting in view of what is to follow, and may prove to have an important bearing on the case. At between nine o'clock and a quarter-past the front-door bell rang, and it was answered by Perkins. There was a man outside who stated that he had come to see Sir John on a very important matter. She told him that Sir John was busy, but when he told her that it was in connection with Sir John's work that he was there, she showed him along the passage to the laboratory. And then she heard the stranger say distinctly, 'I've come from Scotland Yard, Sir John.'

"Now there can be but little doubt that this man was the murderer himself, since no one from Scotland Yard visited Sir John at that hour. And as walking openly into a man's house, killing him, and walking out again requires a nerve possessed by few, the added touch of introducing himself as a member of the police is quite in keeping with the whole amazing case.

"To return, however, to what happened. Perkins, having shown this man into the laboratory, returned to the servants' hall, where she remained till ten o'clock. At ten o'clock she had a standing order to take Sir John a glass of warm milk, if he had not rung for it sooner. She got the milk and took it along to the laboratory. She knocked and, receiving no answer, she entered the room. At first she thought he must have gone out, as the laboratory appeared to be empty, and then, suddenly, she saw a leg sticking out from behind the desk. She went quickly to the place to find, to her horror, that Sir John was lying on the floor with a dagger driven up to the hilt in his heart.

"She saw at a glance that he was dead, and rushing out of the house she called in a policeman, who at once rang up Scotland

Yard. Inspector MacIver, who, it will be recalled, is in charge of
the Robin Gaunt mystery, at once hurried to the scene. And it
was he who elucidated the fact that the bottle containing the
colourless liquid, and the little cardboard box, had completely
disappeared. It seems, therefore, impossible to doubt that at any
rate one motive for the murder of this distinguished savant was
the theft of these two things with their unknown contents. And
further, since we know that Sir John was experimenting with this
mysterious new poison, the connection between this dastardly
crime and the Gaunt affair seems conclusive.

"The matter is in the capable hands of Inspector MacIver, and
it is to be hoped that before long the cold-blooded criminals
concerned will be brought to justice. It is an intolerable and
disquieting state of affairs that two such appalling crimes can be
committed in London within three days of one another."

Which was a fair sample of what they all said. The *Daily
Referee* offered a reward of a thousand pounds to the first person
who discovered a clue which should lead to the arrest of the
murderer or murderers. "Retired Colonel" and "Frankly
disgusted" inflicted their opinions on a long-suffering public;
and as day after day went past and nothing happened, Scotland
Yard began to get it hot and strong in the Press.

Somehow or other MacIver managed to hush up the death of
the woman at Number 12 Ashworth Gardens, but there was no
getting away from the fact that the authorities were seriously
perturbed. Their principal cause of anxiety lay, as I have shown,
in a fact unknown to the public; and whereas the latter were
chiefly concerned with bringing the murderers to book, Scotland
Yard and the Secret Service's chief worry was as to what had
happened to the secret. Had it been disposed of to a foreign
Power? If so, to which?

The only ray of comfort during the weeks that followed lay in
Drummond's happy idea of dividing the antidote – if it was an
antidote – into two portions. For MacIver's specimen had been

analysed, and its exact composition was known. The trouble lay in the fact that it was impossible to carry out further experiments, since we possessed none of the poison. For an antidote to be efficacious it is advisable to know how to use it, and since the most obvious way was not the correct one, we were not much farther advanced. Still, the general opinion was that Drummond's theory was correct, and all the necessary steps were taken to allow its immediate manufacture on a large scale, should occasion arise.

Gradually, as was only natural, public interest died down. Nothing further happened, and it seemed to all of us that the events of those few days were destined to have no sequel. Only Drummond, in fact, continued to do anything: the rest of us slipped back into the normal tenor of our ways. He still periodically disappeared for hours at a time – generally in a disguise of some sort. He was not communicative as to what he did during these absences, and after a time he, too, seemed to be losing interest. But the whole thing rankled in his mind: he made no secret of that.

"Put it how you like," he said to me on one occasion, "we got very much the worst of it, Stockton. They got away with everything they wanted, right under our noses. And positively the only thing we have to show for our trouble is the antidote."

"A pretty considerable item," I reminded him.

He grunted.

"Oh, for ten minutes with gorse bush alone," he sighed. "Or even five."

"You may get it yet," I said.

Off and on we saw a good deal of MacIver, in whose mind the affair rankled also. The comments in the Press concerning Scotland Yard had not pleased him, and I rather gathered that the comments of his immediate superiors had not pleased him either. It was particularly the murder of Sir John Dallas that infuriated him, and over which criticism was most bitter. The other affair contained an element of mystery; a suspicion, almost of the uncanny. There seemed to be some excuse for his failure in connection with Robin Gaunt. But there was no element of mystery over stabbing a man to death. It was just a plain straightforward murder. And yet it remained wrapped in as dense a fog as the other. It was perfectly true that Elizabeth Perkins stated that she would recognise the man again. But, as MacIver said, what was the use of that unless he could first be found? And as she was quite unable to describe him, beyond saying that he was of medium height, clean-shaven and dark, the prospect of finding him was remote. At a conservative estimate her description would have fitted some ten million men.

The case of the man called Doctor Helias held out a little more prospect of success. Drummond and I separately described that human monstrosity to MacIver, and within two days a description of him was circulated all over the world. But, as Major Jackson pointed out a little moodily, it wasn't likely to prove of much use. If our fears were justified: if the secret of the poison had been handed over to a foreign Power, it was clear that Doctor Helias was an agent of that Power. And if so they wouldn't give him away.

It certainly proved of no use: no word or trace of him was discovered. He seemed to have disappeared as completely as everyone else connected with the business.

Another thing MacIver did was to turn his attention to the genuine owner of Number 12. First he tracked the maid, and we found out that part, at any rate, of the story told us by the woman who had died was true. Someone had come round and asked Miss Simpson to let the house: she had talked it over later with the maid. And on a certain morning a wire had come stating that her mother was ill, and summoning the maid to her home in Devonshire. To her surprise she found her mother perfectly fit. The wire had been sent from the village by a woman; that was all they could tell her at the Post Office. And then next morning, when she was still puzzling over the affair, had come a letter in Miss Simpson's handwriting. It was brief and to the point, stating that she had decided after all to let her house, and was proposing to travel. And it enclosed a month's wages in lieu of notice. The maid had felt hurt at such a brusque dismissal, and was shortly going to another place.

"That's really all I got out of her," said MacIver, "except for a description of Miss Simpson. She is short and fat, as Captain Drummond surmised. Also, according to the maid, she has no near relatives and very few friends. She hardly went out at all, and no one ever came to the house. Moreover, the description the maid gave me of the woman who came to ask to rent the house would fit the woman who impersonated Miss Simpson and was killed, which may be poetic justice, but it doesn't help us much."

Inquiries as to Miss Simpson's predecessors helped as little. Messrs. Paul & Paul were the agents right enough; but all they could say, having consulted their books, was that the house had belonged to a Mr Startin, who, they believed, had gone abroad. And they knew absolutely nothing about him.

"A dead end everywhere," said MacIver despondently. "Never in the whole course of my career have I seen every trace so completely covered. They set the whole Press blazing from end to end in the country, and then they disappear as if they were wiped out."

And then on the 20th of June occurred the next link in the chain. It was an isolated one, and it is safe to say that the few people who may have read the paragraph in the papers never connected it with the other issues.

"A fisherman named Daniel Coblen made a gruesome discovery late yesterday afternoon. He was walking over the rocks near the Goodrington Sands at Paignton when he saw something floating in the sea. It proved to be the body of a woman in an advanced stage of decomposition. He at once informed the police. From marks on the unfortunate lady's garments it appears that her name was A. Simpson. Doctor Epping, who made an examination, stated that she must have been dead for considerably over a month."

As I say, the few people who may have read the paragraph would assuredly have traced no connection between it and Sir John Dallas being stabbed to death, but MacIver went down post haste to Paignton. It transpired at the inquest that death was due to drowning: no marks of violence could be found on the body. But the point of interest lay in how it had happened. How had she been drowned? No local boatman knew anything about it: no ship had reported that any passenger of that name was missing. How then had Miss Simpson been drowned?

That it was a question of foul play seemed obvious – but beyond that one bald fact everything seemed blank. The gang had decided to get rid of her, and they had chosen drowning as the method. Why they had done so was a totally different matter.

It was well-nigh inconceivable that they would have taken the trouble to put her on board a boat merely to take her out to sea and drown her, when their record in London showed that they had no hesitation in using far more direct methods. It seemed to add but one more baffling feature to a case that contained no lack of them already.

And the sole result was that Drummond's interest, which had seemed to be waning, revived once more. Sometimes I wonder if Drummond, with that strangely direct brain of his, didn't have a glimmering of the truth. Not the final actual truth – that would have been impossible at that stage of the proceedings; but a glimpse of the open ground through the trees. He said nothing then, and when I asked him the other day he only shrugged his shoulders. But I wonder... Day after day he disappeared by himself until his wife grew quite annoyed about it. As a matter of fact I, too, thought he was wasting his time. What he was doing, or where he went, he would never say. He just departed in the morning or after lunch, and often did not return till two or three in the morning. And since there seemed to be nothing particular to look for, and no particular place to look for it in, the whole thing struck me as somewhat pointless.

It was about that time that I began to see a good deal of Major Jackson. His club had been closed down for structural repairs, and the members had come to mine. So I saw Jackson two or three times a week at lunch. General Darton, too, was frequently there, and sometimes we shared the same table. On the whole I thought they were fairly optimistic: nothing had as yet been heard from any of our agents abroad which led them to suspect any particular Power of having acquired the secret.

"Somebody must have it presumably," said the General. "Crimes of that sort aren't perpetrated for fun. But the great point, Stockton, is this – we've got the antidote. It might be quite useful if we could discover how it worked," he added sarcastically.

"Anyway those squirting machines must have a very small range, and there still are rifles left in the world amidst this mass of filthy chemicals."

The worthy infantryman snorted, and Jackson kicked me gently under the table. He was off on his favourite topic, and he required no assistance from us. Only now as I look back on that conversation, which was only one of many similar ones, that big fundamental mistake of ours looms large. It was a natural mistake, particularly since the War Office had been concerned in the affair from the very beginning. Automatically their gaze was fixed on the foreign target; and it was tacitly assumed by us all that the direction was right. Until, that is, Drummond proved it wrong.

At the time, however, all of us who knew the inner history of the affair had our attention fixed abroad; and for the rest – the great general public – the Robin Gaunt mystery had become a back number. The Press had buried him in a final tirade of obloquy and turned its attention to other things – principally, as will be remembered, the Wilmot dirigible airship.

It was in July, I see after reference to my files, that the Wilmot airship publicity stunt was first started. Up to that date airships were regarded as essentially connected with the fighting services. And it was then that the big endeavour was made to popularise them commercially.

The first difficulty which the promoters of the scheme had to overcome was a distinct feeling of nervousness on the part of the public. Aeroplanes they were accustomed to: the magnificent Croydon to Paris service was by this time regarded as being as safe as the boat train. But airships were a different matter. Airships caught fire and burned: airships broke their backs and crashed: airships had all sorts of horrible accidents.

The second difficulty was financial nervousness in the City, doubtless induced largely by the physical nervousness of the public. Would a fleet of airships – six was the number suggested – pay? They were costly things to construct: a mooring mast worked out at about £25,000 – a shed at more than £100,000. Would it prove a commercial success?

And the promoters of the scheme, rightly realising that the first difficulty was the greater, took every step they could to reassure the public. Who can fail to remember that beautiful, graceful ship circling over London day after day: going long trips over the Midlands and down to the West Country: anchored to the revolving top of the lattice-work mooring mast?

And then came the celebrated trip on July 25th, when representatives from every important London paper were taken for a trial voyage, and entertained to a luncheon during the journey which the Ritz itself could not have beaten.

I have before me a copy of the *Morning Herald* of the 26th in which an account of the trip is given. And I cannot refrain from quoting a brief extract. Having described the journey, and paid a glowing tribute to the beauty and the comfort of the airship, the writer proceeds as follows:

"Then came the culminating moment of this wonderful experience. Lunch was over, a meal which no restaurant *de luxe* could have bettered. The drone of the engines ceased, and, as we drifted gently down wind, the whole gorgeous panorama of English woodland scenery unfolded itself before our eyes. It was the psychological moment of the day: it was the fitting moment for Mr Wilmot to say a few words. He rose, and we tore our eyes away from the view to look at the man who had made that view possible. Tall, thick-set, and with greying hair and eyes gleaming with enthusiasm he stood at the end of the table.

" 'I am not going to say much,' he remarked, in his deep steady voice – a voice which holds the faintest suspicion of American accent, 'but I feel that this occasion may mark the beginning of a new epoch in British aviation. Today you have seen for yourselves something of the possibilities of the airship as opposed to the aeroplane: I want the public to see those possibilities too. The lunch which you have eaten has been prepared entirely on board: not one dish was brought into the kitchen ready-made. I mention that to show that the domestic arrangements are, as I think you will agree, passably efficient. But that, after all, is a detail. Think of the other possibilities. A range of 3000 miles carrying fifty passengers in the essence of comfort. Australia in a fortnight; America in three days. And it is safe, gentlemen – safe. That is the message I want you to give the British public.' "

And at this point I can imagine the reader laying the book down in blank amazement. What, he will say, is the fellow talking about? What on earth has the Wilmot dirigible got to do with the matter? We all know that any hope of success for the scheme was killed when the airship crashed in flames. There were ridiculous rumours of Wilmot going mad, though for some reason or other the thing was hushed up in the papers. Anyway, what has it got to do with Gaunt and his poison?

Don't get irritable, my friend. I warned you that I am no story-teller: maybe if I was I could have averted your anger by some trick of the trade. And I admit it looks as if I had suddenly taken leave of my senses, and that a dissertation on the habits of ferrets would have been equally relevant. I will merely say that at the time I would have agreed with you. The Wilmot dirigible had as little to do with Robin Gaunt in my mind as the fact that my clerk's name was Stevens. If I ever thought of Mr Wilmot, which I presume I must have done, I pictured him as an ordinary business man who saw a great commercial future in the rigid airship. I take it that such was the picture in everybody's mind. I know that I heard of him lunching in the City: I know that I heard rumours of a company being actually floated. (The Duke of Wessex was to be one of the directors.)

The principal thing I did not know at the time was the truth. So bear with me, my irritated friend: in due course you shall know the truth yourself. Whether you believe it or not is a totally different matter.

Furthermore, I'm now going to make you angry again. More apparent red herrings are going to be drawn across the trail: herrings which, I once again repeat, seemed as red to me then as they will to you now.

On the 31st of July the celebrated American multi-millionaire, Cosmo A Miller, steamed into Southampton Water in his equally celebrated yacht, the *Hermione*. He had with him on board the type of party that a multi-millionaire might have been expected to entertain. To take the ladies first, there was his wife, for whom he had recently bought the notorious Shan diamonds. The diamonds of death, they had been christened: strange, wasn't it, how they lived up to their evil reputation! Then there was Angela Greymount, a well-known film star: Mrs Percy Franklin, a New York society woman and immensely wealthy; and finally Mrs James Delmer, the wife of a Chicago millionaire. The feminine side of the party was to be completed by the Duchess of Sussex – also an American, and Lady Agatha Dawkins, an extremely amusing woman whom I knew slightly. These last two were to join the yacht at Southampton, and it was to pick them up that the *Hermione* called there.

The men consisted of the owner, three American business friends, the Duke of Sussex and Tony Beddington, who was, incidentally, a pal of Drummond's. He and the Duke also joined the yacht in England.

Cowes week was in progress at the time, of course – so the eyes of social England and the pens of those who chronicle the doings of the great were already occupied in that quarter. But the arrival of the *Hermione* was something which dwarfed everything else. Never had so much wealth been gathered together in a private yacht before. Mrs Tattle, in that bright and breezy column which she contributed daily to the *Morning Express*, stated that the jewellery alone was worth over two million pounds sterling. And it is, I gather, a fact that a dear friend of Mrs Cosmo Miller's once stated that she'd lunched with Minnie's diamonds and she believed Minnie was inside.

The yacht itself was a miniature floating palace. It had a swimming pool and a gymnasium: it had listening-in sets and an electric piano encrusted in precious stones – or almost. There was gold plate for use at dinner, and the plebeian silver for lunch. In fact it was the supreme essence of blatant vulgarity.

In addition to the guests there were the Wallaby Coon Quartette, the Captain, the wireless operator, four maids, the chef and the writer of *The Three Hundred Best Cocktails* as barman. The crew numbered sixteen.

So that when the *Hermione* steamed slowly down Southampton Water there were in all forty souls on board. The sea was like a mill-pond; the date was August 2nd. On August 4th a marconigram was received in London by the firm of

Bremmer and Bremmer. It was from Mr Miller, and is of interest merely because it is the last recorded message received from the *Hermione*. From that moment she completely disappeared with every soul on board.

At first no one worried. When the *Hermione* failed to arrive at the Azores, which was originally intended, it was assumed that Mr Miller and his guests had changed their route. But when, on August 10th, Bremmer and Bremmer having obtained the information required by Mr Miller proceeded to wireless it to the *Hermione*, no response whatever was received from her. The sea was still beautifully calm: no report of any storms had been received from the Atlantic. And somewhere in the Atlantic the *Hermione* must be, since it was definitely certain she had not passed Gibraltar and entered the Mediterranean.

By August 12th the whole Press – English and American – was seething with it.

"Mysterious Disappearance of Multi-Millionaire's Yacht."

"Cosmo A Miller beats it with Wallaby Quartette."

"SY *Hermione* refuses wireless calls," etc., etc. Still no one took it seriously. The yacht was fitted with a Marconi installation: the sea was still like glass. The general opinion was that there had been a break-down in the engines, and that for some obscure reason the wireless was out of action.

But by August 20th, when the silence was still unbroken, the tone of the Press began to change. Once again I will refer to my file of cuttings, and quote from the *Morning Herald* of that date.

"The mysterious silence of the SY *Hermione* has now become inexplicable. The last communication from her was received more than a fortnight ago. Since then nothing further has been heard, though Mr Cosmo Miller, her owner, has been repeatedly called up on important business matters. It is impossible to avoid a feeling of grave anxiety that all is not well."

But what could have happened? The wireless operator was known to be a first-class man, and it seemed impossible that such damage could have happened to his instruments, in a perfectly calm sea, that he would be unable to effect a temporary cure.

Then some bright specimen had an idea which held the field for quite a while. It was just an advertisement – an elaborate publicity stunt. They were receiving all these messages, and taking no notice of them merely in order to keep the eyes of the world focused on them. Such a thing, it was argued, was quite in keeping with at any rate Mrs Miller's outlook on life. And it wasn't until August 25th came and went that one of the officials at Southampton Docks shattered that theory. The *Hermione*'s bunkers only held sufficient coal for the fortnight, and that only when steaming at her economic speed. And it was now twenty-four days since she had sailed.

By this tune the public on both sides of the Atlantic were very gravely perturbed. The wildest rumours were flying round: from pirates to sea serpents all sorts of suggestions were put forward.

Both the British and American navies despatched light cruisers to discover what they could; and it may be remembered that when Mr Wilmot's patriotic offer to place his airship at the disposal of the authorities was refused, he himself, at his own expense, went far out into the Atlantic to see if he could find out anything.

Nothing was ever discovered; no trace was found of the yacht. And no trace ever will be; for she sank with every soul on board.

Now for the first time I will put down what happened, and show the connection between the two chains of events – the big and the so-called little between the disappearance of the *Hermione* and Robin Gaunt's cry over the telephone. I will tell of the death of Mr Wilmot, and of what happened to the man called Helias in that lonely spot in Cornwall. And, perhaps, most important of all, certainly most interesting, I will set down word for word the last statement of Robin Gaunt.

CHAPTER 8

In which we come to Black Mine

But before I go on to pick up the thread of my story, I wish again to reiterate one thing. On September 5th, when Drummond rang me up at my office asking me to go round to his house at once, there was no inkling in my mind that there was any connection. Nor was there in his. The events I have just recorded were as irrelevant to us as they appear to be on these pages. In fact the last thing known to us which was connected in any way with Robin Gaunt in our minds was the discovery of Miss Simpson's body at Paignton.

So it was with a considerable feeling of surprise that I listened to what Drummond had to say over the telephone.

"Found out something that may be of value: can you come round at once?"

I went, to find, to my amazement, a man with him whom I had never expected to see again. It was little rat face, who had been put to watch Toby Sinclair and whom we had saved from hanging in Number 10. He was sitting on the edge of his chair, plucking nervously at a greasy hat in the intervals of getting outside a quart of Drummond's beer.

"You remember Mr Perton, don't you, old boy?" said Drummond, winking at me. "I happened to meet him this morning, and reminded him that there was a little matter of a fiver due to him."

"Well, gentlemen," said Mr Perton nervously, "I don't know as 'ow I can call it due, for I didn't do wot you told me to. But I couldn't, sir: I 'ad a dreadful time. You won't believe wot them devils did to me. They 'ung me."

"Did they indeed?" said Drummond quietly. "They don't seem to have done it very well."

"Gawd knows 'ow I escaped, guv'nor. They 'ung me, the swine – and left me swinging. I lost consciousness, I did – and then when I come to again, I was laying on the floor in the room alone. You bet yer life I didn't 'alf do a bolt."

"A very sound move, Mr Perton. Have some more beer? Now do you know why they hanged you?"

"Strite I don't, guv'nor. They said to me, they said – 'You're bait, my man: just bait.' They'd got me gagged, the swine: and they was a-peering out of the window. 'Here they come,' says one of 'em: 'trice 'im up!' So they triced me up, and then they give me a push to start me swinging. Then they does a bunk into the next 'ouse."

'How do you know they bunked into the next house?" said Drummond.

"Well, guv'nor, there was a secret door, there was – and they'd brought me from the next house."

He looked at us nervously, as if afraid of the reception of his story.

"How long had you been in the next house, Mr Perton," asked Drummond reassuringly, "before they brought you through the secret door to hang you?"

"Three or four hours, sir: bound and gagged. Thrown in the corner like a ruddy sack of pertaters. Just as I told you, sir."

"I know, Mr Perton; but I want my friend to hear what you have to say also. During those three or four hours whilst you were thrown in the corner, you heard them talking, didn't you?"

"Well, I didn't pay much attention, sir," said Mr Perton apologetically. "I was a-wondering wot was going to 'appen to me too 'ard. But there was a great black-bearded swine, who was swearing something awful. And two others wot was sitting at a table drinking whisky. They seemed to be fair wild about something. Then the other bloke come in – the bloke wot had been in Clarges Street that morning, and the one wot had brought me from the Three Cows to the 'ouse. They shut up swearing, though you could see they was still wild.

" 'You know wot to do,' says the new man, 'with regard to that thing.' He points to me, and I listened 'ard.

" 'We knows wot to do,' says the black-bearded swab, 'but it's damned tomfoolery.'

" 'That's for me to decide,' snaps the new bloke. 'I'll get the others next door, and I'll do the necessary once they're there.' They didn't say nothing then abaht making me swing, you see, so...

"Quite, Mr Perton," interrupted Drummond. "But they did say something else, didn't they?"

"Wot, that there bit about Land's Hend? Wot was it 'e said, now – old black beard? Yus – I know. 'We'll all be in 'ell's end,' he said, 'not Land's Hend if we goes on like this.' And then someone cursed 'im for a ruddy fool."

"You're sure of that, Mr Perton, aren't you? I could hear the excitement in Drummond's voice. "I mean the bit about Land's End?"

"Sure as I'm sitting 'ere, sir."

He took a large gulp of beer, and Drummond rose to his feet.

"Well, I'm much obliged to you, Mr Perton. I have your address in case I want it, and since you had such a rotten time, I must make that fiver a tenner." He thrust two notes into the little man's hand, rushed him through the door, and bawled for Denny to let him out. Then he came back, and his face was triumphant.

"Worth it, Stockton: worth day after day, night after night searching London for that man. Heavens! the amount of liquor I've consumed in the Three Cows."

"Great Scott!" I cried, "is that what you've been doing?"

"That – and nothing else. And then I ran into him this morning by accident outside your rooms in Clarges Street. Still, it's been worth it: we've got a clue at last."

"You mean?" I said, a little bewildered.

"Land's End, man: Land's End," he cried. "I nearly kicked the desk over when he said it first. Then I sent for you: I wanted him to repeat his story for confirmation. He did – word for word. The fog is lifting a little, old boy: one loose end is accounted for at any rate. I always thought they hanged the poor little swine in order to get a sitting shot at us. As they told him – bait. But, anyway, that is all past, and a trifle. He's got a tenner in his pocket and two quarts of beer in his stomach – and we can let him pass out of the picture. We, on the contrary, I hope and trust, are just going to pass into it again."

"You really think," I said a little doubtfully, "that we're likely to find out anything at Land's End?"

"I'm going to have a damned good try, Stockton," he said quietly. "On his own showing the little man was listening with all his ears at that time, and it seems incredible to me that he would invent a thing like that. We know that the rest of his story was true – the part that he would think us least likely to believe. Very well, then: assuming that black beard did make that remark it must have had some meaning. And what meaning can it have had except the obvious one? – namely, that the gang was going to Land's End. Why they went to Land's End, Heaven alone knows. But what this child knows is that we're going there too. I've warned in the boys: Toby, Peter and Ted are coming with us. Algy is stopping behind here to guard the fort."

"What about MacIver?" I asked. Drummond grinned.

"Mac hates leaving London," he remarked.

"And if by any chance we do run into gorse bush, I feel MacIver would rather cramp my style. When can you start?"

"Well," I said doubtfully. "After lunch?"

143

"I've got a rather important brief."

"Damn your brief."

I did, and after lunch we started. We went in the Hispano, and spent the night in Exeter.

"Tourists, old lads," remarked Drummond. That's what we are. Visiting Penzance. Let's make that our headquarters."

And so at four o'clock on the 6th September five tourists arrived at Penzance and took rooms at an hotel. But should any doubting reader who dwells in that charming West Country town search the various hotel registers I can tell him in advance that he will find no record of our names. Further, I may say that mine host at Exeter would have been hard put to it to recognise the five men who got out of the Hispano in Penzance. There was no point in handicapping ourselves unnecessarily, and Drummond and I at any rate would be certainly recognised by the gang, even if the others weren't. .

The next day we split up. The plan of action we had decided on was to search the whole of the ground west of a line drawn from St Ives to Mount's Bay. We split it into five approximately equal parts with the help of a large-scale ordnance map, and each part worked out at about ten square miles.

"To do it properly should take three or perhaps four days," said Drummond. "It's hilly going, and the north coast is full of caves. If anybody discovers anything, report to the hotel at once. Further, in order to be on the safe side we'd better all return here every night."

We drew lots for our beats, and I got the centre strip terminating to the north in the stretch of coast on each side of Gurnard's Head. Having a very mild sketching ability I decided that I would pose as an artist. So I purchased the necessary gear, slung a pair of Zeiss field-glasses over my shoulder and started off. I had determined to work my strip from north to south, since I felt sure that if the gang was there at all they would have chosen the desolate country in the north or centre rather than the comparatively populous part near Penzance itself.

The weather was glorious, and since I happen to love walking I foresaw a very pleasant holiday in store. I admit frankly that I did not share the optimism of the others. It struck me that, considering over four months had elapsed, we were building altogether too much on a chance remark.

This is not a guide-book, so I won't bore my readers with rhapsodies over the scenery. The granite cliffs carved and indented into fantastic shapes by countless centuries of erosion: the wild rugged tors rising from the high moorland – it is all too well known to need any further description from my pen. And the desolation of it! Here and there a deserted mine shaft – tin, I supposed, or copper. No longer a paying proposition: not even worth the labour of dismantling the rusty machinery.

I stopped for a few moments to light my pipe, and a passing shepherd touched his cap.

"Going sketching, sir," he said in his delightful West Country burr. "There certainly do be some fine views round these parts."

I walked with him for a while, listening absent mindedly to his views on men and matters. And, in common with a large number of people in many walks of life, he was of the opinion that things were not what they were. The good old days! Those were the times.

I remember, sir, when each one of them was a working concern." He paused and pointed to a derelict mine below us. "That was Damar Mine – that was, and two hundred men used to work there."

"Bad luck on them," I said, "but I think as far as the scenery is concerned it's better as it is. Didn't pay, I suppose?"

"That's it, sir: didn't pay. Though they do say as how the men that are working Black Mine are going to make it pay. A rare lot of money they're putting into it, so Peter Tregerthen told me. He be one of the foremen."

"Where is Black Mine?" I asked perfunctorily.

"Just over this hill, sir, and you'll see it. Only started in May, they did. Queer people too."

I stared at him: it was impossible, of course – just a coincidence...

"How do you mean – queer people?" I asked.

"Peter Tregerthen he tells me as how they've got queer ideas," he answered. "Scientific mining they're a-going for: carrying out lots of experiments secretly – things which the boss says will revolutionise the industry. But so far nothing seems to have come of them: they just goes on mining in the old way. There it is, sir: that's Black Mine."

We had reached the top of the tor, and below us, a quarter of a mile away, lay the road from Land's End to St Ives. On the other side, half-way between the road and the edge of the cliffs, stood the works, and for a moment or two a sudden uncontrollable excitement took hold of me. Was it possible that our search was ended almost before it had begun? And then I took a pull at myself: I was jumping ahead with a vengeance. To base such an idea on a mere coincidence in dates and a Cornish miner's statement that the owners were queer people was ridiculous. And anything less nefarious than the peaceful appearance of Black Mine would have been hard to imagine. Smoke drifted lazily up from the tall chimney, and lines of trucks drawn by horses passed and repassed.

"How many men are employed there?" I asked my companion.

"Not many, sir, yet," he answered. "It's up in that wooden building yonder on the edge of the cliffs that they be experimenting as I told you. No one aren't allowed near at all. In fact Peter Tregerthen he did tell me that one day he went up and there was a terrible scene. He wanted for to ask the boss something or t'other, and the boss very nigh sacked him. Well, sir, I reckons I must be a-going on. Be you waiting here?"

"Yes," I said. "I think I'll stop here a bit. Good-morning to you."

I watched him go down the hill and strike the road : then, moved by a sudden impulse, I retraced my steps to the reverse slope of the tor, and lying down behind a rock I focused my field-glasses on the wooden building which was so very private in its owners' estimation. It seemed a perfectly ordinary erection, though considerably larger than I had thought when I saw it with the naked eye. I could see now that it stretched back some distance from the edge of the cliff, though, being foreshortened, it was hard to guess any dimensions.

Of signs of life in it I could see none. No one entered or left, and on the land-side – the only one I could observe properly – there were no windows as far as I could make out. And then a sudden glint, such as the sun makes when its light strikes something shining, came from up near the roof. It was not repeated, though I kept my glasses glued on the spot for ten minutes.

It was as I was coming to the conclusion that I was wasting time, and that an inspection from closer range was indicated (after all they couldn't sack me), that a man came out of the building and walked towards the mine. I saw, on consulting the ordnance map, that the mine itself was just over half-a-mile from where I lay, and the cliff's edge was distant a further half-mile. And it was just about ten minutes before the man reappeared on my side of the mine buildings. I watched him idly: he was still too far off for me to be able to distinguish his features. After a while he struck the road, but instead of turning along it one way or the other he came straight on, and commenced to climb the hill. In fact it suddenly dawned on me that he was coming directly for me. I slipped backwards out of sight, and hurriedly set up my easel and camp stool, only to see another man approaching from my right rear. And the second man must have seen my hurried preparations. However, I argued to myself that there is no law that prevents a man admiring a view through field-glasses preparatory to sketching it. And though as an argument it was perfectly sound, the presence of Drummond would have been far more comforting.

"Good-morning."

The man who had come from the mine breasted the rise in front of me, and I glanced up. He was a complete stranger, with a dark rather swarthy face, and I returned the compliment politely.

"Sketching, I see," he remarked affably.

"Just beginning," I answered. And then I took the bull by the horns. "I've been admiring the country through my glasses most of the morning."

"So I perceived," said another voice behind my shoulder. It was the second man, who again I failed to recognise. "You seemed to decide to start work very suddenly."

"I presume," I remarked coldly, "that I can decide to start work when I like, where I like, and how I like. The matter is my business, and my business only."

A quick look passed between the two men, and then the first arrival spoke.

"Of course," he remarked still more affably. "But the fact of the matter is this. By way of experiment a small syndicate of us have taken over Black Mine. We believe, I trust rightly, that we have stumbled on a method which will enable us to make a large fortune out of tin mining. The information has leaked out, and we have had several people attempting to spy on us. Please wait," – he held up his hand as I began an indignant protest. "Now that I have seen you, I am perfectly sure that you are not one of them. But you will understand that we must take precautions."

"I would be obliged," I remarked sarcastically, "if you would tell me how you think I can discover your secret – even granted I knew anything about tin-mining, which I don't – from the range of a mile."

"A very natural remark," he replied. "But, to adopt military terms for a moment, there is such a thing as reconnoitring a position, I believe, before attempting to assault it."

"Which it seems to me, sir, you have been doing pretty thoroughly this morning," put in the other.

I rose to my feet angrily.

"Look here," I said, "I've had about enough of this. I'm an Englishman, and this is England. If you will inform me of any law which prohibits me from looking through field-glasses at anything I like for as long as I like, I shall be pleased to listen to you. If, however, you can't, I should be greatly obliged if you'd both of you go to blazes. I may say that the question of tin-mining leaves me even colder than your presence."

Once again I saw a quick glance pass between them.

"There is no good losing your temper, sir," said the first man. "We are speaking in the most friendly way. And since you have no connection with the tin-mining industry there is no need for us to say any more."

"I certainly have no connection with the tin-mining industry," I agreed. "But for the sake of argument supposing I had. Is that a crime?"

"In this locality, and from our point of view," he smiled, "it is. In fact it is worse than a crime: it is a folly. Several people have proved that to their cost. Good-morning."

I watched them go, and my first thought was to pack up and walk straight back to the hotel. And then saner counsels prevailed. That second man – where had he come from? I felt certain now that that flash had been a signal. Or an answer. He must have been lying up in that high ground behind me on the right. And glancing round I could see hundreds of places where men could lie hidden and watch my every movement.

Was it genuine? that was the whole point. Was all this talk about revolutionising tin-mining the truth, or merely an elaborate bluff? There below me was an actual tin mine going full blast, which substantiated their claim. Anyway the main thing was to give them no further cause for suspicion. And in view of the fact that for all I knew unseen eyes might still be watching me, I decided to stop on for a couple of hours, eat my lunch, and then saunter back to Penzance. Moreover, I determined that I wouldn't use the field-glasses again. I had seen all I could from that distance, so there was no object in rousing further suspicion in the event of my being watched.

Was it genuine? The question went on reiterating itself in my mind. And it was still unanswered when I returned to the hotel about tea-time. I had seen no trace of any other watcher; the high ground on each side of me had seemed silent and deserted while I ate my lunch and sketched perfunctorily for an hour or so. Was it genuine? Or did the so-called secret process cloak something far more sinister?

We weighed up the points for and against the second alternative over a round of short ones before dinner.

Points for – Coincidence of dates and the very special precautions taken to prevent outsiders approaching. Point against – Why come to a derelict tin mine in the back of beyond, and incur all the expense of paying miners, when on the face of it a far more accessible and cheaper location could be found?

"In fact," remarked Drummond, "the matter can only be solved in one way. We will consume one more round of this rather peculiar tipple which that sweet girl fondly imagines is a Martini: we will then have dinner: and after that we will go and see for ourselves."

"Supposing it is genuine?" I said doubtfully.

"Then, as in the case of Aunt Amelia, we will apologise and withdraw. And if they refuse to accept our apologies and show signs of wishing to rough-house, Heaven forbid that we should disappoint them."

We started at nine in the car. There was no moon and we decided to approach from the west, that is, the Land's End direction.

"We'll leave the car a mile or so away – hide it if possible," said Drummond. "And then, Stockton, call up your war lore, for we're going to have a peerless night creep."

"Do we scatter, Hugh, or go in a bunch?" asked Jerningham.

"Ordinary patrol, Ted. I'll lead: you fellows follow in pairs."

His eyes were gleaming with excitement; and if my own feelings were any criterion we were all of us in the same condition. My doubts of the morning had been replaced by a quite unjustifiable optimism: I felt that we were on the track again at last. Undoubtedly the wish was father to the thought, but as we got into the car after dinner I was convinced that these were no genuine experimenters in tin.

"Carry a revolver, but don't use it except as a last resort."

Such were Drummond's orders, followed by a reminder of the stringent necessity for silence.

"On their part as well as our own," he said quietly. "If you stumble on anyone, don't let him give the alarm."

In our pockets we each of us had a gag, a large handkerchief, a length of fine rope, and a villainous-looking weapon which Drummond alluded to as Mary. It was a short, heavily loaded stick, and as he calmly produced these nefarious objects from his suit-case, followed by five decent-sized bottles of chloroform, I couldn't help roaring with laughter.

"Always travel hoping for the best," he grinned. "Don't forget, boys – no shooting. To put it mildly, it would be distinctly awkward if we killed a genuine tin merchant."

It was ten o'clock when we reached a spot at which Drummond considered it sound to park the car. For the last two miles we had been travelling without lights, and with the aid of a torch we confirmed our position on the map.

"I make out that there is another ridge beyond the one in front of us before we get to Black Mine," said Drummond. "If that's so and they've got the place picketed, the sentry will be on the further one. Man-handle her in, boys: she'll make a noise on reverse."

We backed the car off the road into a small deserted quarry and then, with a final inspection to see that all our kit was complete, we started off. Toby and I came five yards behind Drummond, with the other two behind us again, and I soon began to realise that the yarns I had heard from time to time – told casually by his pals about our leader – were not exaggerated. I have mentioned before his marvellous gift of silent movement in the dark; and I had myself seen an exhibition of it in the house in Ashworth Gardens. But that was indoors: that night I was to see it in the open. You could hear nothing: you could see nothing, until suddenly he would loom up under your nose with whispered instructions.

Toby had had previous experience of him, but the first time it happened I very nearly made a fool of myself. It was so utterly unexpected that, never dreaming it was he, I lunged at him viciously with my loaded stick. The blow fell on empty air, and I heard him chuckle faintly.

"Steady, old man," he whispered from somewhere behind me. "Don't lay me out at this stage of the proceedings. We're just short of the top of the first ridge: spread out sideways until we're over. Then same formation. Pass it back."

We waited till the other two bumped into us, I feeling the most infernal ass. And then, even as we were passing on the orders, there came a faint snarling noise away to our left. We stared in the direction it came from, but it was not repeated. All was silent save for the lazy beat of the breakers far below.

"By Gad! you fellows, we've bumped the first sentry." Drummond materialised out of the night. "Fell right on top of him. Had to dot him one. What's that?"

A stone moved a few yards away from us, and a low voice called out – "Martin! Martin – are you there? What was that noise? God! this gives me the jumps. Martin – where are you? Ah – "

The beginnings of a scream were stifled in the speaker's throat, and we moved cautiously forward to find Drummond holding someone by the throat.

"Put him to sleep, Ted," he whispered, and the sickly smell of chloroform tainted the air.

"Lash him up and gag him," said Drummond, and then, with infinite precaution, be switched his torch for a second on to the man's face. He was one of the two who had spoken to me that morning.

"Good," said Drummond cheerfully. "We won't bother about the other: he will sleep for several hours. And now, having mopped up the first ridge, let us proceed to do even likewise with the second. Hullo! what the devil is that light doing? Out to sea there."

Three flashes and a long pause – then two flashes. That was all: after that, though we waited several times, we saw nothing more.

"Obviously a signal of some sort," remarked Drummond. "And presumably it is to our friends in front. By Jove! you fellows, is it possible that we've run into a bunch of present-day smugglers? What a perfectly gorgeous thought. Let's get on with it. There's not likely to be anyone in the hollow in front, but go canny in case of accidents. Same formation as before, and spread out when we come to the next ridge."

Once more we started off. Periodically I glanced out to sea, but there was no repetition of the signal. Whatever boat had made it was lying off there now without lights – waiting. And for what? Smugglers? Possible, of course. But what a coast to choose! And yet was it a bad one? Well out of the beaten track: full of caves: sparsely populated. One thing anyway seemed certain. If the signal had been intended for the present owners of Black Mine, it rather disposed of the genuineness of their claim. The connection between tin-mining secrets and mysterious signals out at sea seemed rather too obscure to be credible.

"Hit him, Stockton."

Toby Sinclair's urgent voice startled me out of my theorising just in time. I had literally walked on a man, and it was a question of the fraction of a second as to whether he got away and gave the alarm.

"Good biff," came in Drummond's whisper as the man crashed. "I've got the other beauty. We're through the last line."

The other two had joined us, and for a while we stood there listening. Ahead of us some three hundred yards away was the Black Mine: to the left, on the edge of the cliff, the wooden house stood outlined against the sky. And even as we stared at it a door opened for a second, letting out a shaft of light as someone came out.

"So our friends are not in bed," said Drummond softly. "There is activity in the home circle. Let's go and join the party. We'll make for the edge of the cliff a bit this side of the house."

It was farther than it looked, but we met no more sentries. No further trace of life showed in the wooden house as we worked our way cautiously forward.

"Careful." Drummond's whisper came from just in front of us. "We're close to the edge." He was peering in front, and suddenly he turned round and gripped my arm. "Look up there towards the house. See anything? Underneath a little – just below the top of the cliff."

I stared at the place he indicated, and sure enough there was a patch which seemed less dark than its surroundings.

"There's a heavily screened light inside there," he muttered. "It's an opening in the cliff."

And then, quite clearly audible over the lazy beat of the sea below, we heard the sound of rowlocks.

"This is where we go closer," said Drummond. "It strikes me things are going to happen."

We crept towards the house, and I know that I at any rate was quivering with excitement. I could just see Drummond in front well enough to conform to his every movement. He paused every now and then, but not for long, and I pictured him peering into the darkness with that uncanny sight of his. Once, I remember, he stopped for nearly five minutes, and while I lay there trying to stop the pounding of my heart I thought I heard voices below. Then he went on again, until the house seemed almost on top of us.

At last he stopped for good, and I saw him beckoning to us to come and join him. He was actually on the edge of the cliff, and when I reached his side and passed over, I very nearly gave the show away in my surprise. Not twenty feet below us a man's head was sticking out of the face of the cliff. We could see it outlined against a dim light that came from inside, and he was paying out something hand over hand. At first I couldn't see what it was. It looked like a rope, and yet it seemed singularly stiff and inflexible.

"Form a circle," breathed Drummond to the other three. "Not too near. For Heaven's sake don't let us be surprised from behind."

"What on earth is it that he's paying out?" I whispered in his ear as he once more lay down beside me.

"Tubing of sorts," he answered. "Don't talk – watch."

From below came a whistle, and the man immediately stopped. Then a few seconds later came another whistle and the man disappeared. Something must have swung into position behind him, for the light no longer shone out; only a faint lessening of the darkness marked the spot where he had been. And then, though it may have been my imagination, I thought I heard a slight gurgling noise such as a garden hose makes when you first turn the water on.

For some time nothing further happened; then again from below came the whistle. He must have been waiting for it from behind the screen, for he reappeared instantly. As before the light shone on him, and suddenly I felt Drummond's hand close on my arm like a vice. *For the man was wearing indiarubber gauntlets.*

Coil by coil he pulled the tubing up until it was all in: then again he disappeared and the screen swung down, shutting out the light.

"Stockton," whispered Drummond, "we've found 'em."

"What are you going to do?" I asked.

"Explore," he said quietly. "If we'd got through without bumping their sentries, I'd have given it a chance till daylight tomorrow. As it is, it's now or never."

"Then I'm coming with you," I remarked.

"All right," he whispered. "But I'm going down to reconnoitre first."

He collected the other three and gave his orders. He, Jerningham and I would go down and force an entrance through the front of the cliff: the other two would guard our retreat and hold the rope for us to ascend again. But Toby was adamant. There was a large post rammed into the ground for some purpose or other to which the rope could be attached, and he and Peter insisted on coming too. And even in the darkness I could see Drummond's quick grin as he agreed.

"As soon as I signal all right, the next man comes down. And if they find the bally rope and cut it we'll fight our way out through the back door. One other thing: instructions *re* revolvers cancelled. It's shoot quick, and shoot often. Great Heavens! what's that?"

From somewhere near by there came a dreadful chattering laugh followed by a babble of words which died away as abruptly as it had started. To the others it was merely a sudden noise, staggering because of the unexpectedness of it, but to me it was a paralysing shock which for the moment completely unnerved me. For the voice which had babbled at us out of the night was the voice of Robin Gaunt.

CHAPTER 9

In which we are entertained strangely in Black Mine

"You're certain of that?" muttered Drummond tensely, for even his iron nerves had been shaken for the moment.

"Absolutely," I answered. "That cry came from Robin Gaunt."

"Then that finally proves that we're on to 'em. Let's get busy: there's no time to lose."

We made fast the rope, and then lay peering over the edge of the cliff as he went down hand over hand. For a moment the light gleamed out as he drew aside the screen, and then we heard his whispered "Come on." One after another we followed him till all five of us were standing in the cave. Behind us a curtain of stout sacking, completely covering the entrance, was all that separated us from a hundred-feet fall into the Atlantic: in front – what lay in front? What lay round the corner ten yards away? Even now, though many months have elapsed since that terrible night, I can still feel the pricking at the back of my scalp during the few seconds we stood there waiting.

Suddenly Drummond stooped down and sniffed at something that lay on the floor. Then he beckoned significantly to me. It was the end of the tubing which we had seen the man paying out, and from it came the unmistakable scent of the poison. More confirmation of the presence of the gang: and another piece in this strange and inexplicable jig-saw.

I straightened up to see that Drummond had reached the corner and was peering cautiously round it. He was flattened against the rough wall, and his revolver was in his hand. Inch by inch he moved forward with Jerningham just behind him, and the rest of us following in single file.

The passage went on bending to the left and sloping downwards. The floor was smooth and made of cement, but the walls and roof were left in their natural condition just as they had been blasted out. It was not new except for the floor, and as we crept forward I wondered for what purpose, and by whom it had been originally made. The illumination came from somewhere in front, and it was obvious through the light getting brighter that that somewhere was very close.

Suddenly Drummond became motionless: just ahead of us a man had laughed.

"Damned if I see what there is to laugh at," snarled a harsh voice. "I'm sick to death of this performance."

"You won't be when you get your share of the stuff," came the answer.

"It's an infernal risk, Dubosc."

"You don't handle an amount like that without running risks," answered the other. "What's come over you tonight? We've been here four months and now, when we're clearing out, you're as jumpy as a cat with kittens."

"It's this damned place, I suppose. No report in from the sentries? No one about?"

"Of course there's no one about. Who would be about in this God-forsaken stretch of country if he hadn't got to be?"

"There was that sketching fellow this morning. And Vernier swears that he was lying there on the hill examining the place for an hour through glasses."

"What if he was? He couldn't see anything."

"I know that. But it means he suspected something."

"It's about time you took a tonic," sneered the other. "We've gone through four months in this place without being discovered; and now, when we've got about four more hours to go at the most, you go and lose your nerve because some stray artist looks at the place through field-glasses. You make me tired. Devil take it, man, it's a tin mine, with several perfectly genuine miners tinning in it."

He laughed once again, and we heard the tinkle of a glass.

There was every excuse if you like for being windy when we were in London. And it served that cursed fool Turgovin right. What did we want anyway with that man – what was his name – Stockton, wasn't it? What was the good of killing him, even if the fool had done it, and not got killed himself? I tell you that when I saw the Chief a week later, he was still apoplectic with rage. And if Turgovin hadn't been dead, the Chief would have killed him, himself. We ought to have done what Helias said, and cleared out as soon as we got Gaunt."

"What are we going to do with that madman when we go?"

"Kill him," said the other callously. "If he hadn't gone mad, and suffered from his present delusion, he'd have been killed weeks ago. Hullo, here he is. Why ain't you tucked up in the sheets, looney?"

And then I heard old Robin's voice.

"Surely it's over by now, isn't it?

"Surely what's over? Oh! the war. No: that's not over. The Welsh have gained a great victory over the English and driven 'em off the top of Snowdon. Your juice doesn't seem to be functioning quite as well as it ought to."

"It must succeed in time," said Robin, and his voice was the vacant voice of madness. "How many have been killed by it?"

"A few hundred thousand," answered the other. "But they're devilish pugnacious fighters, these Englishmen. And the General won't give up until he's got that leg of Welsh mutton for his dinner. By the way, looney, you'll be getting slogged in the neck and hurt if I hear you making that infernal noise again. Your face is bad enough without adding that filthy shindy to it."

"That's so," came in a new deep voice. I saw Drummond's hand clench and he glanced round at me. Doctor Helias had come on the scene. "If it occurs again, Gaunt, I shall hang you up head downwards as I did before."

A little whimpering cry came from Robin, and suddenly the veins stood out on Drummond's neck. For a moment I thought he was going to make a dash for them then and there, which would have been a pity. Sooner or later it would have to come: in the meantime, incomprehensible though much of it was, we wanted to hear everything we could.

"Get out, you fool," snarled Helias.

There was the sound of a heavy blow, and a cry of pain from Robin.

"Let him be, Helias," said one of the others. "He's been useful."

"His period of utility is now over," answered Helias. "I'm sick of the sight of him."

"But there isn't enough," wailed Gaunt. "Too much has gone into the sea, and it is the air that counts"

"It's all right, looney; there's plenty for tonight. Go and put your pretty suit on so as to be ready when he comes."

A door closed and for a time there was silence save for the rustling of some papers. And then Helias spoke again.

"You've neither of you left anything about, have you?"

"No. All cleared up."

"We clear the instant the job is finished. Dubose – you're detailed to fill the tank with water as soon as it's empty. I'll deal with the madman."

"Throw him over the cliff, I suppose."

"Yes; it's easiest. You might search his room, Gratton: I want no traces left. Look at the fool there peering at his gauge to see if there's enough to stop the war."

"By Jove! this is going to be a big job, Helias."

"A big job with a big result. The Chief is absolutely confident. Lester and Degrange are in charge of the group on board the *Megalithic*, and Lester can be trusted not to bungle."

"Boss! Boss! Vernier is lying bound and gagged on the hill outside there."

Someone new had come dashing in and Drummond gave us a quick look of warning. Discovery now was imminent.

"What's that?" We heard a chair fall over as Helias got up. "Vernier gagged. Where are the others?"

"Don't know, boss. Couldn't see them. But I was going out to relieve Vernier, and I stumbled right on him. He's unconscious. So I rushed back to give the warning."

"Rouse everyone," said Helias curtly. "Post the danger signal in the roof. And if you see any stranger, get him dead or alive."

"Terse and to the point," remarked Drummond. "Just for the moment, however, stand perfectly still where you are."

He had stepped forward into the room, and the rest of us ranged up alongside him.

"Well, gorse bush – we meet again. I see you've removed your face fungus. Very wise: the police were so anxious to find you."

"By God! it's the Australian," muttered Helias. He was standing by the table in the centre of the room, and his eyes were fixed on Drummond.

"Have it that way if you like," answered Drummond. "The point is immaterial. What my friends and I are principally interested in is you, Doctor Helias. And when we're all quite comfortable we propose to ask you a few questions. First of all, you three go and stand against that wall, keeping your hands above your heads."

Dazedly they did as they were told: our sudden appearance seemed to have cowed them completely.

"Feel like sitting down, do you, Doctor? All right. Only put both your hands on the table."

He pulled up a chair and sat down facing Helias.

"Now then: to begin at the end. Saves time, doesn't it? What exactly is the game? What are you doing here?"

"I refuse to say," answered the other.

"That's a pity," said Drummond. "It would have saved so much breath. Let's try another. Why have you got Gaunt here, and why has he gone mad?"

"Ask him yourself."

"Look here," said Drummond quietly, "let us be perfectly clear on one point, Doctor Helias. I know you, if not for a cold-blooded murderer yourself, at any rate for a man who is closely connected with several of the worst. I've got you and you're going to the police. What chance you will have then you know best. But if you get my goat you may never get as far as the police. For only a keen sense of public duty restrains me from plugging you where you sit, you ineffable swine."

"In which case you would undoubtedly hang for it," snarled the other. His great hairy hands kept clenching and unclenching on the table: his eyes, venomous with hatred, never left Drummond's face.

"I think not," said Drummond. "However, at present the point does not arise. Now another question, Helias. Who was the woman who impersonated the wretched Miss Simpson the first time?"

"I refuse to say."

"She knew me, didn't she? I see you start. You forget that Stockton was not unconscious like the rest of us. Helias – do you know a man called Carl Peterson?"

He fired the question out suddenly, and this time there was no mistaking the other's agitation.

"So," said Drummond quietly. "You do. Where is he, Helias? Is he at the bottom of all this? Though it's hardly necessary to ask that. Where is he?"

"You seem to know a lot," said Helias slowly.

"I want to know just that one thing more," answered Drummond. "Everything else can wait. Where is Carl Peterson?"

"Supposing I told you, would you let me go free?" Drummond stared at him thoughtfully. "If I had proof positive – and I would not accept your word only – as to where Peterson is, I might consider the matter."

"I will give you proof positive. To do so, however, I must go to that cupboard."

"You may go," said Drummond. "But I shall keep you covered, and shoot without warning on the slightest suspicion of trickery."

"I am not a fool," answered the other curtly. "I know when I'm cornered."

He rose and walked to the cupboard, and I noticed he was wearing a pair of high white rubber boots.

"Been paddling in your filthy poison, I suppose," said Drummond. "You deserve to be drowned in a bath of it."

The other took no notice. He was sorting out some papers, and apparently oblivious of Drummond's revolver pointing unwaveringly at the base of his skull.

"Strange how one never can find a thing when one wants to," he remarked conversationally. "Ah! I think this is it."

He came back to the table, with two or three documents in his hand.

"I have your word," he said, "that if I give you proof positive you will let me go."

"You have my word that I will at any rate think about it," answered Drummond. "Much depends on the nature of the proof."

Helias had reseated himself at the table opposite Drummond, who was looking at the papers that had been handed to him.

"But this has got nothing to do with it," cried Drummond after a while. "Are you trying some fool trick, Helias?"

"Is it likely?" said the other. "Read on."

"Keep him covered, Ted."

And then suddenly Drummond sniffed the air.

"There's a strong smell of that poison of yours, Helias."

I caught one glimpse on Helias' face of unholy triumph, and the next moment I saw it.

"Lift your legs, Drummond," I yelled. "Lift them off the floor."

The advancing wave had actually reached his chair; another second would have been too late. I have said that the passage sloped down abruptly from the opening in the cliff to the room, and pouring down it was a stream of the liquid. It came surging over the smooth floor and in an instant there ensued a scene of wild confusion. Drummond had got on the table: Toby Sinclair and I scrambled on to chairs, and Jerningham and Darrell just managed to reach a wooden bench.

"You devil," shouted the man Dubosc, "turn off the stopcock. We're cut off."

Helias laughed gratingly from the passage into which he had escaped in the general scramble. And then for the first time we noticed the three other members of the gang. They were standing against the wall – completely cut off, as they said. Owing to some irregularity in the floor they were surrounded by the liquid, which still came surging into the room.

And then there occurred the most dreadful scene I have ever witnessed. They screamed and fought like wild beasts for the central position – the place which the poison would reach last. It was three inches deep now under our chairs, and it was within a yard of the place where the three men struggled.

Suddenly the first of them went. He slipped and fell right into the foul stuff, and as he fell he died. Without heeding him the other two fought on. What good they could do by it was beside the point: the frenzied instinct of self-preservation killed all reason. And forgetful of our own danger we watched them, fascinated.

It was Dubosc who managed to wrap his legs round the other's waist, at the same time clutching him round the neck with his arms.

"Carry me to the cupboard, you fool," he screamed. "It's the only chance."

But the other man had completely lost his head. In a last frenzied attempt to get rid of his burden he stumbled and fell. And with an ominous splash they both landed in the oncoming liquid. It was over; and we stared at the three motionless bodies in stupefied silence.

"I don't like people who interfere with my plans," came the voice of Helias from the passage. "Unfortunately I shan't have the pleasure of seeing you die because the thought of your revolver impels me to keep out of sight. But I will just explain the situation. In the cupboard is a stopcock. In the building beyond you is a very large tank containing some tons of this poison. We use the stopcock to allow the liquid to pass through the pipe down to the sea – on occasions. Now, however, the end of the pipe is in the passage, which, as you doubtless observed, slopes downwards into the room where you are. And so the liquid is running back into the room, and will continue to do so until the stopcock is turned off or the tank is empty. It ought to rise several feet, I should think. I trust I make myself clear."

We looked round desperately: we were caught like rats in a trap. Already the liquid was so deep that the three dead men were drifting about in it sluggishly, and the smell of it was almost overpowering.

"There's only one thing for it," said Drummond at length. His voice was quite steady, and he was tucking his trousers into his socks as he spoke.

"You're not going to do it, Hugh," shouted Jerningham. "We'll toss."

"No, we won't, old lad. I'm nearest."

He stood up and measured the distance to the cupboard with his eye.

"Cheer oh! old lads – and all that sort of rot," he remarked. "Usual messages, don't you know. It's my blithering fault for having brought you here."

And Peter Darrell was crying like a child.

"Don't!" we shouted. "For God's sake, man – there's another way. There must be."

And our shout was drowned by the crack of a revolver. It was Drummond who had fired, and the shot was followed by the sound of a fall.

I thought he might get curious," he said grimly. "He did. Poked his foul face round the corner."

"Is he dead?" cried Ted.

"Very," said Drummond. "I plugged him through the brain."

"Good Lord! old man," said Peter shakily. "I thought you meant that other stuff."

"Dear old Peter," Drummond smiled: "I did. And I do. But I'm glad to have paid the debt first. You might – er – just tell – er – you know, Phyllis and all that."

For a moment his voice faltered: then with that wonderful cheery grin of his he turned to face certain death. And it wasn't only Peter who was sobbing under his breath.

His knees were bent: he was actually crouching for the jump when the apparition appeared in the door.

"Hugh," shouted Ted. "Wait."

It was the figure of a man clothed from head to foot in a rubber garment. His legs were encased in what looked like high fishing waders: his body and hands were completely covered with the same material. But it was his head that added the finishing touch. He wore a thing that resembled a diver's helmet, save that it was much less heavy and clumsy. Two pieces of glass were fitted for his eyes, and just underneath there was a device to allow him to breathe.

He stood there for a moment with the liquid swirling round his legs, and then he gave a shout of rage.

"The traitor: the traitor. There will not be enough for the air."

It was Robin Gaunt, and with sudden wild hope we watched him stride to the cupboard. Of us he took no notice: he did not even pause when one of the bodies bumped against him. He just turned off the stopcock, and then stood there muttering angrily whilst we wiped the sweat from our foreheads and breathed again. At any rate for the moment we were reprieved.

"The traitor. But I'll do him yet. I'll cheat him."

He burst into a shout of mad laughter.

"I'll do him. There shall be enough."

Still taking no notice of us, he waded back to the door and disappeared up the passage. What wild delusion was in the poor chap's brain we knew not: sufficient for us at the moment that the liquid had ceased to rise.

Half-an-hour passed – an hour with no further sign of Gaunt. And the same thought was in all our minds. Had we merely postponed the inevitable? The fumes from the poison were producing a terrible nausea, and once Darrell swayed perilously on his bench. Sooner or later we should all be overcome, and then would come the end. One thing – it would be quick. Just a splash – a dive .

"Stockton," roared Drummond. "Wake up." With a start I pulled myself together and stared round stupidly.

"We must keep awake, boys," said Drummond urgently. "In an hour or two it will be daylight, and there may be someone about who will hear us shout. But if you sleep – you die."

And as he spoke we heard Gaunt's voice outside raised in a shout of triumph.

"He is coming: he is coming. And there will be enough."

We pulled ourselves together: hope sprang up again in our minds; though Heaven knows what we hoped for. Whoever this mysterious he proved to be, it was hardly likely that he would provide us with planks or ladders by which we could walk over the liquid.

"What's that noise?" cried Toby.

It sounded like a motor bicycle being ridden over undulating ground, or a distant aeroplane on a gusty day. It was the drone of an engine – now loud, now almost dying away, but all the time increasing in volume. Shout after shout of mad laughter came from Gaunt, and once he rushed dancing into the room with arms outstretched above his head.

"He comes," he cried. "And the war will cease." And now the noise of the engine was loud and continuous and seemed to come from close at hand. Gaunt in a frenzy of joy was shouting meaningless phrases whilst we stood there marooned in his foul poison, utterly bewildered. For the moment intense curiosity had overcome all other thoughts.

Suddenly Gaunt reappeared again, staggering and lurching with something in his arms. It was a pipe similar to the one which had so nearly caused our death, and he dropped the nozzle in the liquid.

"I'll cheat him," chuckled Gaunt. "The traitor."

It was Drummond who noticed it first, and his voice almost broke in his excitement.

"It's sinking, you fellows: it's sinking."

It was true: the level of the liquid was sinking fast. Hardly daring to believe our eyes we watched it disappearing: saw first one and then another of the dead men come to rest on the floor and lie there sodden and dripping. And all the time Robin Gaunt stood there chuckling and muttering.

"Go on, pump: go on. I will give you the last drop."

"But where's it being pumped to?" said Jerningham dazedly. "I suppose we aren't mad, are we? This is really happening. Great Scott! look at him now."

Holding the pipe in his hands, Gaunt went to pool after pool of the poison as they lay scattered on the uneven floor. His one obsession was to get enough, but at last he seemed satisfied.

"You shall have more," he cried. "The tank is still half full."

He lurched up the passage with the piping, and a few seconds later we heard a splash.

"Go on," came his shout. "Pump on: there is more."

"Devil take it," cried Drummond. "What is happening? I wonder if it's safe to cross this floor."

"Be careful, old man," said Jerningham. "Hadn't we better let it dry out a bit more? Everything is still ringing wet."

"I know that. But what's happening? We're missing it all. Who has pumped up this stuff?"

He gave a sudden exclamation.

"I've got it. Chuck me a handkerchief, someone. These two books will do."

He sat down on the table, and tied a book to the sole of each of his shoes. Then he cautiously lowered himself to the ground.

"On my back – each of you in turn," he cried. And thus did we escape from that ghastly room, to be met with a sight that drove every other thought out of our mind. Floating above the wooden hut so low down that it shut out the whole sky was a huge black shape. It was Wilmot's dirigible.

Standing by the tank of which Helias had spoken was Robin Gaunt, and the piping which had drained the liquid from the room was now emptying the main reservoir.

"Enough: there will be enough," he kept on saying. "And this time he will succeed. The war will stop. Instantaneous, universal death. And I shall have done it."

"But there isn't any war, Robin," I cried.

He stared at me vacantly through his goggles.

"Instantaneous, universal death," he repeated. "It is better so – more merciful."

We could see the details of the airship now: pick out the two central gondolas and the keel which formed the main corridor of the vessel. And once I thought I saw a man peering down at us – a man covered with just such a garment as Robin was wearing.

"Pumping it into a ballast tank," said Toby, going to the door. "You see that: they're letting water out as this stuff goes in."

He pointed to the stern of the vessel, and in the dim light it was just possible to see a stream of liquid coming out of the airship.

"To think," he went on dazedly, "that ten days ago I went for one of Wilmot's Celebrated Six-hour Trips and had Lobster à l'Américain for lunch."

Suddenly the noise of the engine increased, and the airship began to move. I glanced at Robin and he was nodding his head triumphantly.

"I knew there would be enough," he cried. "Go: go, and stop the senseless slaughter."

The poor devil stood there, his arms thrown out dramatically while the great vessel gathered speed and swung round in a circle. Then she flew eastwards, and five minutes later was lost to sight.

"Well, I'm damned," said Jerningham, sitting down on the grass and scratching his head.

"You're certain it was Wilmot's?" said Drummond.

"Absolutely," said Toby. "There's no mistaking her."

"Can't we get any sense out of Gaunt?" cried Jerningham. "Where is he anyway?"

And just then appeared. He had taken off his suit of india-rubber, and I gave an exclamation of horror as I saw his face. From chin to forehead ran a huge red scar; the blow that gave it to him must have well-nigh split his head open. He came towards us as we sat on the ground, and stopped a few yards away, peering at us curiously.

"Who are you?" he said. "I don't know you."

"Don't you know me, Robin?" I said gently. "John Stockton."

For a while he stared at me: then he shook his head.

"It doesn't matter," I went on. "Tell us why your poison is pumped up into the airship."

"To stop the war," he said instantly. "It flies over the place where they are fighting and sprays the poison down. And everyone touched by the poison dies."

"It sounds fearfully jolly," remarked Drummond. "And what happens if a shell bursts in the airship; or an incendiary bullet?"

A sudden look of cunning came on Robin's face.

"That would not matter," he answered. "Not one: nor even two. And an incendiary bullet is useless. Just death. Instantaneous, universal death."

He stared out over the sea, and Drummond shrugged his shoulders hopelessly.

"Or better still, as I have told them all," went on Robin dreamily, "is a big city. The rain of death. Think of it! Think of it in London..."

"Good God!" With a sudden gasp Drummond got to his feet. "What are you saying, man? What do you mean?"

"The rain of death coming down from the sky. That would stop the war."

"But there isn't a war," shouted Drummond, and Robin cringed back in terror.

"Steady, Drummond," I said. "Don't frighten him. What do you mean, Robin? Is that airship going to spray your poison on London?"

"I don't know," he said. "Perhaps if the war doesn't stop he will do it. I have asked him to."

He wandered away a few paces, and Jerningham shook his head.

"Part of the delusion," he said. "Why, damn it, Wilmot is trying to float a company."

"I know that," said Drummond. "But why has he got that poison on board?"

"It's possible," I remarked, "that he is taking the stuff over to some foreign Power to sell it."

"Then why not make it over there and save bother?"

To which perfectly sound criticism there was no answer.

"Anyway," said Drummond, "there is obviously only one thing to do. Get out of this, and notify the police. I should think they would like a little chat with Mr Wilmot." And then suddenly he stared at us thoughtfully. "Wilmot! Can it be possible that Wilmot himself is Peterson?"

He shook both his fists in the air suddenly.

"Oh! for a ray of light in this impenetrable fog. Who was down there last night? Whom did we see signalling from the sea? Why did they want the poison? Why does the airship want it? In fact, what the devil does it all mean? Hullo! What's Ted got hold of?"

Jerningham was coming towards us waving some papers in his hand.

"Just been into another room," he cried, "and found these. Haven't examined them yet, but they might help."

With a scream of rage Robin, who had been standing vacantly beside us, sprang at Jerningham and tried to snatch the papers away.

"They're mine," he shouted. "Give them to me."

"Steady, old man," said Drummond, though it taxed all his strength to hold the poor chap in his mad frenzy. "No one is going to hurt them."

"It's gibberish," I said, peering over Jerningham's shoulder. He was turning over the sheets, on which disconnected words and phrases were scrawled. They had been torn out of a cheap note-book and there seemed to be no semblance of order or meaning. Stray chemical formula were mixed up with sentences such as "Too much to the sea. I have told him."

"Just mad gibberish," I repeated. "What else can one expect?"

I turned away, and as I did so Jerningham gave a cry of triumph.

"Is it? "he said. "That's where you're wrong. It may not help us much, but this isn't gibberish."

In his hand he held a number of sheets of paper covered with Robin's fine handwriting. He glanced rapidly over one or two, and gave an excited exclamation.

"Written before he lost his reason," he cried. "It's sense, you fellows – sense."

And the man who had written sense before he lost his reason was crying weak tears of rage as he still struggled impotently in Drummond's grip.

CHAPTER 10

In which we read the Narrative of Robin Gaunt

Many times since then have I read that strange document, the original of which now lies in Scotland Yard. And whenever I do my mind goes back to that September morning, when, sitting in a circle on the short clipped turf two hundred feet above the Atlantic, we first learned the truth. For after a while Robin grew quiet, though I kept an eye on him lest he should try and snatch his precious papers away. But he didn't: he just sat a little apart from us staring out to sea, and occasionally babbling out some foolish nonsense.

Before me as I write is an exact copy. Not a line will be altered: not a comma. But I would ask those who may read to visualise the circumstances under which we first read that poor madman's closely guarded secret with the writer himself beside us, and the gulls screaming discordantly over our heads.

I am going mad.

[Thus it started without preamble.]

I, Robin Caxton Gaunt, believe that I shall shortly lose my reason. The wound inflicted on me in my rooms in London: the daily torture I am subjected to, and above all the final unbelievable atrocity which I saw committed with my own eyes, and for which, so help me God, I feel a terrible personal responsibility, are undermining my brain. I have some rudimentary medical knowledge: I know how tiny is the dividing line between sanity and madness. And I have been seeing things lately that are not there: and hearing things that do not exist.

It may be that I shall never complete this document. Perhaps my brain will go first: perhaps one of these devils will discover me writing. But I am making the attempt, and maybe in the future the result will fall into the hands of someone who will search out the arch monster responsible and kill him as one kills a mad dog. Also – for they showed me the newspapers at the time – it may help to clear my character from the foul blot which now rests on it. Though why John Stockton, who I thought was my friend, didn't say what he knew at the inquest I can't imagine.

[That hurt, as you may guess.]

I will begin at the beginning. During the European war I was employed at Head-quarters on the chemical branch. And just before the Armistice was signed I had evolved a poison which, if applied subcutaneously, caused practically instant death. It was a new poison unknown before to toxicologists, and if it were possible I would like the secret to die with me. God knows, I wish now I had never discovered it. Anyway I will not put down its nature here. Sufficient to say that it is the most rapid and deadly drug known at present in the civilised world.

As a death-dealing weapon, however, it suffered from one grave disadvantage: it had to be applied under the skin. To impinge on a cut or a small open place was enough, but it was not possible to rely on finding such a thing. Moreover, the method of distribution was faulty. I had evolved a portable cistern capable of carrying five gallons, which could be ejected through a fine-pointed nozzle for a distance of over fifty yards when pressure was applied by means of a pump, on the principle of a pressure-fed feed in a motor-car. But a rifle bullet carries considerably more than fifty yards, and therefore rifle fire afforded a perfectly effective counter except in isolated cases of surprise.

The possibilities of shells filled with the liquid, of distribution by aeroplane or airship, were all discussed and rejected for one reason or another. And the scheme which was finally approved consisted of the use of the poison on a large scale from fleets of tanks.

All that, however, is ancient history. The Armistice was signed: the war was over: an era of peace and plenty was to take place. So we thought – poor deluded fools. Six years later found Europe an armed camp with every nation snarling at every other nation. Scientific soldiers gave lectures in which they stated their ideas of the next war: civilised human beings talked glibly of raining down myriads of disease germs on huge cities. It was horrible – incredible: man had called in science to aid him in destroying his fellow-men, and science had obeyed him – at a price. It was a price that had not been contemplated: it was a case of another Frankenstein's monster. Man had now to obey science, not science man: he had created a thing which he could not control.

It was in the summer of 1924 that the idea first came to me of inventing a weapon so frightful that its mere existence would control the situation. The bare fact that it was there would act as the presence of the headmaster in a room full of small boys. One very forgetful lad might have to be caned once, after that the lesson would be learned. At first it seemed a wildly fanciful notion, but the more I thought of it the more the idea gripped me. And quite by chance in the July of that year when I was stopping in Scotland playing golf I met a man called David Ganton – an Australian – whose two sons had been killed in Gallipoli. He was immensely wealthy – a multi-millionaire, and rather to my surprise when I mentioned my idea to him casually one evening he waxed enthusiastic over it. To him war was as abhorrent as it was to me: and he, like I, was doubtful as to the efficacy of the League of Nations. He immediately placed at my disposal a large sum of money for research work, and told me that I could call on him for any further amount I required.

My starting-point, somewhat naturally, was the poison I had discovered during the war. And the first difficulty to be overcome was the problem of the subcutaneous injection. A wound, or an opening of some sort, must be caused on the skin before the poison could act. For months I wrestled with the problem till I was almost in despair. And then one evening I got the solution – obvious, as things like that so often are. Why not mix with the poison an irritant that would cause a blister which would make the little openings necessary?

Again months of work, but this time with renewed hope. The main idea was, I knew, the right one: the difficulty now was to find some liquid capable of blistering the skin, which when mixed with the poison would not react with it chemically and so impair its deadliness. The blister and the poison had, in short, though mixed together as liquids, each to retain its own individuality.

In December 1925 I solved the problem: I had in my laboratory a liquid so perfectly blended that two or three drops touching the skin meant instantaneous death.

Then came the second great difficulty – distribution. The tank scheme, however effective it might have been when a war was actually raging, was clearly an impossibility in such circumstances as I contemplated. Something far more sudden, far more mobile was essential.

Aeroplanes had great disadvantages. Their lifting power was limited: they were unable to hover: they were noisy.

And then there came to my mind the so-called silent raid on London during the war when a fleet of Zeppelins drifted downwind over the capital with their engines shut off. Was that the solution?

There were disadvantages there too. First and foremost – vulnerability. Silent raids by night were not my idea of the function of a world policeman. But by day an airship is a comparatively easy thing to hit; and once hit she comes down in flames.

The solution to that was obvious: helium. Instead of hydrogen she would be filled with the non-inflammable gas helium.

Which brought me to the second difficulty – expense. Hydrogen can be produced by a comparatively cheap process – the electrolysis of water: helium is rare and costly.

I met Ganton in London early in 1926 and told him my ideas. His enthusiasm was unbounded: the question of expense he waved aside as a trifle.

"That's my side of the business, Gaunt: leave that to me. You've done your part: I'll do the rest."

And then, as if it was the most normal thing in the world, he calmly announced his intention of having a rigid dirigible constructed of the Zeppelin type.

For many months after that I did not see him, though I was in constant communication with him by letter. Difficulties had arisen, as I had rather anticipated they might, but with a man like Ganton difficulties only increased his determination. And then there came on the scene the man – if such a being can be called a man – who goes by the name of Wilmot. What that devil's real name is I know not; but if these words are ever read, then to the reader I say, seek out Wilmot and kill him, for a man such as he has no right to live.

From the very first poor Ganton was utterly deceived. Letter after letter to me contained glowing eulogies of Wilmot. He too was heart and soul with me in his abhorrence of war; and, what was far more to the point, he was in a position to help very considerably with regard to the airship. It appeared that a firm in Germany had very nearly completed a dirigible of the Zeppelin type, to be used for commercial purposes. It was to be the first of a fleet, and the firm was prepared to hand it over when finished provided they secured a very handsome profit on the deal. They made no bones about it: they were constructing her for their own use and they were not going to sell unless it was really made worth their while.

Ganton agreed. The exact figure he paid I don't know – but it was enormous. And his idea, suggested again by Wilmot, was to employ the airship for a dual purpose. Ostensibly she was to be a commercial vessel, and, in fact, she was literally to be employed as one. But, in addition, she was to have certain additions made to her water ballast tanks which would enable those tanks to be filled with my poison if the necessity arose. The English Government was to be informed, and the vessel was to be subjected to any tests which the War Office might desire. After that the airship would remain a commercial one until occasion should arise for using her in the other capacity. Such was the proposition that I was going to put before the Army Council on the morning of April 28th of this year. The appointment was made, and mentioned by me to John Stockton when I dined with him at Prince's the preceding evening. Why did he say nothing about it in his evidence at the inquest?

As the reader may remember, on the night of April 27th, a ghastly tragedy occurred in my rooms in Kensington – a tragedy for which I have been universally blamed. That I know: I have seen it in the Press. They say I am a madman, a cold-blooded murderer, a super-vivisectionist. They lie, damn them, they lie.

[In the original document it was easy to see the savage intensity with which that last sentence was written.]

Here and now I will put down the truth of what happened in my rooms that night. It must be remembered that I had never seen Wilmot, but I knew that he was coming round with Ganton to see the demonstration. Ganton had written me to that effect, and so I was expecting them both. He proved to be a big, thick-set man, clean-shaven, and with hair greying a little over the temples. His eyes were steady and compelling: in fact the instant you looked at him you realised that his was a dominating personality.

I let them both in myself – Mrs Rogers, my landlady, being stone deaf – and took them at once up to my room. I was the only lodger in the house at the time, and looking back now I wonder what that devil would have done had there been others. He'd have succeeded all right: he isn't a man who fails. But it would have complicated things for him.

He professed to be keenly interested, and stated that he regarded it as an honour to be allowed to be present at such an epoch-making event. And then briefly I told them how matters stood. Since I had perfected the poison, I had spent my time in searching for an antidote: a month previously I had discovered one. It was not an antidote in the accepted sense of the word, in that it was of no use if applied *after* the poison. It consisted of an ointment containing a drug which neutralised not the poison but the blister. So that if it was rubbed into the skin *before* the application of the poison the blister failed to act, and the poison – not being applied subcutaneously – was harmless. I pointed out that it was for additional security, though the special india-rubber gloves and overalls I had had made were ample protection.

He was interested in the matter of the antidote, was that devil Wilmot.

Then I showed them the special syringes and cisterns I had designed more out of curiosity than anything else, for our plan did not include any close-range work.

And he was interested – very interested in those – was that devil Wilmot.

Then I experimented on two guinea-pigs. The first I killed with the poison: the second I saved with the antidote. And I saw one fool in the papers who remarked that I must obviously be mad since I had left something alive in the room!

"Most interesting," remarked Wilmot. He went to the window and threw it up. "The smell is rather powerful," he continued, leaning out for a moment. Then he closed the window again and came back: he had signalled to his brother devils outside from before our very eyes and we didn't guess it. Why should we have? We had no suspicions of him.

"And tomorrow you demonstrate to the War Office," he said.

"I have an appointment at ten-thirty," I told him.

"And no one save us three at present knows anything about it."

"No one," I said. "And even you two don't know the composition of the poison or of the antidote."

"But presumably, given samples, it would be easy to analyse them both."

"The antidote – yes: the poison – no," I remarked. "The poison is a secret known only to me, though, of course, I propose to tell you. I take it that there will be no secrets between us three?"

"None, I hope," he answered. "We are all engaged on the same great work."

And just then a stair creaked outside. Now I knew Mrs Rogers slept downstairs, and rarely if ever came up at that hour. And so almost unconsciously – certainly suspecting nothing – I went to the door and opened it. What happened then is still a confused blur in my mind, but as far as I can sort it out I will try and record it.

Standing just outside the door were two men. One was the man whom I afterwards got to know as Doctor Helias: the other I never saw again till he was carried in dead to the cellar where they confined me.

But it was the appearance of Helias that dumbfounded me for a moment or two. Never have I seen such an appalling-looking man: never have I dreamed that such a being could exist. Now that a description of him has been circulated by the police he has shaved off the mass of black hair that covered his face; but nothing can ever remove the mass of vile devilry that covers his black soul.

But to go back to that moment. I heard a sudden cry behind me, and there was Ganton struggling desperately with Wilmot. In Wilmot's hand was a syringe filled with the poison, and he was snarling like a brute beast. For a second I stood there stupefied; then it seemed to me we all sprang forward together – I to Ganton's assistance, the other two to Wilmot's. And after that I'm not clear. I know that I found myself fighting desperately with the second man, whilst out of the corner of my eye I saw Wilmot, Helias and Ganton go crashing through the open door.

"Telephone Stockton."

It was Ganton's voice, and I fought my way to the machine. I was stronger than my opponent, and I hurled him to the floor, half stunning him. It was Stockton's number that came first to my head, and I just got through to him. I found out from the papers that he heard me, for he came down at once; but as for me I know no more. I can still see Helias springing at me from the door with something in his hand that gleamed in the light: then I received a fearful blow in the face. And after that all is blank. It wasn't till later that I found out that little Joe – my terrier – had sprung barking at Wilmot as he came back into the room and had been killed with what was left of the poison after Ganton had been murdered in the next room.

How long afterwards it was before I recovered consciousness I cannot say. I found myself in a dimly-lit stone-floored room which I took to be a cellar. Where it was I know not to this day. At first I could not remember anything. My head was splitting, and I barely had the strength to lift a hand. Now I realise that the cause of my weakness was loss of blood from the wound inflicted on me by Helias: at the time I could only lie in a kind of stupor in which hours were as minutes and minutes as days.

And then gradually recollection began to come back – and with it a blind hatred of the treacherous devil who called himself Wilmot. What had he done it for? The answer seemed clear. He wished to get the secret of the poison in order to sell it to a foreign Power. Ganton had confided in him believing him to be straight, and all the time he had been waiting and planning for this. And if once the secret was handed over to a nation which could not be trusted to use it in the way I intended – God help the world. I imagined Russia possessing it – Russia ruled by its clique of homicidal alien Jews. And it would be my fault – my responsibility.

In my agony of mind I tried to get up. It was useless: I was too weak to move. And suddenly I happened to look at my hands in the dim light and I saw they were covered with blood. I was lying in a pool of it, and it was my own. Once again time ceased, but I did not actually lose consciousness. Automatically my brain went on working, though my thoughts were the jumbled chaos of a fever dream. And then out of the hopeless confusion there came an idea – vague at first but growing in clearness as time went on. I was still in evening clothes, and in the pockets of my dinner jacket I had placed the two samples – the bottle containing the poison, and the box full of the antidote. Were they still there? I felt, and they were. Would it be possible to hide them somewhere in the hopes of them being found by the police? And if they were found, then at any rate my own country would be in the possession of the secret too.

But where to hide them? Remember, I was too weak to even stand, much less walk, so the hiding place would have to be one which I could reach from where I sat. And just then I noticed, because my hand was resting on the ground, that some of the bricks in the floor were loose.

Now I know from what Wilmot has told me since that the hiding-place was discovered by the authorities. Was it my handkerchief, I wonder, on which I scrawled the clue in blood with my finger? But oh! dear Heavens, why did they lose the antidote? Why didn't they guard John Dallas? He was murdered, of course: you know that. He was murdered by Wilmot himself. He was murdered by that devil – that devil – that...

I must take a pull at myself. I must be calm. But the noises are roaring in my head: they always do when I think that it was all in vain. Besides, I'm going on too fast.

I buried the two things under two bricks, and I pushed the handkerchief into a crack in the wall behind me. And then I think I must have slept – for the next thing I remember was the door of the cellar opening and men coming in carrying another in their arms. They pitched him down in a corner, and I saw he was dead. Then I looked closer, and I saw it was the man I had fought with at the telephone.

But how had he died? Why did his eyes stare so horribly? Why was he so rigid?

It was Helias who told me – he had followed the other two in.

"Well, Mr Pacifist," he remarked, "do you like the effects of your poison? That man died of it."

Until my reason snaps, which can't be long now, I shall never forget the horror of that moment. It was the first time I had seen the result of my handiwork on a human being. Since then, God help me, I have seen it often – but that first time, in the dim light of the cellar, is the one that haunts me.

For a while I could think of nothing else: those eyes seemed to curse me. I think I screamed at them to turn his head away. I know that Helias came over and kicked me in the ribs.

"Shut that noise, damn you," he snarled. "We've got quite enough to worry us as it is without your help. I'll gag you if you make another sound."

Then he turned to the other two.

"That fool has brought the police into the next house," he raved, and wild hope sprang up in my mind. "That means we must get these two out of it tonight. Get his clothes."

One of the men went out, to come back almost at once with a suit of mine.

"Look here, Helias," he said, "if we're to keep him alive we'd better handle him gently. He's lost about two buckets of blood."

"Handle him how you like," returned Helias, "but he's got to be out of this in an hour."

And so they took off my evening clothes and put on the others. Then one of them put a rough bandage on my head and face, and here and now I would say – if ever that vile gang be caught – that I hope mercy will be shown him. I don't know his name, and I have never seen him since, but he is the only one who has treated me with even a trace of kindness since I fell into their clutches.

I think I must have become unconscious again: certainly I have no coherent recollection of anything for the next few hours. Dimly I remember being put into a big motor-car, seeing fields and houses flash past. But where I was taken to I have no idea. Beyond the fact that it was somewhere in the country and that there were big trees around the house I can give no description of the place in which I was kept a prisoner for the next few weeks.

Little by little I recovered my strength, and the ghastly wound on my face healed up. But I was never allowed out of doors, and when I asked any question, no answer was given. The window was barred on the outside: escape was impossible even had I possessed the necessary strength.

But one night, when I was feeling desperate, I determined to chance things. I flashed my electric light on and off, hoping possibly to attract the attention of some passer-by. And two minutes later Helias came into the room. I had not seen him since the night in the cellar, and at first I did not recognise him, for he had shaved his face clean.

"You would, would you?" he said softly. "Signalling! How foolish. Because anyway no one could see. But you obviously need a lesson."

He called to another man, and between them they slung me up to a hook in the wall by my feet, so that I hung head downwards. And after a while the pressure of blood on the partially healed wound on my face became so terrible that I thought my head would burst.

"Don't be so stupid another time," he remarked as they cut me down. "If you do I'll have your window boarded up."

They left me, and in my weakness I sobbed like a child. Had I had any, I would have killed myself then and there with my own poison. But I hadn't, and they took care to see that I had no weapon which could take its place. I wasn't allowed to shave: I wasn't even allowed a steel knife with my meals.

The days dragged on into weeks, and weeks into months, and still nothing happened. And I grew more and more mystified as to what it was all about. Remember that then I had seen no papers, and knew nothing. I wasn't even sure that David Ganton was dead. Why did they bother to keep me alive? was the question I asked myself again and again. They had the secret: at least I assumed they must have, for the paper on which I had written the formula of the poison was no longer in my possession. So what use could I be to them?

And then one day – I'd almost lost count of time, but I should say it was about the 10th of June – the door of my room opened and Helias came in, followed by Wilmot.

"You certainly hit him pretty hard, Doctor," said Wilmot, after he'd looked at me for some time. "Well, Mr Gaunt – been happy and comfortable?"

"You devil," I burst out, and then, maddened by his mocking smile, I cursed and raved at him till I was out of breath.

"Quite finished?" he remarked when I stopped. "I'm in no particular hurry, and as I can easily understand a slight feeling of annoyance on your part, please don't mind me. Say it all over again if it comforts you in any way."

"What do you want?" I said, almost choking with sullen rage.

"Ah! that's better. Will you have a cigar? No. Then you won't mind if I do. The time has come, Mr Gaunt," he went on, when it was drawing to his satisfaction, "when you must make a little return for the kindness we have shown you in keeping you alive. For a while I was undecided as to whether I would dispose of you like your lamented confrère Mr Ganton, but finally I determined to keep you with us."

"So Ganton is dead," I said. "You murdered him that night."

"Yes," he agreed. "As you say, I killed him that night. I have a few little fads, Mr Gaunt, and one of them is a dislike to the word murder. It's so coarse and crude. Well – to return, Mr Ganton's sphere of usefulness as far as I was concerned was over the moment he had afforded me the pleasure of meeting you. But for the necessity of his doing that, he would have – er – disappeared far sooner. He had very kindly paid a considerable sum of money to acquire an airship, and as I wanted the airship and not Mr Ganton, the inference is obvious. You've no idea, Mr Gaunt, how enormously it simplifies matters when you can get other people to pay for what you want yourself."

I found myself staring at him speechlessly: in comparison with this cold, deadly suavity Helias seemed merely a coarse, despicable bully.

"In addition to that," he went on quietly, "the late Mr Ganton presented me with an idea. And ideas are my stock-in-trade. For twenty years now I have lived by turning ideas into deeds, and though I have accumulated a modest pittance I have not yet got enough to retire on. I trust that with the help of Mr Ganton's idea – elaborated somewhat naturally by me – I shall be able to spend my declining years in the comfort to which I consider myself entitled."

"I don't understand what you're talking about," I muttered stupidly.

"It is hardly likely that you would at this stage of the proceedings," he continued. "It is also quite unnecessary that you should. But I like everyone with whom I work to take an intelligent interest in the proceedings. And the thought that your labours during the next few weeks will help to provide me with my pension should prove a great incentive to you. In addition you must remember that it will also repay a little of the debt you owe to Doctor Helias for his unremitting care of you during your period of convalescence."

"For God's sake, don't go on mocking," I cried. "What is it you want me to do?"

"First, you will move from here to other quarters which have been got ready for you. Not quite so comfortable, perhaps, but I trust they will do. Then you will take in hand the manufacture of your poison on a large scale, a task for which you are peculiarly fitted. A plant has been installed which may perhaps need a little alteration under your expert eye: anything of that sort will be attended to at once. You have only to ask."

"But what do you want the poison for?" I asked.

"That, as Mr Gilbert once said – or was it Mr Sullivan? – is just like the flowers that bloom in the spring, tra-la-la. It has nothing to do with the case. In time you will know, Mr Gaunt: until then, you won't."

"Is it for a foreign country?" I demanded.

He smiled. "It is for me, Mr Gaunt, and I am cosmopolitan. But you need have no fears on that score. I am aware of the charming ideal that actuated you and Mr Ganton, but, believe me, my dear young friend, there's no money in it."

"It was never a question of money," I cried.

"I know." His voice was almost pained. "That is what struck me as being so incredible about it all. And that is where my elaboration comes in. Now there is money in it: very big money if things work out as I have every reason to hope they will."

"And what if I refuse?" I said.

He studied the ash on the end of his cigar.

"In the course of the twenty years I have already mentioned, Mr Gaunt," he said, "I wouldn't like to say how many people have made that remark to me. And the answer has become monotonous with repetition. Latterly one of your celebrated politicians has given me an alternative reply, which I will now give to you. Wait and see. We've been very kind to you, Gaunt, up to date. You gave me a lot of trouble over that box of antidote which you hid in the cellar" – how my heart sank at that – "though I realise that it was partially my fault – in not remembering sooner that you had it in your pocket. In fact, I had to dispose of an eminent savant, Sir John Dallas, in order to get hold of it."

"Then the authorities got it?" I almost shouted.

"Only to lose it again, I regret to say. By the way," he leaned forward suddenly in his chair – "do you know a man called Drummond – Captain Hugh Drummond?"

From beside me as I read, Drummond heaved a deep sigh of joy.

"It is Peterson," he said. "That proves it. Go on, Stockton."

"Hugh Drummond! No, I've never heard of the man. But do you mean to say you murdered Sir John?"

"Dear me! That word again. I keep on forgetting that you have been out of touch with current affairs. Yes, Sir John failed to see reason – so it was necessary to dispose of him. Your omission of the formula for the antidote on the paper containing that of the poison has deprived the world, I regret to state, of an eminent scientist. However, during the sea-voyage which you are shortly going to take I will see that you have an opportunity of perusing the daily papers of that date. They should interest you, because really, you know, your discovery of this poison has had the most far-reaching results. Still, if you will give me these ideas…"

He rose shrugging his shoulders.

"Am I to be taken abroad?" I cried.

"You are not," he answered curtly. "You will remain in England. And if I may give you one word of warning, Mr Gaunt, it is this. I require your services on one or two matters, and I intend to have your services. And my earnest advice to you is that you should give that service willingly. It will save me trouble, and you – discomfort."

With that they left me, if possible more completely bewildered than before. I turned it over from every point of view in my mind, and I could see no ray of light in the darkness. The only point of comfort was that at any rate I was going to change my quarters, and it was possible that I might escape from the new ones. Vain hope! It is dead now, but it buoyed me up for a time.

It was two days later that Helias entered the room and told me to get ready.

"You are going in a car," he said. "And I am going with you. If you make the slightest endeavour to communicate or signal to anyone I shall gag you and truss you up on the floor."

And that brings me to the point... Eyes, those ghastly staring eyes. And the woman screaming...Oh! God, my head...

At this point the narrative as a narrative breaks off. It is continued in the form of a diary. But it has given rise to much conjecture. Personally I think the matter is clear. I believe, in fact from a perusal of the original it is obvious, that "head" was the last coherent word written by Robin Gaunt. The rest of the sheet is covered with meaningless scrawls and blots. In fact I think that at that point the poor chap's reason gave way. How comes it, then, that the diary records events which occurred after he had been taken away in the motor-car? To me the solution is clear. The diary, though its chronological position comes after the narrative given above, was actually written first.

Surely it must be so. Up to the time when he was removed in the car he was in such a dazed physical and mental condition that the mere effort of keeping a diary would have been beyond him. Besides, what was there to record? His mind, as he says, was hopelessly fogged. He knew nothing when he left the house in which he had been confined as to what had happened in his rooms in London – or rather shall I say he knew nothing as to what had been reported in the papers? And yet the narrative already given was obviously written with a full knowledge of those reports.

Besides – take his first paragraph, "Daily torture." There had been no question of daily torture. "Final unbelievable atrocity." There had been none. No: it is clear. When things began to happen Gaunt kept a diary. And when, at the end he felt his reason going, he wrote the narrative to fill in the gap not covered by the subsequent notes. Had he not gone mad we might have had the whole story in the form in which he presented the first half.

I know that certain people hold a different view. They agree with me that he went mad at this point, but they maintain that the diary was written by him when he was insane. They say, in fact, that he scrawled down the disordered fancies of his brain, and for confirmation of their argument they point to the bad writing – sometimes well-nigh illegible: to the scraps of paper the notes were made on: to the general untidiness and dirt of the record.

I can only say that I am utterly convinced they are wrong. The bad writing, the scraps of paper were due, I feel certain, to the inherent difficulties under which they were written. Always was he trying to escape detection: he just scribbled when he could and where he could. Then for some reason which we shall never know he found himself in the position of being able to write coherently and at length. And the fortunate thing is that he brought his narrative so very close to the point where his diary starts.

CHAPTER 11

In which we read the Diary of Robin Gaunt

I am on board a ship. She is filling with oil now from a tanker alongside. No lights. No idea where we are. Thought the country we motored through resembled Devonshire.

They're Russians – the crew – unless I'm much mistaken. The most frightful gang of murderous-looking cut-throats I've ever seen. Two of them fighting now: officers seem to have no control. Difficult to tell which are the officers. Believe my worst fears confirmed: the Bolsheviks have my secret. May God help the world!

Under weigh. Just read the papers Wilmot spoke about. Is Stockton mad? Why did he say nothing at the inquest? And Joe – poor little chap. How dare they say such things about me? The War Office knew; why have they kept silent?

The murderers! The foul murderers! There was a wretched woman on board, and these devils have killed her. They pushed her in suddenly to the cabin where I was sitting. She was terrified with fear, poor soul. The most harmless little short fat woman. English. They hustled her through – three of them, and she screamed to me to help her. But what could I do? Two more of the crew appeared, and one of them clapped his hand over her mouth. They took her on deck – and with my own eyes I saw

them throw her overboard. It was dark, and she disappeared at
once. She just gave one pitiful cry – then silence. Are they going
to do the same to me?

Four men playing cards outside the door. Certain now that they
are Russians. What does it all mean?

It is incomprehensible. There must be at least fifty rubber suits
on board with cisterns and everything complete for short-range
work with my poison. An officer took me to see them, and one
of the men put one on.
  "Good?" said the officer, looking at me.
  I wouldn't answer, and a man behind me stuck a bayonet into
my back.
  "Good now?" snarled the officer.
  I nodded. Oh! for a chance to be on equal terms...

But they are good: far too good. They have taken my rough idea,
and improved upon it enormously. A man in one of those suits
could bathe in the poison safely. But what do they want them for,
on board a ship?

Thank Heavens! I am on shore again. They dragged me up on
deck and I thought it was the end. A boat was alongside, and
they put me in it. Then some sailors rowed me away. It was dark,
and the boom of breakers on rocks grew louder and louder. At
last we reached a little cove, and high above me I could see the
cliffs. The boat was heaving, and then the man in charge switched
on an electric torch. It flashed on the end of a rope ladder
dangling in front of us, and swaying perilously as the swell
lapped it and then receded. He signed to me to climb up it, and
when I hesitated for a moment, he struck me in the face with his
boat-hook. So I jumped and caught the ladder, and immediately
the boat was rowed away, leaving me hanging precariously. Then

a wave dashed me against the cliff, half stunning me, and I started to climb. An ordeal even for a fit man... Exhausted when I reached the top. I found myself in a cave hewn out of granite. And Helias was waiting for me.

"Your quarters," he said. "And no monkey tricks."

But I was too done in to do anything but sleep.

The mystery deepens. This place is too amazing. Today I have been shown the plant in which my poison is to be made. It is a huge tank capable of holding I know not how many tons concealed from view by a wooden building built around it. The building is situated on the top of the cliff and the cliff itself is honeycombed with caves and passages. One in particular leads down from the tank to a kind of living-room, and thence up again to another opening in the cliff similar to the one by which I entered. And from the bottom of the tank there runs a pipe – yards and yards of it coiled in the room. Enough to allow the end to reach the sea. There is a valve in the room by which the flow can be stopped. It must be to supply the vessel below. But why so much? I will not make it: I swear I will not make it, even if they torture me.

Dear God! I didn't know such things were known to man. Four days – four centuries. Don't judge me... I tried, but the entrance was guarded.

[In the original this fragment was almost illegible. Poor devil – who would judge him? Certainly not I. Who can even dimly guess the refinements of exquisite torture they brought to bear on him in that lonely Cornish cave? And I like to think that behind that last sentence lies his final desperate attempt to outwit them by hurling himself on to the rocks below. "But the entrance was guarded."]

It is made. And now that it is made what are they going to do with it? They've let me alone since I yielded, but my conscience never leaves me alone. Night and day: night and day it calls me "Coward." I am a coward. I should have died rather than yield. And yet they *could* have made it themselves: they said so. They knew the formula. But they thought I'd do it better. If any accident took place I was to be the sufferer.

Should I have ended it all? It would have been so easy. It would be so easy now. One touch: one finger in the tank and everything finished. But surely sooner or later this place must be discovered. I lie and look out over the grey sea, and sometimes on the far horizon there comes the smoke of a passing vessel.

Always far out – too far out. Anyway I have no means of signalling. I'm just a prisoner in a cave. They don't even give me a light at night. Nothing to do but think and go on thinking, and wonder whether I'm going mad. Is it a dream? Shall I wake up suddenly?

Yesterday I had a strange thought. I must be dead. It was another world, and I was being shown the result of my discovery on earth. Cruelty, death, torture – that was all that the use of such a poison as mine could lead to. It was my punishment. It's come back to me since – that thought. What was that strange and wonderful play I saw on earth? "Outward Bound." Rather the same idea: no break – you just go on. Am I dead?

[Undoubtedly to my mind the first time that Robin Gaunt's reason began to totter. Poor devil – day after day – brooding alone.]

Things are going to happen. There's a light at sea – signalling. Is it the ship, I wonder? They're letting down the pipe from the cave above me. It's flat calm: there is hardly a murmur from the sea below.

At last I know the truth. At last I know the reason for the tank on the top of the cliff, and all that has happened in the last three months. With my own eyes I have seen an atrocity, cold-blooded and monstrous beyond the limits of human imagination.

Six thousand feet below me gleams the Atlantic: I am on board the dirigible that Wilmot murdered Ganton to obtain. I have locked my cabin door: I hope for a few hours to be undisturbed. And so whilst the unbelievable thing that has happened is fresh in my mind I will put it down on paper.

[I may say that this final portion of Robin Gaunt's diary was written in pencil in much the same ordered and connected way as the first part of his narrative. It shows no trace of undue excitement in the handwriting: nor, I venture to think, does it show any mental aberration as far as the phraseology is concerned.]

I will start from the moment when I saw the signal from the sea. The pipe was hanging down the cliff, and after a while there came a whistle from below. Almost at once I heard the gurgle of liquid in the pipe: evidently poison from the tank was being lowered to someone underneath. Another whistle and the gurgling ceased. Then came the noise of oars; the pipe was drawn up, and for some time nothing more happened.

It was about half-an-hour later that Helias appeared and told me to come with him. I went to the main living-room, where I found Wilmot, and a man whom I recognised as having seen on board. They were talking earnestly together and poring over a chart that lay between them on the table.

"The 2nd or 3rd," I heard Wilmot say, "and the first port of call is the Azores."

The other man nodded, and pricked a point on the chart.

"That's the spot," he said. "A bit west of the Union Castle route."

And just then I became aware of the faint drone of an engine. It sounded like an aeroplane, and Wilmot rose.

"Then that settles everything. Now I want to see how this part works." He glanced at me as I stood there listening to the noise, which by this time seemed almost overhead. "One frequently has little hitches the first time one does a thing, Mr Gaunt. You will doubtless be able to benefit from any that may occur when you proceed yourself to stop the next war."

They all laughed, and I made no answer.

"Let's go and watch," said Wilmot, glancing at his watch. "I'll just time it, I think."

He led the way up the passage towards the tank, and I followed. That there was some devilish scheme on foot I knew, but I was intensely eager to see what was going to happen. Anything was better than the blank ignorance of the past few weeks.

We approached the tank, and then to my amazement I saw that there was a large open space in the roof through which I could see the stars. And even as I stared upwards they were blotted out by a huge shape that drifted slowly across the opening so low down that it seemed on top of us.

"The dirigible that Mr Ganton so kindly bought for me," said Wilmot genially. "As I say, it is the first time we have done this and I feel a little pardonable excitement."

And now the huge vessel above us was stationary, with her engines going just sufficiently to keep her motionless in the light breeze. One could make out the two midship gondolas, and the great central keel that forms the backbone of every airship of her type. And as I stared at her fascinated, something hit the side of the wooden house with a thud. A man clad in one of the rubber suits who was standing on the roof slipped forward and caught the end of a pipe similar to the one in the cave. This he dropped carefully into the tank.

"Ingenious, don't you think, Mr Gaunt?" said Wilmot. "We now pump up your liquid into the ballast tanks, at the same time discharging water to compensate for weight. You will see that by keeping one tank permanently empty there is always room for your poison to be taken on board. When the first empty tank is filled, another has been emptied of water and is ready."

I hardly listened to him: I was too occupied in watching the level of the liquid fall in the gauge of the tank: too occupied in wondering what was the object of it all.

"Twelve minutes," he remarked as the pump above began to suck air in the tank. "Not so bad. We will now go on board. Another little device, Gaunt, on which we flatter ourselves. It looks alarming, but there is no danger."

Swinging above us was a thing that looked like a cage, which had evidently been let down from the airship. In a moment or two it came to rest on the roof, and Wilmot beckoned to me to go up the steps.

"Room for us both," he remarked.

I made no demur: it was useless to argue. Why he wanted me on board was beyond me, though doubtless I should know in time. So I followed him into the cage, and he shut the door. And the next moment we were being drawn up to the dirigible.

It was the first time I had been outside and I stared round eagerly, but in the faint grey light that precedes dawn it was difficult to see much. Far below us lay the sea, whilst inland the ground was hilly. I saw what I took to be a road in the distance: also a tall chimney which stuck up from the midst of low-lying buildings. And then the cage came to rest: it had been drawn right into the keel of the airship. A metal plate closed underneath us with a clang, and we both stepped out into the central corridor.

"Something to eat and drink, Mr Gaunt," said Wilmot, and I followed him in a sort of dull stupor.

He led the way to a luxurious cabin which was fitted up as a dining-room. On the table were champagne and a variety of sandwiches.

"We will regard this as a holiday for you," he remarked. "And if you behave yourself there is no reason why it shouldn't prove a very pleasant one. After it is over you will have to refill the tank for us, but for the next three or four days let us merely enjoy ourselves."

We were flying eastwards – I could tell that by the light; and I peered out of the window, trying to see if I could spot where we were.

"A beautiful sight, isn't it?" said Wilmot. "And when the sun rises it is even more beautiful. Lord Grayling and the Earl of Dorset both agreed that to see the dawn from such a vantage-point was to see a very wonderful sight."

"In God's name," I burst out, "what does it all mean?"

He smiled as he selected a sandwich.

"Just your scheme, my dear fellow," he answered. "Your scheme in practice."

"But there's no war on," I cried.

"No. There's no war on," he agreed.

"Then why have you filled the ballast tanks with poison?"

"You may remember that I once pointed out to you the weak point in your scheme," he answered. "There was no money in it. In the course of the next few days you are going to see that defect remedied, I trust.

"Of course," he went on after a while, "this is only going to be quite a small affair. It's in the nature of a trial run: just to accustom everyone to what they have to do when the big thing comes along. And that's why I've brought you along. You have had, I gather, a little lesson over not doing what you're told, and I feel sure that you will give me no further trouble. But one never knows that some little hitch may not occur, and should it do so in your particular department, it will be up to you to rectify it."

But I haven't the time to give that devil's conversation in full. I can see him now, suave and calm, seated at the table smoking a cigar whilst he played with me as a cat plays with a mouse.

Utterly ignorant then as to what was going to happen, much of it was lost on me. Now I can see it all.

It conveyed nothing to me then that the British public was keenly interested in the airship: that tours at popular prices were given twice a week: that there was talk of floating a company in the City.

"Not that that is ever likely to come of, my dear Gaunt," he remarked, "though if it did, of course, I should have no objection to taking the money. But it instils confidence in the public mind: makes them regard me as an institution. And an institution can do no wrong. You might as well suspect the Cornish Riviera express of robbing the Bank of England."

There lies the diabolical ingenuity of it all. Did I not hear from the cabin where they kept me bound and gagged – guarded by two men – did I not hear him showing two members of the Royal Family over the vessel? That was while we were tied up to the mooring mast before we started.

Did we not go for a four-hour trip with thirty people on board, amongst them some of the highest in the land? He told me their names that night, with a vile mocking smile on his face.

"But why," I shouted at him, "why?"

"All in good time," he answered. "I am just showing you what an institution I am."

That's it: and will anyone believe what I am going to write down? I see it all now: the tin mine ostensibly being worked as a tin mine; in reality merely a cloak to disguise the making of the poison. As he said, it had to be in a deserted place by the sea, because the ship had to take supplies on board.

He's told me everything: he knows I'm in his power. He seems to take a delight in tormenting me: in exposing for my benefit the workings of his vile brain. But he's clever: diabolically clever.

It was two days ago that they let me out of my cabin. The airship was in flight, and looking out I saw that we were over the sea. They took me into the dining-cabin, and there I saw Wilmot and a woman. She was smoking a cigarette, and I saw she was very beautiful. She stared at me with a sort of languid interest: then she made some remark to Wilmot at which he laughed.

"Our friend Helias has a strong right arm," he remarked. "Well, Gaunt – very soon now your curiosity is going to be satisfied. We have ceased to be commercial: we're going to go and stop your war. But we still remain an institution. Have you ever heard of Mr Cosmo Miller?"

"I have not," I said.

"He is an American multi-millionaire, and at the moment he is some forty miles ahead of us in his yacht. If you look through that telescope you will be able to see her."

I glanced through the instrument, and saw away on the horizon the graceful outlines of a steam yacht.

"A charming boat – the *Hermione*," he went on. "It goes against the grain to sink her."

"To do what?" I gasped.

"Sink her, my dear Gaunt. She is, one might say, your war. She is also the trial run to give us practice for other and bigger game."

I stared at him speechlessly: surely he must be jesting.

"Considerate of Mr Miller to select this moment for his trip, wasn't it? Otherwise we might have had to try our 'prentice hand on less paying game. At any rate he has sufficient jewellery on board to pay for our running expenses if nothing more."

"But, good God!" I burst out, "you can't mean it. What is going to happen to the people on board?"

"They are going to sink with her," he replied, getting up and looking through the telescope.

A man came into the cabin and Wilmot swung round.

"No message been sent yet, Chief."

Wilmot nodded and dismissed him.

"A wonderful invention – wireless, isn't it? But I confess that it renders modern piracy a little difficult. In this case the matter is not one of vital importance, but when we come to the bigger game the question will have to be very carefully handled. Now on this occasion it may be that the two excellent and reliable men who took the place of two members of the *Hermione's* crew at Southampton have broken up the instrument already; or it may be that the wireless operator hardly considers it worth while to broadcast the information that he has seen us. However, we shall soon know. My dear!" he added to the girl, "we're getting very close. I think it might interest you now."

She got up and stood beside him, whilst I stood there in a sort of stupor. I watched Wilmot go to a speaking-tube: heard him give directions to fly lower. And then, drawn by some unholy fascination, I too went and looked out.

Half-a-mile ahead of us was the yacht, steaming slowly ahead. The passengers were lining the rail staring up at us, and in a few seconds we had come so close that I could see the flutter of their pocket handkerchiefs.

"Come with me, Gaunt," snapped Wilmot. "Now comes the business. My dear, you stay here."

He rushed me along the main corridor till we came to one of the central ballast tanks. The engines were hardly running, and I realised that we must be directly over the yacht and just keeping pace with her. Two men clad in rubber suits stood by the tank: two others were by the corresponding tank on the opposite side of the gangway. Wilmot himself was peering into an instrument set close by the first tank, and I saw a duplicate by the second. I went to it and found it was an arrangement of mirrors based on the periscope idea: by looking into it I saw directly below the airship.

And of the next ten minutes how can I tell? Straight underneath us – not a hundred feet below – lay the yacht. Everyone – guests, crew, servants – were peering up at the great airship, which must have seemed to fill the entire sky. And then Wilmot gave an order. Two levers were pulled back, and the rain of death began to fall. The rain that I had invented – Oh, God! – it was unbelievable...

I saw a woman who had been waving at us fall backwards suddenly on the deck and lie there rigid, her face turned up towards us. A man rushed forward to her help: he never reached her. The poison got him first. And all over the deck it was the same. Men and women ran screaming to and fro, only to crash forward suddenly and lie still as the death rain went on falling. I saw three niggers, their black faces incongruous against their white ducks. They had rushed out at the sound of the pandemonium on deck, and with one accord, as if they had been pole-axed simultaneously, they died. I saw a man in uniform shaking his fist at us. He only shook it once, poor devil...

And then as if from a great distance I heard Wilmot's voice – "Enough."

The rain of death ceased: it was indeed enough. No soul moved on the yacht: only a white-clad figure at the wheel kept her on her course.

Stumbling blindly, I went back to the central cabin. The girl was still there, staring out of the window, and I think I screamed foolish curses at her. She took no notice: she was watching something through a pair of glasses.

"Quite well timed," she remarked as Wilmot entered. "She's only about a mile off."

I looked and saw a vessel tearing through the water towards us: coming to the rendezvous of death.

"I would never have believed," said Wilmot, "that with her lines she would have been capable of such speed."

Then he turned to me.

"Put on that suit," he said curtly. "We're going down on deck."

He was getting into one himself, and half unconsciously I followed his example. I was dazed: stunned by the incredible atrocity I had just witnessed.

And if it had been terrible from above, what words can paint the scene on deck as we stepped out of the cage? In every corner lay dead bodies; and one and all they stared at me out of their sightless eyes. They cursed me for having killed them: everywhere I turned they cursed me.

The deck was ringing wet: the smell of the poison lay heavy in the air. And again and again I asked myself – What was the meaning of this senseless outrage? I didn't know then of the incredible wealth of the wretched people who had been killed: of the marvellous jewels that were on board.

The other vessel lay alongside: a dozen of the crew clothed in rubber suits had come on board the yacht. It was the ruthless efficiency of it all that staggered me: they worked like drilled soldiers. One by one they carried the bodies below and piled them into cabins. And when a cabin was full they shut the door. They damped down the stoke-room fires: they blew off what head of steam remained. They stove in the four ship's boats and sank them: they moved every single thing that would float and put it below in such a place that when the ship sank everything would go down with her. And all the while the dirigible circled overhead.

Once, and only once, did anything happen to interrupt them. Heaven knows where he had been hidden or how he had escaped, but suddenly, with a wild shout, one of the crew darted on deck. In his hands he held a pick: he was a stoker evidently. Gallant fellow: he got one of them before he died. In the head – with his pick, and then another of the pirates just laid his glove wet with the poison against the stoker's face. And the work went on.

At last Wilmot appeared again. He was carrying a suit-case, and I saw him signal to the airship. She manoeuvred back into position and the cage was lowered on to the deck of the yacht. And a minute later we were in the dirigible once more.

"A most satisfactory little experiment," said Wilmot. "We will now examine the spoils more closely."

Sick with the horror of it all, I stood at the cabin window, whilst he and the woman went over the jewels on the table behind me. We had circled a little away from the yacht, and the other vessel no longer lay alongside, but a hundred yards or so away. And suddenly there came a dull boom, and the yacht rocked a little on the calm sea.

"A sight, my dear, which I don't think you've ever seen," said Wilmot, and he and the woman came to the window. "A ship sinking."

Slowly the yacht settled down in the water: they had blown a great hole in her bottom. And then at last with a sluggish lurch her bows went under and she turned over and sank. For a time the water swirled angrily to mark her grave: then everything grew quiet. No trace remained of their devilish handiwork: the sea had swallowed it up.

"Most satisfactory," repeated Wilmot. "Don't you agree, Gaunt?"

He laughed evilly at the look on my face.

"And you have committed that atrocious crime for those," I said, pointing at the jewels.

"Not altogether," he answered. "As I told you before, this is merely in the nature of a trial trip. Of course it's pleasant to have one's expenses paid, but the principal value of this has been practice for bigger game... That is what we are out for, my dear Gaunt: bigger game."

I watched him with a sort of dazed fascination as he lit a cigar. Then he began to examine through a lens the great heap of precious stones in front of him. And after a while the thought began to obsess me that he was not human. His complete air of detachment: his amused comments when he discovered that a beautiful tiara was only paste: above all the languorous indifference of the girl who only an hour before had witnessed an act of wholesale murder made my head spin.

They are devils – both of them: devils in human form; and I told them so.

They laughed, and Wilmot poured me out a glass of champagne.

"You flatter us, Gaunt," he remarked. "Surely you have not been listening to the foolish remarks of the crew. They, poor simple-minded fellows, do, I understand, credit me with supernatural powers, but I am surprised at you. Merely your antidote, my friend: that's all."

"I don't understand what you're talking about," I muttered.

"There now," he said genially, "I am always forgetting that your knowledge of past events is limited. An amusing little story, Gaunt, and one which flatters your powers as a chemist. I may say that it also flatters my powers as a prophet. My men, as you may know, are largely Russians of the lower classes. Docile, good fellows as a general rule, with a strong streak of superstition in them. And realising that in a concern of this sort one has to control with an iron hand, I anticipated that possibly an occasion might arise when some foolish man would question that control. It was because of that, my dear Gaunt, that I took so much trouble to procure that admirable ointment of yours, the existence of which is not known to the members of my crew. In that point lay the little element of – if I may say so – genius, which separates a few of us from the common herd. Though I admit that it was with some trepidation – pardonable I think you will allow – that I put the matter to the test. Of the efficacy of your poison I had no doubt, but with regard to the antidote I had only seen it in action once, and then on a guinea-pig. If I remember aright, my darling," he said to the girl, "we drank to Mr Gaunt's skill as a chemist in one of our few remaining bottles of Imperial Tokay, at the conclusion of the episode. A wonderful wine, Gaunt; but I fear extinct. These absurd revolutions that take place for obscure reasons do a lot of harm."

That's how he talked: the man is not human. Then he went on.

"But the episode in question will, I am sure, interest you. As I had foreseen, some stupid men began to question my authority. In fact, though you will hardly believe it, it came to my ears that there was a conspiracy to take my life. It is true I had had a man flogged to death, but what is a Russian peasant more or less? Apparently this particular fellow sang folk-songs well, or tortured some dreadful musical instrument better than his friends. At any rate he was popular, and his death was a source of annoyance to the others. So, of course, it became necessary to take the matter in hand at once in a way which should restore discipline, and at the same time prevent a recurrence in the future. My dearest, this caviare is not so good as the last consignment. Another devastating example of the harm done by revolutions, I fear. Even the sturgeons have gone on strike.

"However, to return to my little story. I bethought me of your antidote. 'Here,' said I to myself, 'is an opportunity to test that dear chap Gaunt's excellent ointment in a manner both useful and spectacular.' So I rubbed it well into my face and hands – even into my hair, Gaunt – and strode like a hero of old into the midst of the malcontents. You perceive the beauty of the idea. A man not gifted with our brains might reasonably remark, 'Why not don a rubber suit, which you know is quite safe?'

"True, but besides being hot and uncomfortable – I think we shall have to try and improve those suits, Gaunt – it is very clumsy in the event of the wearer being attacked with a knife. And though I anticipated from what I had heard that they proposed to use your poison, one has to allow for all eventualities. Also there was that mystic vein in them which I wanted to impress.

"Behold me then, my dear fellow, apparently as I am now, striding alone and unarmed to their quarters. For a moment they stared at me dumbfounded – my sudden appearance had cowed them. And then one of them pulled himself together and discharged a syringe full of the liquid at me. It hit me in the cheek – a most nervous moment, I assure you. I apologise deeply to you now for my qualms; I should have trusted your skill better.

"Nothing happened, and the men cowered back. I said no word; but step by step I advanced on the miscreant who had dared to try and rob the world of one of its chief adornments. And step by step he retreated till he could retreat no further. Then I took his hand and laid it on my cheek. And that evening we tied him in a weighted sack, and buried him at sea."

He smiled thoughtfully and studied the ash on his cigar.

"It was most successful. Rumours about me vary amongst these excellent fellows. The one I like best is that I am a reincarnation of Rasputin. But there has been no further trouble."

He rose from the table and swept the jewels carelessly into the suit-case.

"Not a bad haul, my little one. We shall have to be very careful over the disposal of the Shan diamonds: they're notorious stones."

They both walked over to one of the windows together, and...

[At this point the narrative breaks off abruptly. Evidently Gaunt was interrupted and crammed the papers hurriedly into his pocket. And the only other document – the most vital of all – was scrawled almost illegibly on a torn scrap of paper. Whether it was written on the airship or at Black Mine will never be known. Of how he got back to the mine there is no record. Who were the men alluded to as "them" is also a mystery, though I have no doubt that one of them was Wilmot. Possibly the other was Helias.]

I heard them today. They didn't know I was listening. The *Megalithic* with thirty of the gang on board. Attack by night.

The bigger game. He will succeed: he is not human... Hydrogen not helium... Not changed... Sacrifice ship... Fire...

That is all. Those are the papers that we read, sitting on the edge of the cliff with the writer beside us staring with vacant eyes over the grey sea below. Those were the papers, stumbled on by the merest accident, on which we had to base our plans. Was it true or were we the victims of some gigantic delusion on the part of Gaunt? That was the problem that faced us as the first rays of the early sun lit up Black Mine on the morning of September 8th.

CHAPTER 12

In which the final count takes place

How much of it was true? We had confirmation of a certain amount with our own eyes. We had seen the pipe, lowered over the cliff: we had seen the mysterious signal from the sea. Above all we had seen Wilmot's dirigible actually filling up with the poison. So much, therefore, we knew. But what of the rest?

What of the astounding story of the *Hermione*? Had we discovered the solution of the yacht's disappearance, or had we been wasting our time reading the hallucination of a madman's brain? Had Gaunt – having read in the papers of the loss of the *Hermione* – imagined the scene he had described?

Against that theory was the fact – as I have mentioned before – that neither in the writing nor the phraseology could we detect any sign of insanity. And surely if the whole thing was a delusion, traces of incoherence and wildness would have been bound to appear.

So we reasoned, and still could come to no conclusion. It seemed so wildly fantastic: so well-nigh incredible. And if those epithets could be used in connection with the *Hermione*, what was to be said concerning the amazing fragment about the *Megalithic*? Even granted for the moment that the description of the loss of the *Hermione* was correct, were we seriously to imagine that the same thing could be done to a great Atlantic liner?

From the very first moment Drummond made up his mind and never changed it. I admit that I was sceptical until the last damning proof came to us, but he never hesitated.

"It's the truth," he said quietly. "I am convinced of it. The mystery of the *Hermione* is solved. And with regard to the *Megalithic* it is the truth also."

I suppose he saw my look of incredulity, for he then addressed himself exclusively to me.

"Stockton, ever since the time in Ashworth Gardens when that woman recognised me, I've known that we were up against Peterson. I've felt it in every fibre of my being. Now it's proved beyond a shadow of doubt. Whatever may or may not be true in that diary of Gaunt's, that fact is obvious. Wilmot is Peterson: nothing else could account for his asking Gaunt if he knew me."

He lit a cigarette, and I was struck by the gravity of his face.

"You've asked once or twice about Peterson," he went on after a while. "But though we've told you a certain amount, to you he is merely a name. To us, and to me particularly, he's rather more than that. That is why I am certain in my own mind that that scrawled message about the *Megalithic* is true. And the principal reason for making me think it is true lies in the last few words. That is Peterson all over."

I glanced at the scrap of paper.

"Hydrogen not helium... Not changed... Sacrifice ship... Fire..."

"My God! you fellows" – Drummond was almost shouting in his excitement – "it's stupendous. Don't you see the tear in the paper there between sacrifice and ship? Ship doesn't refer to the *Megalithic*: the word 'air' has been torn out. It's the airship he is going to sacrifice. It is still full of hydrogen: Peterson wasn't going to the expense of refilling with helium."

He was pacing up and down, his hands in his pockets.

"That's it: I'll swear that's it. It's the Peterson creed. It's the loophole of escape that he always leaves himself. He has decided to attack the *Megalithic*; why, we don't know. Possibly a boatload of American multi-millionaires on board. He's got thirty of his own men in the ship, and that strange craft of his alongside. Let's suppose the attack is successful. The liner disappears: sinks with all hands. Right: there's nothing further to worry about. But supposing it isn't successful. With the best of luck and arrangement it's a pretty big job to tackle – even for Peterson. What's going to happen then? In a few seconds the astounding news will be wirelessed all over the world that Wilmot's dirigible is carrying out an act of piracy on the high seas of such unbelievable devilry that it would make our old pal Captain Hook rotate in his coffin if he heard of it. Suppose another thing too. Suppose it is successful, but that the wireless people in the *Megalithic* manage to get a message through before their gear is put out of action. Peterson gets that message on his own installation. What's he going to do? He may be an institution all right at the moment, but he won't have the mayor and a brass band out to welcome him on his return once the truth is known. So he descends from his airship either into this mysterious vessel of his, or else on to dry land. We know he can do that. What he does with the crew is immaterial. Probably leaves them with a few ripe and fruity instructions, and a bomb timed to explode a little later. And so Wilmot's dirigible pays the just retribution for an astounding and diabolical crime, while Wilmot himself retires to Monte Carlo on the proceeds thereof. It's what he has always said: there's nothing like dying to put people off the scent. No police in the world are going to bother to look for the blighter if they think he is a perfectly good corpse in his own burnt-out airship. It's a pity in a way," he concluded regretfully, "a great pity. I should have liked to deal with him personally."

"Well, why not?" said Jerningham.

"It's too big altogether, Ted," answered Drummond. "I never mind chancing things a certain amount with MacIver, but I don't think we'd be justified this time. The consequences of failure would be too appalling. Let's dump the sentries inside the hut, and then push off and have some breakfast. After that we'll make for London and MacIver. Whatever is believed or is not believed, there's one thing that Peterson is going to find it hard to explain. Why are his ballast tanks full of Gaunt's poison?"

So we carried the men, who still lay bound and gagged, into the wooden hut. And there, having locked the door, we left them, with the scent of death still heavy in the air and their four gruesome companions.

"It breaks my heart," said Drummond disconsolately as we strolled towards the car, "to think that we've got to pull in Scotland Yard. Still, we've had a bit of fun…"

"We have," I agreed grimly. "Incidentally what on earth are we going to do with Gaunt?"

"Well, since the poor bloke is bug house, I suppose we'll have to stuff him in a home or something. Anyway that comes later: the first thing is to lead him to an egg or possibly a kipper. We can pretend he's eccentric, if the staff go up the pole when they see him."

And so we returned to the hotel, which I certainly had never expected to see again. Now that it was all over the reaction had set in, and I even found myself wondering whether it hadn't all been some terrible nightmare. Only there sat Robin Gaunt to prove the reality, and in my pocket I could feel the sheets of his diary.

Sleep! I wanted it almost more than food: sleep and something to get rid of the racking headache which the fumes of that foul liquid had produced. And even as I waited for breakfast I found my head nodding on to the table. It was over: the strain and tension was past. One could relax…

"Good Lord!" Drummond's startled exclamation roused us all. He was staring at a newspaper, whilst his neglected cigarette burnt the table-cloth beside him.

"What's the day of the week?"

"Thursday," said someone sleepily.

"Look here, you fellows," he said gravely, "pull yourselves together and wake up. The *Megalithic* sails today from Liverpool for New York."

We woke up all right at that, and his next remark completed the arousing process.

"Today, mark you – carrying thirty million in bullion on board."

"Instantaneous, universal death," babbled Gaunt, but we paid no attention. We just sat there – all ideas of sleep banished – staring at Drummond.

"They must be warned," he said decisively. "Even at the risk of making ourselves look complete and utter fools. The *Megalithic* must be wirelessed."

He put his hand into his pocket and pulled out some letters.

"Give me a pencil: I'll scribble down a message."

And then suddenly he broke off, and sat looking blankly at something he held.

"Well, I'm damned," he muttered. "I'd forgotten all about that. Tonight is the night of Wilmot's Celebrated Farewell Gala Night Trip. Somebody sent me two complimentary tickets for it. Couldn't think who'd done it or why. Phyllis was keen on going."

Once more he fell silent as he stared at the two tickets.

"I've got it now," he said at length, and his voice was ominously quiet. "Yes – I've got it all now. Peterson sent me those two tickets, and there's no need to ask why."

He turned to the girl, who was putting the breakfast on the table.

"How long will it take to get through to London on the telephone? Anyway I must do it. Get me Mayfair 3XI. Now then, you fellows – food. And after that we'll drive to London as even the old Hispano has never moved before."

"What are you ringing up Algy for?" said Darrell.

"I want four more tickets, Peter, for tonight's trip. And above all I want some of that antidote. Peterson is not the only man who can play that particular game."

"What about wirelessing the *Megalithic*?" I asked.

He looked at me with a queer smile.

"No necessity now, Stockton. If there is one thing in this world that is certain beyond all others it is that Wilmot's dirigible will be at the aerodrome when we get back to London. For I venture to think – without undue conceit – that there is one desire in Mr Wilmot's heart that runs even the possession of thirty million fairly close. And that desire is my death."

I stared at him incredulously, but he was perfectly serious.

"Had I not known that he was going to be there, it would have been imperative to warn the *Megalithic*. Now the situation is different. If we wireless, don't forget that he will get the message. We warn him equally with the ship."

"Yes, but even so," I objected, "dare we run the risk?"

"There is no risk," said Drummond calmly. "Now that I know who Wilmot is – there is no risk. And tonight I'm going to have my final settlement with the gentleman."

He would say no more: all the way back to London, when he drove like a man possessed with ten devils, he hardly opened his lips. And sitting beside him, busy with my own thoughts, the spell of his extraordinary personality began to obsess me. Never had he seemed so completely sure of himself – so absolutely confident.

And yet the whole thing was bizarre and strange enough to cause all sorts of doubts. I, too, had forgotten the much-advertised final trip of the airship, until Drummond had pulled the tickets out of his pocket. The dinner was to be even more wonderful than usual, and every guest was to receive a memento of the occasion from Mr Wilmot himself. The thing that defeated me was why Wilmot should waste the time. Granted that

Drummond's theory was correct, and that after having attacked the *Megalithic* the airship was to come down in flames, why fool around with a two or three hours' cruise beforehand? There was no longer any necessity to pose as an "institution".

Drummond smiled at my remarks.

"Why of necessity should you assume that it's going to be three hours wasted? You don't imagine, do you, that a man like Peterson would consider it necessary to return to the aerodrome and deposit his passengers?"

"But, great Scott, man," I exploded, "he can't carry out an attack on the *Megalithic* with fifty complete strangers on board his airship."

"Can't he? Why not? Once granted that he's going to carry out the attack at all, I don't see that fifty or a hundred and fifty strangers would matter. You seem to forget that an integral part of his plan is that none of them should return alive to tell the tale."

"It's inconceivable that such a man can exist," I said.

"He's mother's bright boy all right is Carl Peterson," agreed Drummond. "I confess that I'm distinctly intrigued to see what is going to happen tonight."

"But surely, Drummond," I said, "we're not justified in going through with this. An inspection of his ballast tanks will prove the presence of the poison. And then the matter passes into the hands of Scotland Yard."

"I'm perfectly aware that that is what we ought to do," he said gravely. "Moreover, it is what we would do if it was possible."

"But why isn't it possible?" I cried.

"Think, man," he answered. "At a liberal estimate we shall have an hour in which to change and get to the aerodrome. If we puncture we shan't have as much. Let us suppose that during that hour we can persuade MacIver and Co. that we are not mad – a supposition which I think is very doubtful. But for the sake of argument we will suppose it. What is going to happen then?

MacIver appears at the aerodrome with a bunch of his pals, and attempts to board the airship. Peterson, who can spot MacIver a mile off, either sheers off at once in his dirigible, leaving MacIver dancing a hornpipe on the ground; or, what is just as likely, lets him come on board and then murders him. Don't you see, Stockton, the one fundamental factor of the whole thing is that that airship is never going to return. It doesn't matter one continental hoot to Peterson whether he is suspected or whether he isn't suspected – once he has started. He may be branded as the world's arch-devil: what does he care? A just retribution has overtaken him: he has perished miserably in the flames of his machine. No – I've thought it over, and I'm convinced that our best chance is to let his plans go on as he has arranged them. Don't let him suspect that we suspect. It won't seem strange to him that I turn up: he'll merely assume that I've utilised the ticket he sent me in utter ignorance of who he is. And then…"

"Yes," I said curiously as he paused. "And then – what?"

"Why – just one thing. The one vital thing, Stockton, which knocks the bottom out of his entire scheme. If we're right, and I know we're right, his whole plan depends on his ability to leave the airship. And he's not going to leave the airship…"

"For all that," I argued, "he may cause the most ghastly damage to the *Megalithic.*"

"I think not," said Drummond quietly. "I've made out a rough time-table, and this is how I see it. He plans to attack her somewhere off the south coast of Ireland, probably in the early hours of tomorrow morning. Long before that the guests will have realised that something is wrong. The instant that occurs he will show his hand, and matters will come to a head. One way or another it will be all over by eleven o'clock."

"My God! it's an awful risk we're running," I muttered.

"And an unavoidable one," he answered.

"There's not a human being in England who would not believe us to be absolutely crazy if we told them what we know.

So that any possibility of preventing people going on board that airship tonight may be ruled out of court at once."

It was half-past five when we arrived, and we found Algy Longworth waiting for us at Drummond's house.

"Done everything you told me, old lad," he cried cheerfully. "They thought I was mad at the War House. Great Scott!" he broke off suddenly as he saw Gaunt, "who's your pal?"

"Doesn't matter about him, Algy. You've got the antidote?"

"A bucket of it, old boy. Saw Stockton's pal – one Major Jackson."

"And you've got four tickets for Wilmot's dirigible this evening?"

"Got 'em at Keith and Prowse. What is the fun and laughter?"

"Peterson, Algy. Our one and only Carl. He's Wilmot."

Algy Longworth stared at him incredulously.

"My dear old bird," he said at length, "you're pulling my leg."

"Wilmot is Carl Peterson, Algy. Of that there is no shadow of doubt. And that's why you've got four tickets. We renew our acquaintance tonight."

"Good Lord! Well, the tickets are a tenner each, including dinner, and I got the last. So we must get our money's worth."

"You'll get that all right," said Drummond grimly. "Have you brought everybody's clothes round? Good. Get changed, you fellows: we start at six."

And now I come to the final act in the whole amazing drama. Though months have elapsed, every detail of that last flight is as clear in my mind as if it had happened yesterday.

We started at six, leaving Denny in charge of Robin. Each of us had in our pockets a pot of the antidote and a revolver; and no one talked very much. Drummond, his face set like granite, stared at the road in front of him. Algy Longworth polished and repolished his eyeglass ceaselessly. In fact, in sporting parlance –

I don't know about Drummond, but as far as the rest of us were concerned – we had got the needle.

The evening was calm and still as we motored into the aerodrome. Great flaring arc lights lit up everything with the brightness of day: whilst above our heads, attached to the mooring mast, floated the graceful vessel, no longer dark and sinister as we had seen her the night before, but a blaze of light from bows to stern.

She was due to start at seven o'clock, and at ten minutes to the hour we stepped out of the lift at the top of the mast into the main corridor of the dirigible. Everywhere the vessel was gaily decorated with festoons of brightly coloured paper and fairy-lights. And in the first of the big cabins ahead we caught a glimpse of a crowd of fashionably dressed women gathered round a thick-set good-looking man in evening clothes. Mr Wilmot was welcoming his guests.

"Is that Peterson?" I whispered to Drummond.

He laughed shortly.

"Do you mean – do I recognise him? No, I don't. I never have yet, by looking at his face. But it's Peterson all right."

Drummond was handing his coat and hat to a diminutive black boy in a bright red uniform, and I glanced at his face. A faint smile was hovering round his lips, but his eyes were expressionless. And even the smile vanished as he strolled towards the group in the ante-room: he was just the ordinary society man attending some function.

And what a function it proved. It was the first time that I had ever been inside an airship, and the thing that impressed me most was the spaciousness of everything – and the luxury. Even granting that it was a special occasion, one had to admit that the whole thing was marvellously well done. The lighting effect was superb; and in every corner great masses of hot-house flowers gave out a heavy scent.

"It's Eastern," I said to Drummond. "Oriental."

"Peterson has always been spectacular," he answered. "But I agree that he has spared no pains with the coffin."

"I simply can't believe it," I said. "Now that we're actually here, surrounded by all this, it seems incredible that he proposes to sacrifice it all."

"There are a good many things about Peterson that strike one as incredible," said Drummond quietly. "But I wish I had even an inkling of what he's going to do."

Suddenly the eyes of the two men met over the heads of the women. It was the moment I had been waiting for and I watched Wilmot intently. For perhaps the fraction of a second he paused in his conversation and it seemed to me that a gleam of triumph showed on his face: then once again he turned to the woman beside him with just the correct shade of deference which is expected of those who converse with a Duchess.

Drummond also had turned away and was chatting with someone he knew, but I noticed that he continually edged nearer and nearer to the place where Wilmot was standing a little apart from the others. At last he stopped in front of them and bowed.

"Good-evening, Duchess," he remarked. "Why aren't you slaughtering birds up North?"

"How are you, Hugh? Same thing applies to you. By the way-do you know Mr Wilmot? – Captain Drummond?"

The two men bowed, and Jerningham and I, talking ostensibly, drew closer. I know my hands were clammy with excitement, and I don't think the others were in much better condition.

"Your last trip, Mr Wilmot, I believe," said Drummond.

"That is so," answered the other. "In England, I regret to say, the weather is so treacherous that after the early part of September flying ceases to be a pleasure."

"He has got some wonderful surprise for us, Hugh," said the Duchess.

"Merely a trifling souvenir, my dear Duchess," answered Wilmot suavely.

"Of what has become quite an institution, Mr Wilmot," put in Drummond.

Wilmot bowed.

"I had hoped perhaps to have made it even more of an institution," he answered. "But the public takes to new things slowly. Ah! we're off."

"And what," asked Drummond, "is our course tonight?"

"I thought we would do the Thames Valley. Duchess – a cocktail?"

A waiter with a row of exquisite glasses containing an amber liquid was handing her a tray.

"Captain Drummond? You, I'm sure, will have one."

"Why, certainly, Mr Wilmot. I feel confident that what the Duchess drinks is safe for me."

And once again the eyes of the two men met.

Personally I think it was at that moment that the certainty came to Wilmot that Drummond knew. But just as certainly no sign of it showed on his face. All through the sumptuous dinner that followed, when he and Drummond sat one on each side of the Duchess, he played the part of the courteous host to perfection. I was two or three places away myself, so much of their conversation I missed. But some of it I did hear, and I marvelled at Wilmot's nerve.

Deliberately Drummond brought up the subject of the Robin Gaunt mystery, and of the fate of the *Hermione*. And just as deliberately Wilmot discussed them both. But all the time he knew and we knew that things were moving inexorably towards their appointed end. And what was that end going to be?

That was the question I asked myself over and over again. It seemed impossible, incredible that the suave, self-possessed man at the head of the table could possess a mind so infamously black that, without a qualm, he would sacrifice all these women. And yet he had not scrupled to murder the women in the *Hermione*.

It seemed so needless – so unnecessary. Why have brought them at all? Why not have flown with his crew alone? Why have drawn attention to himself with his much-advertised gala night?

"Have you noticed the rate at which we are going? She's positively quivering."

Jerningham's sudden question broke in on my thoughts, and I realised that the whole great vessel was vibrating like a thing possessed. But no one seemed to pay any attention: the band still played serenely on, scarcely audible over the loud buzz of conversation.

At last dinner was over, and a sudden silence fell as Wilmot rose to his feet. A burst of applause greeted him, and he bowed with a faint smile.

"Your Grace," he began, Ladies and Gentlemen. It is, believe me, not only a pleasure but an honour to have had such a distinguished company tonight to celebrate this last trip in my airship. I am no believer in long speeches, certainly not on occasions of this sort. But, before distributing the small souvenirs which I have obtained as a memento of this – I trust I may say – pleasant evening, there is one thing which as loyal subjects of our gracious Sovereign it is our duty to perform. Before, however, requesting the distinguished officer on my right" – he bowed to Drummond, and suddenly with a queer thrill I noticed that Drummond's face was shining like an actor's with grease paint – "to propose His Majesty's health, I would like to mention one fact. The liqueur in which I would ask you to drink the King is one unknown in this country. It is an old Chinese wine the secret of which is known only to a certain sect of monks. Its taste is not unpleasant, but its novelty will lie in the fact that you are drinking what only two Europeans have ever drunk before. One of those is dead – not, I hasten to assure you, as a result of drinking it: the other is myself. I will now ask Captain Drummond to propose the King."

In front of each of us had been placed a tiny glass containing a few drops of the liqueur, and Drummond rose to his feet, as did all of us.

"Ladies and Gentlemen," he said mechanically, and I could tell he was puzzled – "the King."

The band struck up the National Anthem, and we stood there waiting for the end. Suddenly on Drummond's face there flashed a look of horror, and he swung round staring at Wilmot. And then came his mighty shout – drowning the band with its savage intensity.

"Don't drink. For God's sake – don't drink. It's death."

Unconsciously I sniffed the contents of my glass: smelt that strange sickly scent: realised that the liquid was Gaunt's poison.

The band stopped abruptly, and a woman started to laugh hysterically. And still Drummond and Wilmot stared at one another in silence, whilst the great vessel drove on throbbing through the night.

"What's all this damned foolery?" came in angry tones from a red-faced man half-way down the table. "You're frightening the women, sir. What do you mean – death?"

He raised the glass to his lips, and before any of us could stop him, he drained it. And drinking it he crashed forward across the table – dead.

It was then that real pandemonium broke loose. Women screamed and huddled together in little groups, staring at the man who had spoken – now lying rigid and motionless with broken glass and upset flower vases all round him.

And still Drummond and Wilmot stared at one another in silence.

"The doors, you fellows." Drummond's voice reached us above the din. "And line up the servants and keep them covered."

With a snarl that was scarcely human Wilmot sprang forward. He snatched up the Duchess' liqueur glass and flung the contents in Drummond's face. And Drummond laughed.

"Your mistake, Peterson," he said. "You only got half the antidote when you murdered Sir John Dallas. Ah! no – your hands above your head."

The barrel of his revolver gleamed in the light, and once again silence fell as, fascinated, we watched the pair of them. They stood alone, at the head of the table, and Drummond's eyes were hard and merciless, while Peterson plucked at his collar with hands that shook.

"Where are we driving to at this rate, Carl Peterson?" said Drummond.

"There's some mistake," muttered the other.

"No, Peterson, there is no mistake. Tonight you were going to do to the *Megalithic* what you did to the *Hermione* – sink her with every soul on board. There's no good denying it: I spent last night in Black Mine."

The other started uncontrollably, and the blazing hatred in his eyes grew more maniacal.

"What are you going to do, Drummond?" he snarled.

"A thing that has been long overdue, Peterson," answered Drummond quietly. "You unspeakable devil: you damnable wholesale murderer."

He slipped the revolver back in his pocket, and picked up his own liqueur glass.

"The good host drinks first, Peterson." His great hand shot out and clutched the other's throat. "Drink, you foul brute: drink."

Never to my dying day shall I forget the hoarse yell of terror that Peterson uttered as he struggled in that iron grip. His eyes stared fearfully at the glass, and with a sudden stupendous effort he knocked it out of Drummond's hand.

And once again Drummond laughed: the contents had spilled on the other's wrist.

"If you won't drink – have it the other way, Carl Peterson. But the score is paid."

His grip relaxed on Peterson's throat: he stood back, arms folded, watching the criminal. And whether it was the justice of fate, or whether it was that previous applications of the antidote had given Peterson a certain measure of immunity, I know not. But for full five seconds did he stand there before the end came. And in that five seconds the mask slipped from his face, and he stood revealed for what he was. And of that revelation no man can write...

Thus did Carl Peterson die on the eve of his biggest coup. As he had killed, so was he killed, whilst, all unconscious of what had happened, the navigator still drove the airship full speed towards the west.

And now but little remains to be told. It was Drummond who walked along the corridor and found the control cabin. It was Drummond who put a revolver in the navigator's neck, and forced him to swing the airship round and head back to London. It was Drummond who commanded the dirigible till finally we tied up once more to the mooring mast.

And then it was Drummond who, revolver in hand to stop any rush of the crew, superintended the disembarkation of the guests. Lift load after lift load of white-faced women and men went down to the ground till only we six remained. One final look did we take at the staring glassy eyes of the man who sprawled across the chair in which he had sat to entertain Royalty, and then we too dropped swiftly downwards.

News had already passed round the aerodrome, and excited officials thronged round us as we stepped out of the lift. But Drummond would say nothing.

"Ring up Inspector MacIver at Scotland Yard," he remarked curtly. "Leave all the rest of them on board till he comes. I will stop here."

But, as all the world knows, it was decreed otherwise. Barely had we sat down in one of the waiting rooms when an agitated man rushed in.

"She's off," he cried. "Wilmot's dirigible is under weigh."

We darted outside to see the great airship slowly circling round. She still blazed with light, and from the windows leaned men, waving their arms mockingly. Then she headed north-east. And she was barely clear of the aerodrome when it happened. What looked to me like a yellow flash came from amidships, followed by a terrible rending noise. And before our eyes the dirigible became a roaring furnace of flame. Then, splitting in two, she dropped like a stone.

What caused the accident no one will ever know. Personally I am inclined to agree with Drummond that one of the crew, realising that Wilmot was dead, decided to ransack his cabin to see what he could steal. And in the cabin he found some infernal device for causing fire, which in his unskilful hands exploded suddenly. It is a possible solution: that is all I can say for it. Anyway the point is immaterial. For twelve hours no man could approach the wreckage, so intense was the heat. And when at length it was possible, the bodies were so terribly burned as to be unrecognisable. Two only could be traced: the two in evening clothes. Though which was the red-faced man who had drunk and which was Wilmot no one could say. And again the point is immaterial. For when a man is dead he's dead, and there's not much use in worrying further. What did matter was that one of those two charred corpses was all that remained of the super-criminal known to the world as Wilmot – and known to Drummond as Carl Peterson.

CHAPTER 13

In which I lay down my pen

I have finished. To the best of my ability I have set down the events of that summer. At the outset I warned my readers that I was no literary man: had there been anyone else willing to tackle the job I would willingly have resigned in his favour.

There will be many even now who will in all probability shrug their shoulders incredulously. Well, as I have said more than once, I cannot *make* any man believe me. If people choose to think that Gaunt's description of the sinking of the *Hermione* is a madman's delusion based on what he had read in the papers, they are welcome to their opinion. But the *Hermione* has never been heard of again, and it is now more than a year since she sailed from Southampton. And I have, at any rate, put forward a theory to account for her loss.

What is of far more interest to me is what would have happened had the attack been carried out on the *Megalithic*. What would have happened if Drummond had not chanced to pick out the scent of death in his glass, from the heavy languorous smell of the hot-house flowers that filled the cabin in which we dined? Can't you picture that one terrible moment, as with one accord every man and woman round that table pitched forward dead, under the mocking cynical eyes of Wilmot, and the great airship with its ghastly load tore on through the night?

And then – what would have happened? Would the attack have been successful? I know not, but sometimes I try to visualise the scene. The dirigible – no longer blazing with light – but dark and ghostly, keeping pace with the liner low down on top of her. Those thirty desperate men: the shattered wireless: and over everything the rain of death. And then the strange craft capable of such speed in spite of her lines, alongside. Everywhere panic-stricken women and men dashing to and fro, and finding no escape. Perhaps the siren blaring madly into the night, until that too ceased because no man was left to sound it.

Then in the grey dawn the transfer of the bullion to the other vessel: the descent of Wilmot from the airship: perhaps a torpedo. A torpedo was all that was necessary for the *Lusitania*.

And then, last of all, I can see Wilmot – his hands in his pockets, a cigar drawing evenly between his lips – standing on the bridge of his ship. The swirling water has calmed down: only some floating wreckage marks the grave of the *Megalithic*. Suddenly from overhead there comes a blinding sheet of flame, and the doomed airship falls blazing into the sea.

Guess-work, I admit – but that is what I believe would have happened. But it didn't, and so guesswork it must remain to the end. There are other things too we shall never know. What happened to the vessel with the strange lines? There is no one known to us who can describe her save Robin Gaunt, and he is incurably insane. Where is she? What is she doing now? Is she some harmless ocean-going tramp, or is she rotting in some deserted harbour?

What happened to the men we had left bound in Black Mine? For when the police got there next day there was no sign of them. How did they get away? Where are they now? Pawns – I admit; but they might have told us something.

And finally, the thing that intrigues Drummond most. How much did Peterson think we knew?

Personally I do not think that Peterson believed we knew anything at all until the end. Obviously he had no idea that we had been to Black Mine the night before, until Drummond told him so. Obviously he believed himself perfectly safe, and but for the discovery of Gaunt's diary he would have been. Should we, or rather Drummond, ever have suspected that liqueur except for the knowledge we had? I doubt it, and so does Drummond. Even though we knew that smell so well – the smell of death – I doubt if we should have picked it out from the heavy exotic scent of the flowers.

They are questions which for ever will remain unanswered, though it is possible that some day a little light may be thrown on them.

And now there is but one thing more. Drummond and his wife are in Deauville, so I must rely on my memory.

It was four days after the airship had crashed in flames. The scent of the poison no longer hung about the wreckage: the charred bodies had all been recovered. And as Drummond stood looking at the debris a woman in deep black approached him.

"You have killed the man I loved, Hugh Drummond," she said. "But do not think it is the end."

He took off his hat.

"It would be idle to pretend, Mademoiselle," he said, "that I do not know you. But may I ask why you state that I killed Carl Peterson? Is not that how he died?"

With his hand he indicated the wreckage.

She shook her head.

"The airship came down in flames at half-past one," she said. "It was at ten o'clock that Carl died."

"That is so," he said gravely. "I said the other to spare your feelings. You have seen, I presume, someone who was on board?"

"I have seen no one," she answered.

"But those details have been kept out of the papers," he exclaimed.

"I have read no paper," she replied.

"Then how did you know?"

"He spoke to me as he died," she said quietly. "And as I said before, it is not the end."

Without another word she left him. Was she speaking the truth, or was there indeed some strange *rapport* between her and Peterson? Did the personality of that arch-criminal project itself through space to the woman he had lived with for so many years? And if so, what terrible message of hatred against Drummond did it give to her?

He has not seen her since: the memory of that brief interview is getting a little blurred. Perhaps she too has forgotten: perhaps not. Who knows?

SAPPER

THE BLACK GANG

Although the First World War is over, it seems that the hostilities are not, and when Captain Hugh 'Bulldog' Drummond discovers that a stint of bribery and blackmail is undermining England's democratic tradition, he forms the Black Gang, bent on tracking down the perpetrators of such plots. They set a trap to lure the criminal mastermind behind these subversive attacks to England, and all is going to plan until Bulldog Drummond accepts an invitation to tea at the Ritz with a charming American clergyman and his dowdy daughter.

BULLDOG DRUMMOND

'Demobilised officer, finding peace incredibly tedious, would welcome diversion. Legitimate, if possible; but crime, if of a comparatively humorous description, no objection. Excitement essential... Reply at once Box X10.'

Hungry for adventure following the First World War, Captain Hugh 'Bulldog' Drummond begins a career as the invincible protector of his country. His first reply comes from a beautiful young woman, who sends him racing off to investigate what at first looks like blackmail but turns out to be far more complicated and dangerous. The rescue of a kidnapped millionaire, found with his thumbs horribly mangled, leads Drummond to the discovery of a political conspiracy of awesome scope and villainy, masterminded by the ruthless Carl Peterson.

SAPPER

Bulldog Drummond at Bay

While Hugh 'Bulldog' Drummond is staying in an old cottage for a peaceful few days duck shooting, he is disturbed one night by the sound of men shouting, followed by a large stone that comes crashing through the window. When he goes outside to investigate, he finds a patch of blood in the road, and is questioned by two men who tell him that they are chasing a lunatic who has escaped from the nearby asylum. Drummond plays dumb, but is determined to investigate in his inimitable style when he discovers a cryptic message.

The Female of the Species

Bulldog Drummond has slain his arch-enemy, Carl Peterson, but Peterson's mistress lives on and is intent on revenge. Drummond's wife vanishes, followed by a series of vicious traps set by a malicious adversary, which lead to a hair-raising chase across England, to a sinister house and a fantastic torture chamber modelled on Stonehenge, with its legend of human sacrifice.

SAPPER

THE RETURN OF BULLDOG DRUMMOND

While staying as a guest at Merridale Hall, Captain Hugh 'Bulldog' Drummond's peaceful repose is disturbed by a frantic young man who comes dashing into the house, trembling and begging for help. When two warders arrive, asking for a man named Morris – a notorious murderer who has escaped from Dartmoor – Drummond assures them that they are chasing the wrong man. In which case, who on earth is this terrified youngster?

THE THIRD ROUND

The death of Professor Goodman is officially recorded as a tragic accident, but at the inquest, no mention is made of his latest discovery – a miraculous new formula for manufacturing flawless diamonds at negligible cost, which strikes Captain Hugh 'Bulldog' Drummond as rather strange. His suspicions are further aroused when he spots a member of the Metropolitan Diamond Syndicate at the inquest. Gradually, he untangles a sinister plot of greed and murder, which climaxes in a dramatic motorboat chase at Cowes and brings him face to face with his arch-enemy.

OTHER TITLES BY SAPPER AVAILABLE DIRECT
FROM HOUSE OF STRATUS

Quantity	£	$(US)	$(CAN)	€
ASK FOR RONALD STANDISH	6.99	11.50	15.99	11.50
THE BLACK GANG	6.99	11.50	15.99	11.50
BULLDOG DRUMMOND	6.99	11.50	15.99	11.50
BULLDOG DRUMMOND AT BAY	6.99	11.50	15.99	11.50
CHALLENGE	6.99	11.50	15.99	11.50
THE DINNER CLUB	6.99	11.50	15.99	11.50
THE FEMALE OF THE SPECIES	6.99	11.50	15.99	11.50
FINGER OF FATE	6.99	11.50	15.99	11.50
THE ISLAND OF TERROR	6.99	11.50	15.99	11.50
JIM BRENT	6.99	11.50	15.99	11.50
JIM MAITLAND	6.99	11.50	15.99	11.50
JOHN WALTERS	6.99	11.50	15.99	11.50
KNOCK-OUT	6.99	11.50	15.99	11.50
MUFTI	6.99	11.50	15.99	11.50
THE RETURN OF BULLDOG DRUMMOND	6.99	11.50	15.99	11.50
SERGEANT MICHAEL CASSIDY RE	6.99	11.50	15.99	11.50
TEMPLE TOWER	6.99	11.50	15.99	11.50
THE THIRD ROUND	6.99	11.50	15.99	11.50

ALL HOUSE OF STRATUS BOOKS ARE AVAILABLE FROM GOOD BOOKSHOPS
OR DIRECT FROM THE PUBLISHER:

Internet: www.houseofstratus.com including author interviews, reviews, features.

Email: sales@houseofstratus.com please quote author, title and credit card details.

Hotline: UK ONLY: 0800 169 1780, please quote author, title and credit card details.
INTERNATIONAL: +44 (0) 20 7494 6400, please quote author, title and credit card details.

Send to: House of Stratus Sales Department
24c Old Burlington Street
London
W1X 1RL
UK

Please allow for postage costs charged per order plus an amount per book as set out in the tables below:

	£(Sterling)	$(US)	$(CAN)	€(Euros)
Cost per order				
UK	2.00	3.00	4.50	3.30
Europe	3.00	4.50	6.75	5.00
North America	3.00	4.50	6.75	5.00
Rest of World	3.00	4.50	6.75	5.00
Additional cost per book				
UK	0.50	0.75	1.15	0.85
Europe	1.00	1.50	2.30	1.70
North America	2.00	3.00	4.60	3.40
Rest of World	2.50	3.75	5.75	4.25

PLEASE SEND CHEQUE, POSTAL ORDER (STERLING ONLY), EUROCHEQUE, OR INTERNATIONAL MONEY ORDER (PLEASE CIRCLE METHOD OF PAYMENT YOU WISH TO USE)
MAKE PAYABLE TO: STRATUS HOLDINGS plc

Cost of book(s): —————————— Example: 3 x books at £6.99 each: £20.97

Cost of order: —————————— Example: £2.00 (Delivery to UK address)

Additional cost per book: ————— Example: 3 x £0.50: £1.50

Order total including postage: ——— Example: £24.47

Please tick currency you wish to use and add total amount of order:

☐ £ (Sterling)   ☐ $ (US)   ☐ $ (CAN)   ☐ € (EUROS)

VISA, MASTERCARD, SWITCH, AMEX, SOLO, JCB:

☐☐☐☐☐☐☐☐☐☐☐☐☐☐☐☐☐☐☐☐

Issue number (Switch only):

☐☐☐

Start Date: **Expiry Date:**

☐☐ / ☐☐   ☐☐ / ☐☐

Signature: ————————————

NAME: ——————————————————

ADDRESS: ——————————————————

————————————————————

POSTCODE: —————————

Please allow 28 days for delivery.

Prices subject to change without notice.
Please tick box if you do not wish to receive any additional information. ☐

House of Stratus publishes many other titles in this genre; please check our website (**www.houseofstratus.com**) for more details.